THE LONG ROAD TO LOVING JACKSON

ALICIA HOPE

ACKNOWLEDGMENTS

This story is written in Australian English.

The situations, organisations and characters in this book are fictional. Any resemblance to an existing or past entity is entirely coincidental.

DEDICATION

For Biddy, Oigle, Comanchee, Trooper, Shorty, Jacko, and all the horses in my life – you each deserve a story.

ABOUT THE AUTHOR

Once you choose HOPE, anything is possible....

Horse riding, bass playing, and bird watching Alicia Hope lives on coastal acreage dotted with Australia's famous gum trees and frequented by a delightful variety of birds and animals. Alicia also shares her Queensland home with an author husband, Frank H Jordan, and a feathered larrikin, cockatiel Kewbie Kewberton.

Inspiration for *The Long Road to Loving Jackson* came from a display of trick riding at a country show, and from glimpses of a gracious old homestead on sweeping cattle country with the Great Diving Range at its back door, viz 'Granger Farm'.

Writing this novel gave Alicia a chance to re-live the joys of farming life, and she hopes readers also enjoy this very country, very Aussie story.

1

The sound woke him first. Then came rumbling vibrations through the ground beneath his swag. He folded down the flap and raised an arm, the half moon casting a silvery glow on the ripple of well-defined muscles beneath his skin. Blinking, he focused on his watch's illuminated dial.

Almost midnight.

Wafts of night air carried the sounds closer, and the vibrations became pounding hoof beats. Lifting himself to his elbows, he tilted his head to listen.

A mob of brumbies going past?

A small mob at best.

Peering toward the sound he glimpsed movement, and rose to his feet. In the distance, the hazy silhouettes of three riders flew toward the ridge.

Funny time to be out riding.

He watched until they disappeared. Rubbing a large, rough-skinned hand over his face, he settled back down with a grunt.

Way too early for a coffee. Anyway, he needed more sleep after the long, tiring hike north. While the views from the summits of mounts Dromedary and Colosseum had proven more than sufficient reward for his efforts, scaling two mountain ranges had left him needing a breather and a recharge.

And so he'd headed east. By his reckoning, he was camped about twenty kilometres inland from the Central Queensland coast. A little too close to *that* place perhaps, but if he didn't stray any closer he should avoid rekindling the old pain ... the worst of it at least. He still couldn't traverse good cattle country without experiencing the sting of regret.

Would that always be the case or would he eventually get over the loss?

With his thirtieth birthday on the horizon he needed to set new, realistic goals, to focus his energies ahead, and let go of what was lost to the past. This hiking trip was a step in that direction. And his discovery of an ideal camping spot, close to water and bordered on three sides by state forest, felt like another reward. Especially when his reconnoitre of the area revealed only one nearby residence, a country homestead that appeared unoccupied.

Perfect.

Abbey paused to squint up at the woman standing by the horse's head. 'Something bothering you, Margot?'

After a quick glance into the dark-ringed grey eyes gazing at her, Margot Boyce went back to absently fingering the fancy stitching in the gelding's bridle. 'You *do* realise how important this performance is?' Rubbing the back of her neck with a sun-spotted hand, she watched the slender young woman position the roller around the gelding's stout grey belly. 'I mean ... I don't need to remind you how much is hanging on getting it right ... do I?'

Swallowing a flutter of pre-show nerves, Abbey flicked her manager a fond glance. 'No, you don't have to remind me.' Her voice took on a sing-song quality. 'This is the Ekka, the chance you've been waiting for to show the state what our team can do.' She gave a teasing grin. 'How often have I heard those words?'

'Some things deserve repeating.' Margot crossed her arms over her wiry midriff, making the fringes on her satin shirt dance.

'You're not nervous, are you Mu— ... er ... Margot?' It was the second time that day she'd almost called her manager 'Mum'. Abbey frowned. She was in her twenties, *way* too old to be pining for her mother. And yet the subject of family, and her distance from what remained of it, kept pricking at her like a burr under a thin blanket.

At Margot's unimpressed 'Humph,' Abbey went back to fitting the roller, saying, 'Who was it said we should never let nerves get in the way of a first-rate performance?'

'Yeah, I know. I need to take my own advice.'

When the gelding shifted his feathered hooves in the straw and swished his salt-and-pepper tail at her, Abbey murmured, 'Steady mate, nearly done.' After positioning the handles and Cossack stirrups just behind his withers, where they'd be within easy reach from his back, she threw Margot an impish glance and turned to the horse again. 'Hope you're not nervous too, Star. One of us has to keep a level head.'

Margot arched an eyebrow. 'Very funny.'

As though sharing the joke, the chestnut in the next stall

gave a snort to clear its nostrils of lucerne chaff and shook itself, flapping its stiff new day rug. The noise reverberated off the corrugated-iron roofing of the day stalls in the Brisbane Exhibition Ground.

Queensland's premier agricultural show, fondly nicknamed 'the Ekka', always attracted the best the state had to offer. The long rows of stalls behind the spectator-filled grandstands held horseflesh of various breeds – some rugged, some saddled, some plaited and primped with checkerboard-patterned rumps, others *au naturel* but gleaming with good health. Most picked at hay nets or dozed, one rear hoof resting on a toe. Others whinnied and tossed their heads, or pawed the ground with frustrated eagerness. Warm, earthy aromas of horse, hay, saddle-soaped leather and trampled grass hung in the air, a horse lover's pot-pourri.

Margot took hold of Star's bridle again and clipped the lunge rein to the padded noseband. As she fiddled with one of the neat plaits in his mane she muttered, 'Just ... ace that final movement, okay? We want cameras clicking during the performance, and a standing ovation as you leave the ring.'

'That's the plan.' Abbey wrapped her arms around Star's neck and pressed her full, lightly glossed lips against his velvety greyness in a quick kiss. 'We know what we're doing, don't we mate?' She turned to give the older woman's arm a reassuring squeeze. 'We've got this.'

Margot gave a pensive nod. 'Just remember there's bound to be some talent scouts in the audience. And a few cashed-up potential backers if I'm lucky.' Seeing Abbey's indulgent grin, her tone grew first defensive and then mildly reproving. 'Which is why your getting it right is so important. The other girls did well in their performances, though maybe not well enough to get the kind of attention we're hoping for. So it's down to you to leave the crowd gasping.'

After a final tug of her sparkling blue bodysuit, Abbey vaulted onto the gelding's back, the movement making the suit's short, filmy skirt float around her slim hips and well-defined thighs. The afternoon sun gleamed off her hair and caught the jiggling sequins on her suit and purpose-made ballet flats, making them twinkle.

Margot crinkled her chin and gave a satisfied dip of her head. She counted herself lucky to have a rider who not only displayed sound work ethics, but was also talented and eye-catching, with a sunny 'girl next door' appeal. It was a hard mix to find in young women these days. Swallowing a scowl, she recalled having to brush potato chip crumbs off Stacey's costume – while leading her into the arena for a performance, no less! The silly girl drew eyes but could be so crass....

Tipping up the brim of her pink cowboy hat, Margot noticed Abbey smiling down at her.

'I know how much this means to you and the team, Margot, which is why we put in all the preparation and practice.' She leaned forward to run a loving hand along the horse's neck. 'Star and I have it down, and we're raring to go.'

'Good.' After tucking her hair behind her ears and straightening her hat, Margot took up the slack on the long lunge rein and led the horse out of the stall. Astride his broad grey back, Abbey did some warm-up stretches and vaults, focusing herself in preparation.

As they approached the entrance to the show ring, a voice over the PA announced, 'Now for the event we've all been waiting for, the final performance by Margot Boyce's fabulous trick riding team, *The Equestriennes*. Let's hear it for Abbey Rae Miller on Starlifter!'

With a glance over her pink-fringed shoulder at Abbey and a quiet, 'Let's give 'em a show to remember,' Margot extended the lunge rein. Jogging to the centre of the ring, she took up position as lunger.

Clicking Star into a controlled circular canter at the end of the rein, Abbey smiled and raised both hands to wave at the cheering crowd, her slender, well-muscled legs holding her firm in the saddle. As the sweet notes of the *Je T'aime* instrumental flowed from the arena's speakers, she twirled her arms out to the sides, palms down and fingers arched elegantly upward like she was flying. Closing her eyes as if in rapture, she put her head back and let her long dark hair cascade behind her.

You and me Star, 'together as one'.

A burst of applause greeted the graceful manoeuvre. Before it died, Abbey lifted herself to her knees while Star maintained his smooth gait beneath her, his movements almost in time with the poignant music. Extending one slim leg behind her, toes pointed, she reached the opposing arm out in front. With a flourish of the extended hand she lifted her chin, and her vivacious smile widened at the resulting ovation.

The announcer gushed, 'Beautifully executed! Now you know why they call this "ballet on horseback", folks.' He went on, reading from notes Margot had given him earlier. 'That was a Flag movement. Next Abbey will perform a Mill. In this vault she has to let go of the grips and swing her legs in a full turn twice, all while the horse is moving beneath her. Let's hope she doesn't slip, folks, it's a long way down from that big fella.'

Amid the energetic applause that followed Abbey's faultless

Mill, the announcer's voice boomed from the speakers again. 'And now for a Scissors movement. Rising into a handstand – on a moving platform remember, folks – our rider will come down facing the horse's tail. From there she'll swing her legs around to face forward again.'

The crowd's loud whistles and applause drowned him out until his voice cut through the din.

'Next, the Stand and Flank movements....'

In the centre of the circle Margot worked the lunge rein as her star performer went through the carefully choreographed routine. Even her eagle eyes found little to criticise in Abbey's well-executed vaults and acrobatic tumbles. Her smooth transitions appeared effortless, her grip changes precise. She kept her legs straight and toes neatly pointed in the passes, and her body adjustments imperceptible to all but the trained eye. Throughout the performance she maintained a focused, happy expression even as the movements gained complexity, building to the finale.

The music changed. *Je T'aime* faded, replaced by the rousing orchestral theme from *The Man from Snowy River*. As the stirring melody poured from the speakers, Abbey urged Star into a faster canter. He responded, nostrils fluttering and hooves pounding the packed earth of the show ring.

It was time for the finale.

As the announcement came over the speakers, Abbey raised her right arm in a flourish for half a circle, before twisting her upper body to grip the roller with her left hand. A hush fell over the crowd and even Margot held her breath, as Abbey lowered herself until she was lying upside down along Star's bobbing nearside. Suspended by one hand and a leg in a harness loop above the fast-moving earth, her sky-blue bodysuit with its sheer, fluttering skirt standing out against Star's greyness and her flowing hair a dark plume against his pale shoulder and chest, Abbey extended her right hand forward in a 'ta-da!' flourish. Her grin widened at the burst of rousing applause and cheers from the spellbound crowd.

Margot couldn't help smiling too when she looked toward the grandstands and saw people – members of the media with any luck – on their feet, taking photographs.

As a beaming Abbey began her final inverted circuit to the appreciative roar of the crowd, Margot said under her breath, 'That's my girl,' and peered into the audience again.

An instant later the lunge rein slackened in her grip and then jerked taut, throwing her off-balance. Whipping her shocked gaze back to the arena as she lurched forward, she glimpsed the disaster unfolding in front of her. Then the rein tore from her grasp, burning through her hands, and she fell forward with a strangled cry.

Abbey's eyelids fluttered and opened a slit, only to squeeze shut against the glare.

'Hello there. How're you doing?' A reassuring hand touched her shoulder.

She blinked, trying to fix her gaze on the face hovering above hers. It moved in and out of focus, but she recognised the Aegean-blue uniform and red Maltese cross on the paramedic's sleeve. When she sucked in a lungful of air it was full of the scents of horse, trampled grass, and sawdust. From the corner of her eye she caught a hazy glimpse of a light-coloured horse being led away, limping.

Star?

Limping?

Oh no....

Through the dusty grit in her mouth and throat she managed to croak, 'Star?'

'Do you know where you are?' The words seemed to come from far away.

She needed to get up....

Pain knifed through her as she made to lift her head. She cried out and felt the paramedic put both hands on her shoulders.

'You need to lie still.'

His words merged into a compressed hum in her ears as pain dulled her senses. Her breathing quickened as she tried to clear her head of fog, only to slow again as she sank into a pain-free blackness.

The next time she surfaced, Abbey managed to focus on her surroundings, frowning at their unfamiliarity. The distinctive smell of antiseptic, the sounds of hushed, urgent voices, and the squeak of hurrying shoes registered in her foggy brain.

Hospital?

She made to sit up but there was something heavy against her neck. Lifting a tentative hand, she touched fingertips to the hard sides of a cervical collar, as pain radiated from low in her back. It throbbed up to her neck and into her head, making her gasp. She squeezed her eyes tightly shut as her body stiffened in response.

All except her legs, which lay motionless and ... numb.

Numb?

Numb!

Her stomach clenched and her eyes snapped open. She clawed at her thigh with a shaking hand.

Nothing.

She thumped a fist into one thigh and then the other as though to wake them. At their lack of feeling her eyes widened in horror.

Oh no.

No.

NO!

2

As daylight inched above the horizon he got the campfire going, set the blackened billy to boil, and dug around in his khaki backpack. Taking out a rolled-up tube of blended coffee and condensed milk, he pressed the last creamy remnant into a battered metal cup.

Just enough for a morning heart-starter.

He sucked the last sweet dregs from the flattened tube, and sighed.

Time for a supply trip.

He hadn't restocked for a while, his hiking trail hadn't taken him through many towns. Some he'd avoided on purpose....

At a sudden vibration in his pocket, he took out his mobile and saw another text message on screen, in all capitals this time.

PLEASE JAX
WE HAVE TO TALK

His mouth hardened. The continued silence must be frustrating the hell out of Johnno.

Too bad.

The time for talk was *before* Johnno did what he did.

After deleting the text he checked the battery indicator, snapped the phone closed, and slipped it back into his pocket. He'd need to recharge it next time he was near a power supply.

When his ears caught sounds of hissing from the fire, he glanced up to see a low grey cloud spreading across the sky. Droplets fell on his upturned face. A damp breeze ruffled the sun-bleached hairs on his arms and tugged at his cotton shirt.

The edges of the horizon still held a promising glow, so the rain probably wouldn't last all day.

He ran a hand over his stubbled chin.

Looks like it'll be an afternoon trip.

Not that it mattered what time he went for supplies.

Jackson Granger was no longer on the clock, was free to do as he pleased, and answered to no one.

Abbey's anguished cry brought a nurse to her bedside.

'My legs!' She clutched at the nurse's arm. 'W-what's wrong —' Her breath caught in her throat.

'You're safe, you're in hospital.'

'My legs ... I c-can't move them—'

'Don't worry.' The nurse patted her shoulder. 'We're taking care of you.'

'What....' Abbey sucked in a ragged breath, released her grip and sagged back against the pillows. She licked her lips and strove to rein in her panic. 'What happened to me?'

'You don't remember?'

At her tearful headshake, the nurse soothed, 'Just relax, Miss Miller. The doctor's on his way. After I check your vitals I'll give you something for the pain.'

A while later a thin man wearing a white coat and purposeful expression bustled into the room. When Abbey glanced his way he said crisply, 'Good, you're awake.'

She watched him pick up her chart, her grey eyes wide and fearful. 'W-what happened to me?'

'You had a fall and the ambos brought you here, to hospital. You're in the spinal unit.'

'A fall? *Spinal* unit?' She fingered the cervical collar and took a deep breath. 'How bad...?'

Without looking up from the chart he said, 'The initial examination revealed a suspected fractured pelvis, and severe bruising to your limbs and torso. The ER doctor also discovered some abnormalities in your leg reflexes.' He flicked her a glance. 'You might've noticed some numbness in them?'

'Y-yes.'

'This can be indicative of spinal trauma, hence the collar and your being referred to me. I'm Dr Hughes, resident neurologist.' At the alarm on her face he said quickly, 'The collar's mostly a precaution. Spinal cord trauma sounds scary, and in severe cases it *can* result in permanent deficits, but it can also heal over time without complications. Depending on the location and severity of the injury, of course.'

She gulped and forced her stunned mind to focus on the specialist's words as he continued with practiced evenness.

'In your case, the damage appears to be in the lumbar sacral region,' and he indicated the area on his own back. 'Injuries to this lower part of the spinal column tend to have less serious complications. Even in severe cases, surgery can be used to stabilise damaged areas and clear any clots pressing on the spinal cord.'

Seeing hope creep into her expression, he raised a pale, freshly-scrubbed finger. 'Before I can confirm anything in your case, though, I need to ascertain the full extent of the trauma. I've ordered neurological tests, a CT scan and MRI.' He gazed at the chart again. 'If the tests confirm the initial diagnosis, I don't expect there'll be any permanent loss of function. And you appear to be in strong physical condition, which will help with the healing. Any return of feeling or movement in your legs within the next few days will be a promising sign.' Lifting his head, he fixed her with an intense gaze. 'However, you should know that full recovery from *any* sort of spinal trauma can take some time.'

Her rush of hope froze. She murmured through tight lips, 'How much time?'

'Weeks, months, possibly even a year or more.' Whipping a pen out of his top pocket, he scribbled notes on her chart. 'Treatment of spinal cord injuries involves a wait-'n-see approach for the most part.'

Her face crumpled. 'A *year* or more?'

'I'll have a better idea of timeframe after I've seen the test results.' He replaced the chart. 'Try not to worry. You're in good hands. For now, the best thing you can do is rest.'

Waking from a broken sleep the following morning, she blinked at the familiar face staring down at her. At her drowsy, 'Margot?' the visitor grasped her raised hand.

'Yes love, I'm here.'

Abbey blinked and licked her lips. 'The fall ... what happened? Is Star alright?' Her eyes darted around the room. 'Is Jesse with you?'

Margot gave a small shake of her head. 'Star's okay but will be out of action for a while. He took some skin off both his front legs and strained his nearside fore. The vet says the strain should heal after a spell, and we're poulticing his legs to prevent them from scarring too badly.' She tapped her chin and murmured absently, 'Though I guess we could bandage him for each performance ... in colours to match the riders' outfits. That could be quite eye-catching.'

'Oh, thank goodness he's going to be alright. I was worried....' Abbey let her voice trail off. They both knew what it was she feared.

'Yeah.' Margot winced. 'Having to put him down, what a disaster that would be.' She blew a breath through pursed lips. 'All those years of training....'

Abbey let her head sink into the pillow and stared at her manager. 'So, what happened?'

'You don't remember?' At Abbey's raised brows Margot said slowly, 'Star stumbled during the finale and caught his foot in the lunge rein. Went nose-first into the dirt, with you still hanging at his side, dangling by one leg after losing your grip on the roller. You were flapping around like a rag doll.' She took a breath and went on. 'At that speed he could've gone rump over nose, but instead he ploughed through the dirt on his front knees – trying his damnedest not to hurt you, I'd reckon. Still, as he floundered you were ... dragged through the dirt and under his back feet.' She shuddered at the memory.

Abbey's eyes took on a faraway look as she recalled snatches of sounds....

Star's startled grunt and laboured breathing, the sensation of falling, gusts of air as sturdy limbs flailed close by her ears, a sharp blow, stab of pain, blackness....

She bit her bottom lip as Margot continued. 'You got pretty knocked about before Star managed to regain his footing. Then he just stood still as stone while people rushed over to help you.' She thumped her thigh with a fist. 'I should've *known* the Clydesdale team that went before us would chop up the ground with their dinner-plate hooves. I could've found another spot for our performance. Though the centre of the ring does give the audience the best view....' After a thoughtful pause, she said, 'We're lucky the horse is going to be okay. And you're lucky to be alive, kiddo.'

'My back....' Abbey swallowed to clear the lump in her throat.

'Yeah.' Margot's expression grew pained. 'I guessed as much when they told me you were in the Spinal Unit.'

'The doctor said it'll be a promising sign if I start to regain feeling in my legs, and ... I think I already am ... a little.'

'I'm pleased for you, love.'

'Margot?'

'The insurance will cover your medical bills.'

'Yeah, but—'

'So you don't need to worry about that.'

Abbey frowned. Why was Margot fast-talking, and why wouldn't she meet her eyes? Grasping the other woman's hand, she said again, 'Margot?'

'I'm ... sorry, kiddo.' The words seemed to catch in Margot's throat.

'It's not your fault, accidents happen.'

'Yes, but...'

'But what?'

'You see, love ... we ... we've got to keep moving.' Margot's gaze roved over the wall behind the bed and travelled down to the floor. 'The team has other commitments, as you know.'

'What are you saying?'

When Margot's eyes finally met hers, Abbey could see the toughness beneath the sympathy, like the steel belt beneath a tyre's rubber tread.

'I'm sorry, kiddo,' she said again, 'but I'm gonna have to leave you here. The team sends wishes for a quick recovery, and asked me to pass on their goodbyes to you.'

Goodbyes?

'You're *leaving* me here?' Abbey tried to blink away her dismay.

Neither of them said anything for a long moment.

Finally Abbey murmured, 'You have to go ... of course ... you have show commitments.' She paused before adding with forced pluck, 'Don't worry, I'll be fine, especially once Jesse gets here.' She gave a nervous titter. 'I'm surprised he's not *already* here, fussing over me.'

Margot looked away.

'And as soon as I'm fit again, I'll join you, wherever you are.'

Margot's perfunctory, 'Sure you will,' held a bleakness that vaporised Abbey's bravado. Before she could say anything more, though, the older woman sprang to her feet and leaned in to kiss her cheek. 'Get well soon and take care, love.' She made to pull her hand from Abbey's grasp only to feel the grip tighten.

Fixing her with entreating eyes, Abbey croaked, 'Where's Jesse? Why isn't he here with you?' She saw Margot's expression harden and went on in a rush. 'He hasn't been to see me that I know of, and I've only heard from him once ... a brief text message....' She bit her lip to stop from blurting that instead of cheering her, his short message, devoid of a kiss sign-off or heart emoticon, left her with a hollow sense of abandonment.

'Jesse did great,' Margot was saying. 'Rushed to your side when you fell. Phoned the Ambos. Sat beside you the whole time, holding your hand....' Her tongue darted over her lips. 'There ... wasn't much more he could do once you were carted away.'

Despite her efforts, tears welled in Abbey's eyes. 'So why hasn't he come to visit me?'

'He never did like hospitals.'

'That's no excuse—'

'Sorry love.' Margot backed away from the bed, tugging her hand free. 'I've ... gotta go.'

Abbey's outstretched arm dropped limply to her side as she watched her manager, the woman she'd come to regard as a second mother, give a flick of fingers in farewell and hurry from the room.

The knot of fear in her stomach swelled like an aggressive, malignant tumour.

I don't care that you hate hospitals, Jesse, just hurry up and get here.

I need you.

3

Sitting in a back corner of the roadhouse, stubbled face in shadow beneath the turned-down brim of his weathered Akubra, Granger took out a hip flask and poured a nip of amber liquid into the cola can in front of him. He was about to take a drink when the roadhouse proprietor turned up the radio and the lyrics of *Travelin' Soldier* drifted from the speakers.

Granger paused with the can half-way to his mouth. He couldn't hear that song without thinking of Laura ... was the *only* time he thought of her now, in fact. She didn't want to end up like the girl in the song, her letter had said, couldn't face months of waiting on a man who may or may not come home. And while he thought she was being a tad dramatic, he didn't blame her for giving up on him. In truth, at that point it hadn't occurred to him to include her in his long-term plans.

The breakup had stung, as most do, but losing Laura soon came a poor second to another, more devastating loss.

Heaving a sigh, he took a long pull from the can and glanced at his mobile phone. It was almost finished charging....

At the approaching thumps of heavy boots, he raised his eyes to see three men in dark oilskins saunter to the counter. One of the men grabbed a major newspaper off the stand and opened it, revealing the headline:

TRICK RIDING TROUPE ENJOYS BUMPER SEASON OF BOOKINGS.
Equestriennes manager Margot Boyce 'quietly optimistic' about the future despite Ekka accident.

The proprietor nodded a greeting at the nearest man. 'Gidday, mate. That'll be one-fifty for the diesel, plus the paper.'

As the man dug a credit card out of his wallet, one of his companions peered into the gloom. 'Who's that?'

All four glanced at Granger, sitting quietly drinking in the corner.

The proprietor bent over the counter to rest on his elbows. 'Been comin' in on and off for a week or so. Youngish bloke, keeps to himself. Spends a bit of money here, so I'm not complainin'.'

Indicating for them to lean in, he lowered his voice further. 'He's one big dude, and handy if I'm any judge of character. I wouldn't be pickin' a fight with him for quids, I'll tell you that for nothin'.' Straightening, he took the card the front man handed him and said conversationally, 'Say, did ya hear about the accident?'

When Granger's eyes swivelled toward the group, he noticed the front man visibly stiffen.

'Local farmer fell off the edge of the escarpment,' the

proprietor went on, launching into the tale without any prompting. 'Horse 'n all.'

'Is that so?'

His customer's disinterested tone didn't deter the proprietor. 'Yeah, in the spot folks call Carson's Ridge, after the kid who died there back in the late sixties.' He gave a sad shake of his head. 'Long drop from there. A *real* long drop.'

Granger saw a glance pass between the other two men while their leader mumbled, 'That's no good.'

'Yeah, a real shame. You know, I always reckoned it was only a matter of time before that ridge claimed another life.' The proprietor finalised the transaction and returned the credit card.

Taking it from him, the man said smoothly, 'Yep, damn shame.'

'I'll say. He was a top bloke. Will be missed around these parts.'

With a dip of his head the man turned and strode out, followed by his two companions. One of them gave an audible snort, which was quickly smothered when it earned him a forbidding scowl.

Granger watched them roar off in a late model Landcruiser, before rising and approaching the counter. 'Which night?'

At the sound of the deep, gravelly voice the proprietor whirled around, to be met with a level gaze from a pair of hooded, smoky-blue eyes. 'Oh, sorry mate, forgot you were there. What did y'say?'

'When did this happen?'

'The accident, you mean?'

Granger nodded.

'One night last week, accordin' to the cops.'

'Where?'

'On *Clearwater Downs,* a local cattle station. Think that cursed ridge forms one of the property's boundaries. Why do ya ask?'

Granger merely bent his head, touched a finger to the brim of his hat, and dissolved once more into the shadows.

'Hey, Abs.'

At the sound of his voice, Abbey's heart gave a thump that reverberated through her whole body. She pressed the phone tighter against her ear. 'Oh ... *finally.*' The words came out in a relieved whoosh. 'I've been leaving messages for days—'

'Yeah,' Jesse cut in, sounding distracted. 'So, how're you doin'?'

'Sore, but improving ... I think.'

'Great. Look, I can't really talk right now, just wanted to check you're doin' okay.'

Only a few words in and he wanted to go already?

'Hang on, Jesse.' She tried to keep her tone light, knowing she mustn't sound needy or accusing. He wouldn't like that ... wouldn't like it at all. 'I can't wait to see you. When can you come visit?'

After a highly-charged pause he said, 'Bit hard at the mo. Lots of bookings thanks to all the attention we got from the Ekka performance.'

Yeah, for which I'm paying the price.

As if he could guess her thoughts he said quickly, 'You know we've moved on?'

'You went too?'

'Of course, the troupe needs me. Someone's gotta handle things behind the scenes, you know that.'

He sounded defensive. Worse, his tone was offhand, like a stranger's.

She swallowed to keep the pleading note out of her voice. 'It's only ... I thought ... you would want to be with me ... seeing's how I'll be in here for a while.'

'Oh sure, I'd *like* to be there, but we have to follow the shows, you know that too. And we're even more short-staffed now you're outta the picture. Mum needs us all to pitch in and go the extra mile.'

Out of the picture.

She clutched at the bedclothes with her free hand. 'Of course, but—' Her voice thickened.

I'll feel stronger if I sit up.

The attempt to haul herself into a seated position left her gasping from an excruciating back spasm. Slumping down again, she punched a limp thigh in frustration, earning herself another stab of pain.

Unaware of her struggles, Jesse drawled, 'Gotta go. I'll call again later, okay?'

'Jesse—' Her voice rose as she battled to keep him on the line.

'Oh, and get better soon, mate.'

Mate.

What he'd call another bloke, or someone who meant nothing to him.

As the phone's screen went blank, she lay staring at it until it blurred into a watery glow. Finally, with a strangled sob, she opened her hand and let the phone drop to the bed.

Life appeared so rosy mere days ago, now here she was,

lying seriously injured in hospital. And the team she had come to think of as family had moved on, taking with them the man who claimed to love her; claimed to have 'fallen head over heels for her at first sight'.

She thought back to the day she arrived in the sprawling, feverish city of Brisbane. Feeling like a hayseed blown a long way from home, she had stayed glued to her seat for the whole trip, as if clinging to what was familiar and safe. Some time after their arrival at the Roma Street terminal, the bus driver had stuck his head inside to stare pointedly at her, the one passenger still on board. She'd come *this* close to telling him she wanted to stay on the bus and make the return journey! Then she recalled how she'd left things at home. That spurred her to rise on unsteady legs and make her hesitant way down the aisle.

The whole troupe was on the bus platform to greet her.

Despite first receiving a disheartening, 'It's *Margot,* Abbey, not *Marg,*' response to her effusive greeting, she found her new manager's otherwise warm welcome a balm to her ragged nerves. But when introduced to the other girls as the troupe's 'new rising star', their forced smiles set her stomach churning again with what Bill would call a 'dose of the collywobbles'. Their expressions hardened further the instant Margot looked away, leaving Abbey in no doubt of her position within the troupe.

The unwelcome interloper.

The revelation had sent her once more digging in her bag for the Greyhound bus timetable. When her shaking fingers failed to locate it, she headed for the doors into the terminal, intending to grab another. That was when she noticed Jesse leaning against a nearby wall, arms crossed, pale blue eyes studying her.

Flashing a toothy grin he'd stepped forward to shake her hand. 'Gidday Abs, welcome to the troupe.'

The warmth in his Aussie drawl had re-ignited her earlier optimism.

'Bet you're keen to get riding?'

Trick riding, the reason she'd taken this bold step.

At her eager, new-kid-on-the-block nod, his smile widened. 'Thought so. I've readied Star for you, back at the complex. He's our best horse so you should feel honoured.'

To her chagrin, his wink made her blush.

Appearing not to notice her rising colour, he pointed to her case, still tightly clutched in both her hands. 'Want me to take your bag?'

After telling herself she could always go home later if it didn't work out; that it wouldn't hurt to let Uncle Bill stew for a while, she had handed over her case with a shy smile.

How much Jesse's kindness had meant to her at that crucial point! It stopped her turning tail, rushing back to the farm, and abandoning her dream of becoming a professional trick rider.

She had tried to tell him later what a help he'd been, only to have him laugh it off. 'It worked, didn't it?' he'd drawled. 'Got me in good with you!'

Lying in her hospital bed, she found herself mulling over those words.

Had his warm welcome been simply a tactic, a way to 'get in good' with her? Had he used it on other newbies too, not just her?

Surely not. We had something special, Jesse and me.

Abbey blinked the insistent moisture from her eyes.

I think the pain in my back is sending me crazy.

She took a calming breath.

Jesse was an integral part of the troupe, they would struggle without having him to care for the horses, gear, vehicles, and everything else, pretty much. And the troupe *had* to move on to meet their commitments in towns along the show circuit. Without a cashed-up backer they lived from performance to performance, with the money Margot received keeping them all clothed, housed, and fed.

They had no choice but to leave.

Abbey took a deep breath.

I'll re-join them once I've recovered, accept Jesse's apology for being a lousy boyfriend, and everything will be okay again.

'I'm seeing definite improvement.' Dr Hughes raised his eyes from the chart. 'And the suspected fracture turned out to be just a contusion. You should be pleased.'

'I am.'

He frowned, thinking she appeared more dejected than pleased. But it wasn't his job to jolly patients, just to fix their injuries.

'Right. Let me know if you feel any discomfort during my examination.'

She made no sound while he manipulated her torso this way and that, not the slightest mew of protest. Inside, she was kicking herself for once more giving in to the impulse to phone Jesse. He hadn't answered ... again. On the odd occasion she did manage to reach him, he always seemed distracted and worry-ingly offhand.

And what was the deal with Uncle Bill? Why wasn't he answering his mobile or the landline either?

'Given your improvement thus far,' Dr Hughes said as he finished his examination, 'and with plenty of rest over the coming weeks, I'm confident you'll make a full recovery.' Replacing her chart, he paused to eye her intently. 'That's provided you take things easy and give the injury time to heal. You may also need continued pain management for a while.'

She gazed up at him hopefully. 'Will I be able to ride again?'

'Ride?'

'Horses.'

He thought a while before answering. 'I should think so, though not until you're completely healed. Of course you will have to take it slowly at first.'

'Oh.' Her face fell.

'I'll look in on you again in a day or so.'

After he left she lay still, willing herself to be patient. Then her mobile chimed, bringing on a rush of hope.

It was dashed by the caller's first words.

'Hey Abs, how're you doing?'

The girlish voice didn't belong to Jesse, Uncle Bill, or Margot. It was familiar though…

Abbey's heart fell. 'Stacey?'

'Yeah. Thought you'd wanna know the team's new star performer – that's me, by the way – *blitzed* the final movement in our latest show. And I didn't make a fool of myself by falling off in the middle of it.' Her tone held the relish of victory made sweeter by long-held jealousy. 'It looks like I've scored us a financial backer too. Everyone's so proud of me, *especially* Jesse.' Her voice took on a triumphant purr. 'Oh, and he gave me a message for you. Wants you to quit calling him all the time. *We're* very busy, with bookings pouring in. He can't spend every waking hour talking on the phone. Anyway, he'll call you,' she added breezily, 'if he gets time.' With a final snigger and an offhand, 'Gotta go, I'm a busy girl. Bye for now,' she ended the call.

Abbey lay once again gaping at a blank screen.

What the—?

Stacey must be lying. She'd always had a 'thing' for Jesse, the whole troupe knew that. They also knew she could be a vindictive little so-'n-so.

One way to be sure.

Abbey punched in Jesse's number and got his voice mail message again.

And again.

And again.

Next she tried Margot's number.

Same story.

It didn't make sense. Margot was devoted to her phone. As the troupe's lifeline, the deliverer of the all-important show bookings, it was never out of reach, *never* ignored. So why wasn't she answering it now?

The furrow in Abbey's brow deepened. Why was it suddenly so hard to get in touch with people? Had she become some sort of pariah? *Damn* caller ID!

Setting her lips in a mulish line, she tried Margot's number again.

And again.

And again.

When her call was eventually answered, she didn't waste time on pleasantries. 'Stacey rang me, Margot.'

'Oh ... right.'

'She said Jesse doesn't want me to call him, and made out like he's kind of ... moved on ... from me.' She gave a nervous laugh. 'Of course I figured that's not true, that she's just being a little b—'

'I can't....'

'Can't what?'

An awkward silence followed.

'Can't what, Margot? Talk about it? Can't say it's not true? What?'

A resigned sigh crackled across the phone connection. 'I'm sorry, Abbey, I can't get involved.'

After another drawn-out silence, Abbey snapped, 'I see. Well then ... I guess there's nothing more to say.' Still she waited for Margot to speak, to tell her of course it wasn't true, that Stacey *was* a vindictive little cow, that Jesse was just exceptionally busy. More than that, she waited for the assurance she was still a valued member of the *Equestriennes* 'family'.

Instead, she heard the click of the call ending.

4

I *fell so easily for the Jesse Boyce charm offensive. Margot's too,
come to think of it. What a gullible fool.*

Abbey scowled at the ceiling.

Everything was rosy while she was celebrated trick rider
Abbey Rae Miller. Different story now her star had crashed and
burned, revealing in its dying embers the true colours of people
she'd come to trust....

*I should've realised that things easily gained could be just as
easily lost.*

The lump rose in her throat again.

But was she reading too much into the Boyces' insensitivity,
expecting too much of them perhaps? After all, the troupe *was*
Margot's bread and butter, and hard-headedness just part of
who she was. She had the ever-affable Jesse to counter-balance
her pragmatism. At least that's how Abbey saw things ... *used* to
see things.

In Bill's opinion, the Boyces were all show and no

substance, motivated always by the prospect of personal gain. Had he been spot-on about them? Was Jesse's relationship with her merely one of convenience?

At the time, it felt grown-up and noble to ignore her uncle's advice and stick up for the Boyces.

Now...?

She swallowed.

Was she overthinking things? Did she just need to give them time? The accident *had* come as a shock to them all.

Another of Bill's sayings sprang to mind. He first recited it to her the day she ran home from school crying, having been ditched by her grade three best friend. Tugging a wrinkled handkerchief from the pocket of his stained work shirt, he lowered himself to one knee and dried her eyes. 'If you love something,' he'd said in his dear, gravelly voice, 'let it go. If it comes back to you, it's yours. If it doesn't, it never was.'

She came to see the truth of it with her rescued strays. LB, who stayed on after being set free to become a feathered sibling; the lame young brumby, who chose to remain at the farm and repay her with more blue ribbons among her Pony Club wins.

'If it comes back, it's yours.'

Would Jesse come back to her, once he realised what he stood to lose?

Would *she* be the one to 'come back', to the troupe?

She swiped a hand across her stinging eyes as a nurse bustled into the room.

'This came for you.'

'Oh?' Abbey took the proffered satchel and frowned.

Who would be mailing her in hospital?

For that matter, who apart from the troupe knew she was in

here? Not even Uncle Bill. She still hadn't been able to reach him.

With a distracted, 'Thanks,' to the nurse's departing back, she gazed at the scrawled address on the satchel.

Margot's handwriting.

Of course.

With hope and dread fighting for dominance inside her, she tore the satchel open. A bundle of mail tumbled onto her lap. The envelopes, some bearing week-old postmarks, were addressed to the modest Bowen Hills apartment complex that housed Margot's troupe.

Abbey wondered idly who the current occupant of her old unit might be. There was no way sharp-nosed Margot would let it sit empty, not after 'sweating blood' to cut a bulk rental deal with the body corporate. 'It's all a question of economies,' she was fond of saying. 'Something you youngsters don't understand yet.'

Pulling a face at the memory, Abbey flicked through the mostly window-faced envelopes. A folded note slipped out of the pile and fluttered to the mattress. It too bore Margot's hurried scrawl. Snatching it up, she unfolded it with unsteady fingers.

Dearest Abbey, it read, *I hope your recovery is going well. We miss you and are all thinking of you here. You'll be pleased to know we scored write-ups in the Chronicle and Courier Mail newspapers after the Toowoomba performance. The publicity sparked more book-ings, and even interest from another potential backer. So things are looking promising.*

At this point the tone of the letter changed, as though Margot had taken a break before writing the rest.

I'm sorry about this kiddo, but you've now exhausted all your leave entitlements. And in light of current budgetary constraints, I've been forced to reassign your apartment.

Big surprise. Abbey gave a scornful huff.

So you'll need to arrange for redirection of your mail, and collection of your car and other personal items at some stage.

Well, at least there wouldn't be a lot to collect. She had learned from a young age to travel light.

A *very* young age.

Her thoughts skittered to the night her bruised and bleeding mother dragged her out of bed, whimpering and clutching her teddy bear. The night a terrified Leah Miller fled with her daughter into the darkness....

For now, we've stashed everything of yours in the garage. It'll be safe till you collect it. We're heading off on tour again soon, so just lock your apartment keys in the garage when you go.

Her top lip curled. Margot didn't even have the guts to face her.

Like mother, like son.

I hope you'll be able to take up performing again one day, Abbey. It would be such a shame to waste all that wonderful talent. You were my favourite prodigy.

Were.

If she needed confirmation her link with *The Equestriennes* was severed, it was there in that one word.

Her jaw clenched.

I wish you all the best for the future, kiddo. Just remember, often when a stable door shuts another one opens.

Your friend, Margot Boyce.

Scrunching the note into a ball, Abbey hurled it at the nearby partition, wincing at the flare of pain that followed the imprudent move.

Don't you mean ex-friend, Margot-not-Marg?

She resisted the urge to bang her head against the pillow, instead making herself lie still until the throbbing in her back subsided. Hot, angry tears tumbled down both sides of her face and soaked into the bed linen.

And to think I was even contemplating a return to the troupe – does my gullibility have no bounds?

The Boyces' 'investment' in her had clearly ended the moment they had nothing more to gain from it.

The ultimate fair-weather friends. Right again, Uncle Bill.

She sniffed, and blinked. Sniffed again.

Uncle Bill.

The farm.

Her spirits lifted.

If she went home she would be welcomed with open arms, regardless of the nature of their parting. A proper, face-to-face reconciliation was long overdue in any case. Facing up to her mistakes would sting, but there was nothing else for it. Anyway, she wouldn't have to openly admit Bill was right to mistrust the Boyces, her tail-between-the-legs return would tell the story for her.

How much time had passed since the day she stormed out, to take up Margot's offer to join the troupe?

After a quick mental calculation, incredulity creased her brow.

No ... not as long as all that, surely?

The months had stretched into years with alarming speed. And while they had kept in touch by phone, neither she nor Bill had mentioned the sore point between them, allowing the rift to remain.

The last time she phoned, he was in the middle of a muster.

Mobile reception wasn't brilliant in the area and even worse down at the cattle yards, so she had promised through the static to ring back on the landline later.

And promptly forgot.

Oh well, she would just have to apologise for being a slacko when she got through to him. Wasn't another of his sayings, 'Loving someone doesn't mean living in their pockets or having to gas-bag every five minutes'?

Her lips softened.

Returning to the pile of mail, she was about to grab another envelope when her mobile rang, making her heart thump.

Was it Jesse? Calling to apologise and explain?

She snatched up the phone and checked the caller ID.

Unknown.

Kicking herself for being a hopeful – make that hope*less* – fool, she pressed ANSWER and snapped, 'Hello?'

An officious male voice, sounding mildly affronted at the brusqueness of her greeting, said, 'I was given this number for a Miss Abbey Rae Miller. May I speak with her please?'

'Speaking.'

'Abbey Rae Miller of *Clearwater Downs* in Central Queensland?'

'Yes, that's my uncle's farm. Who's this? And who gave you my number?'

'My name is Ferris Dolcher, of legal firm Dolcher and Dolcher. I was given your number by....' There were rustling noises. 'Your manager, one Margot Boyce, in response to an urgent telegram sent to your last known address.'

After an anxious pause, Abbey said warily, 'You sent me a telegram?'

'I did, when earlier attempts to contact you proved unsuccessful.' The man cleared his throat before going on. 'Miss Miller, with no other family to advise you, I'm afraid it falls to me to be the bearer of bad news.' He took a breath. 'As his duly appointed legal representative, it is my sad duty to inform you ... of the death of your uncle, William Wallace Miller.'

Abbey's mouth fell open and her heart stopped ... and then banged hard in her chest. 'W-WHAT?'

'Please accept my sincere condolences on your loss.'

'No ... wait.' Her voice rose a notch. 'There must be some mistake.'

Dolcher sighed. 'If only that were the case, but I'm afraid there can be no doubt.' He pronounced each word carefully as though addressing a slow learner. 'Your uncle died unexpectedly, in a tragic accident. I'm terribly sorry, Miss Miller.'

'But....' Her voice sounded strangled. She gulped despite the sudden dryness of her mouth. 'I don't—'

'A memorial service has been arranged,' he went on, sounding eager to get the conversation over with, 'in accordance with Mr Miller's instructions in his Final Will and Testament. It is to be held three days from now. I assume you'll want to attend.'

She managed to croak through stiff lips, 'Yes. Hang on ... no. Wait....' She shook her head, trying to clear it.

He charged on in the same starchy monotone. 'It also falls to me to advise that as his sole beneficiary, you stand to inherit Mr Miller's entire estate; including the property, all its chattels and livestock.'

She shook her head again. And again. And again.

Each shake wider and more ardent than the last.

Uncle Bill ... *dead?*

It can't be true.

She *must've* misunderstood.

Even as she clutched at that thought, all the unanswered phone calls to home flashed across her mind. Her heart swelled and anguish filled her chest and throat, making further speech impossible.

'In regard to your inheritance, documentation outlining the details can be collected from this office, or sent via post if you prefer. I will await your instructions in that regard.' When she didn't respond, Dolcher said with an air of relieved finality, 'Once again, Miss Miller, please accept our condolences. And don't hesitate to contact this office if we can be of further assistance.'

Greeted only with the sound of ragged breathing, he murmured, 'Goodbye, Miss Miller,' and ended the call.

With the mobile still jammed against her ear, Abbey felt pinned under a crushing sense of loss; her body like chilled granite, her face contorted by shock.

Not Uncle Bill, not him.

Please, let it be someone else, anyone else. PLEASE. He's all I have left....

The years fell away, and she was once again the teary-eyed, bewildered toddler clinging to her mother's hand on Bill's doorstep. Her uncle had been a total stranger then. But it had felt so good, so *right,* to be wrapped in his strong arms and carried inside the farmhouse. She recalled breathing in his wood-smoke scent and listening to his gravelly voice soothing her traumatised mother.

And then she was a giggling six-year-old being piggy-backed around the house, while her mount, Bill, warbled the chorus of *My Girl Bill.* That was the song her mother Leah sang to him whenever she thought he was becoming too possessive of his young niece. It had been *their* song, the three of them ... until three became two.

Bill sang it for the last time at Leah's bedside the day she died, softly so only she and Abbey could hear. And after Leah slipped away he held his niece at arm's length, looked intently into her face, and promised that no matter what, she would always be his girl.

I'm still your girl, Bill.

A low moan escaped her as her whole body convulsed in an intense wave of grief. She tried to swallow but her throat was too tight to let more than ragged breaths past. The envelope in her hand blurred in front of her eyes. She made a fist, scrunching the envelope in it, uncaring when her fingernails dug into her palms.

A tortured moment later, she opened her hand and let the crumpled correspondence fall.

I'm so sorry, Uncle Bill, for turning my back on you and the farm. Please give me a chance to tell you that in person; to tell you how much I love you.

Please be alive.

Please.

When she curled herself into a tight ball, the resulting blast of back pain was nothing compared to the anguish in her heart. Dragging the bedclothes over her head, she buried her drowning face in the pillow.

The proprietor of the Gympie motel sat at the reception desk, one hand under his grey-stubbled chin, a cup of congealing coffee at his elbow. When the local news came on the old-fashioned, small-screen TV tucked beneath the overhanging counter, he turned up the volume.

'A Queensland trick riding troupe has won the honour of opening the new *Australiana Extravaganza* show on the Gold Coast,' a young reporter announced. 'I'm here with troupe manager of *The Equestriennes*, Margot Boyce.'

The camera panned to a heavily made-up Margot who beamed, revealing candy-pink lipstick-smudged teeth. Leaning in to make sure she was in the shot, she gushed, 'We're over the moon at being selected as the opening act for such a prestigious show.' Her smile widened and she fluttered mascara-laden lashes at the lens. 'Over the moon, and so very, *very* honoured.'

When a battered four wheel drive rattled to a stop outside the office, the proprietor's expression brightened and he turned down the volume on the TV.

At last, a late evening check-in to relieve the boredom.

He watched as a dark-haired, petite young woman in fitted jeans, checked shirt, and riding boots stepped down from the dusty dual-cab ute. Nice looking in a girl-next-door kinda way, her lightly freckled face when she moved under the light was clouded, her cheeks hollow.

He ran his eyes over the rest of her. She had an athletic figure but her movements were constrained, careful. Recently injured, perhaps? Maybe a sports injury? The bad ones could be debilitating; take that bloke in the wheelchair with the stomach-turning twisted limbs. A chatty type, he had been happy to share all the gory details of his cycling accident....

The proprietor squirmed at the memory and focused his attention on the ute.

No one else in there that he could see.

If indeed travelling alone, the young woman might be keen

for a chat. From the looks of things, she was bound to have a story, maybe more than one. Could make for an interesting interval in an otherwise dull evening, if she were the talkative type.

Sitting straighter in his seat, the proprietor watched her compose herself before entering the office. When she stood before him, he saw the stricken, closed-off look in her darkly-lashed grey eyes.

No, this pretty country girl didn't look the type to bare her soul to a stranger. And he'd take an odds-on bet she just wanted to break a journey for one night. With a resigned headshake, he flicked the motel register open to a new page.

'Hello there, love. You wantin' a room?'

5

The waning sun cast long shadows over the landscape as Granger trekked back to camp. After emptying his bulging backpack he loaded the supplies into his hanging camp cupboard, alongside the lightweight cooking, eating and drinking utensils. Dumping his backpack under the camouflage-coloured tarp strung adeptly between trees, he paused to take stock of the still, clear evening.

Good time for a hunt.

Tinned baked beans, tuna, and Spam did the job as staples, but nothing could beat fresh meat. And if he'd learned anything about surviving on the land, it was to conserve rations whenever he could.

Among its other benefits, this campsite offered a bountiful supply of game within easy reach – rabbits grown plump on the station's improved pastures. Although some farmers opted to use baits to control the declared pests, that wasn't the case here, luckily.

He swept a glance over his bivouac. Not every location provided such effective shelter or easy access to potable water. Five Mile Creek was just over the crest, its water clear and sweet even before he ran it through the filtering jug in his kit. And he had the place pretty much to himself, could even belt out some songs without anyone hearing.

Dipping his head beneath the tarp, he moved to the rear of the covered area to kneel in front of a dense shrub. After a quick check of his surroundings, he reached under the foliage to pull out a rolled khaki bundle. Unwrapping the canvas folds, he removed his current hunting weapon of choice, a compact crossbow. Light and easy to carry thanks to its collapsible carbon-fibre construction, the bow perfectly suited long-distance hiking. It was also effective, and didn't need a silencer.

Moving to his backpack he took out a pair of night-vision goggles. Once geared up, he set off in the direction of the home-stead. He had earlier scoped out a sizeable warren over that way, where the tree line met the open paddocks. By now, the first of his well-rested and adventurous prey would be emerging. He licked his lips, picturing a roast crackling to golden-brown on a spit over his campfire.

'Feed the man meat,' as his father used to say.

Jim Granger, gentleman grazier, staunch traditionalist ... felled by his own, big heart.

Not the time for reminiscing.

Blowing a drawn-out breath, Granger lengthened his stride. Twenty metres from the warren he dropped to crawl on his belly. When he reached the edge of the tree line he could see rabbits already frolicking around the entrance of the warren. After loading a bolt in the crossbow, he settled in to wait for the right moment to strike.

The closest rabbit, a plump young buck, thumped the ground with its oversized back feet. Granger waited until it relaxed and began preening, before focusing his scope's crosshairs on its furry chest. He slowed his breathing, preparing to take the shot, when the rabbit's head suddenly bobbed up, ears pricked. The animal stretched to its full height to see over the tall grass, appearing to stare right at him.

Had his quarry made him?

Keeping his movements slight, Granger wet the tip of a finger and held it out.

Definitely down-wind, and over fifteen metres from his prey. No way the rabbit could smell him.

Then he felt them, tremors through the ground. The drumming vibrations increased, followed by sounds.

He glanced back at the warren. The rabbits had gone.

Damn.

Following their lead, he hunkered down as the horses thundered past in the gloom, spooking the cattle and sending them in all directions as they went.

Three riders again, heading for the homestead.

Overcome with a sense of déjà vu, Granger removed the bolt from the crossbow and rose from his hiding spot. On impulse, he slipped on his night vision goggles and set off after the riders.

His energy-efficient, long-legged lope moved him swiftly and surely over the uneven terrain. As he approached the homestead he saw a light flare on the porch. It took the shape of a hurricane lamp. Instead of being set in place, the glowing lamp moved lengthways along the veranda and back again.

As he drew nearer, keeping to the shadows, Granger heard ominous splashing sounds, accompanied by a distinctive odour.

In the lamp's light he glimpsed the vandal's face. The man was smirking as he shook the last drops from a kerosene tin over the veranda floorboards. Still holding the lamp in his other hand he gave a coarse laugh, tossed the tin to the side, and leaped off the porch onto his wild-eyed horse.

Amid hoots from his two mates he yelled, 'Burn, baby, burn!' and raised the lamp above his head.

In that instant, a menacing hiss through the air preceded a metallic *thwhack!*

The lamp exploded in the man's hand, spraying him in burning kerosene. His shocked bellow rose above the shouts of his two companions as the shattered lamp hit the ground in a ball of fire, a crossbow bolt lodged in what remained of its metal base.

The man's horse squealed and reared as its rider frantically slapped his burning sleeve to douse the flames. The other two horses snorted in fear, spinning on their hooves as their riders peered into the blackness, straining to catch a glimpse of their attacker.

When one of the men reached for the rifle in his saddle's leather scabbard, another bolt slammed into the rifle's timber stock. With a yelp he jerked his hand away as his horse shied violently, almost unseating him.

Granger lowered the crossbow and crouched in the darkness, one hand wrapped around the hilt of the hunting knife strapped to his right calf. He withdrew his hand only after the third rider reefed his horse's head around and dug his heels into its side, yelling, 'Come on, let's go!'

As all three pounded away, Granger stepped out of the shadows and kicked dirt over the remaining flames. After watching the riders' dark silhouettes disappear into the blackness, he stood listening as the night-time sounds resurfaced; the odd grassy rustle, chirps of crickets, and the distant eerie wail of curlews. As his adrenaline level dropped to normal, he gave a grunt and turned to climb the homestead's front stairs. Perching on the top step he leaned against the railing, settling in to stay a while in case the horsemen returned for another attempt.

His head swivelled at a noise close by, and he saw a dark shape emerge from the shadows and hug the ground as it approached. Crawling on its belly toward him, the dog whimpered and wagged its tail hopefully.

At his gentle, 'Gidday muttly,' and click of fingers, the dog leaped to its feet and bounded to him. Lifting his head away from the eagerly licking pink tongue, Granger murmured, 'Alright, alright. Settle down.' Running a hand over its body, he could feel ribs beneath the fur. 'You're a bit skinny, mate. You live here or just visiting? Either way, you picked a bad night to be around. There are mongrels afoot.'

He glanced behind at the house. 'Who'd want to burn such a great old place?' Beside him, the wriggling dog dropped to its belly and lay its front paws across his lap, whining with delight when he scratched its head. 'But then mongrels will be mongrels, especially in a pack. Lucky you're a loner, boy. There's a lot to be said for keeping to yourself.'

They stayed that way a long time, the dog contentedly wagging its tail while the man stroked its dark head.

A while later, with a final pat and a gruff, 'Seeya, mate,' Granger pushed the dog to the side and rose to his feet. Although it gave a soft whine, the dog didn't attempt to follow as he descended the stairs and strode off.

On the way back to camp he found the paddock gates

hanging open, chain fasteners dangling from the posts. Another legacy of the three unwelcome visitors, no doubt.

With his father's growled admonition, 'Farm gates are there for a reason, boys, and good country folk don't leave 'em hanging open,' ringing in his ears, he made sure to close all the gates behind him.

After fastening the last chain, he looked back with an irate grunt.

'Good country folk' also don't try to torch what is obviously someone's home.

Abbey blinked hard and pulled her ute to a stop in the gateway, sending a cloud of dust into the air.

No more tears. I've cried enough.

She blew a breath through pursed lips. Action and distance hadn't provided the hoped-for respite. No matter how far or fast she ran from it, grief dogged her every move, every thought, every impulse. If she'd only had the chance to say a proper goodbye....

Despite chafing at being stuck in a hospital bed, she hadn't blamed Dr Hughes for predicting dire, life-altering outcomes if she discharged herself too soon; he was only doing his job. She could still see his appalled expression when she let slip how long it would take her to drive home after collecting her gear from the Bowen Hills complex.

'A *six* hour drive on your own, after first loading up the car with your possessions?' He'd stared at her aghast, before collecting himself to say stiffly, 'Of course it's your choice, Miss Miller. However, if you go against my advice, I will not be held responsible for the consequences. You will also cease to be a patient of mine.'

In spite of his grim warnings she was still determined to go, until a particularly tough physiotherapy session left her virtually incapacitated for two days.

That was from a *therapy* session. What repercussions could she expect from *underestimating* her injuries?

Although Dr Hughes may have been exaggerating a little, what if her back *did* seize up again while she was on the road, leaving her stuck in the middle of nowhere? And even if she made it to the farm, what if she was unable to do anything except lie around swallowing pain killers every four hours while the farm deteriorated around her?

Choosing what Dr Hughes called the 'wisest and safest' option had felt like admitting defeat, and left her flattened and despondent. The day of the funeral, when she should've been there, paying her respects to Uncle Bill, was the worst. For those dreadful twenty-four hours, all she could do was submit to therapy, try not to fret, wish like hell she could be prescribed something to ease her *emotional* pain, and count the days until she could return home.

The rattle of the Hilux's idling diesel engine roused her from her musings. While irritating, the noise was preferable to the sense of loss and loneliness that silence brought on. She swiped the back of a hand across her eyes and raised her head to blink through the windscreen. In front of the ute's grille, the metal entrance gate emerged from the settling dust. Pushed inward, it hung askew with the punched steel sign bearing the station's name dangling by one tenacious screw. The heavy chain meant to keep the gate closed lay in the dirt, obviously where it fell when the gate was pushed in.

She frowned.

Who would've done that?

Bill was a stickler for keeping the gate shut, to stop his stock from wandering onto the road and to keep the farm entrance looking neat. The gate hanging skewwhiff like that gave a down-at-heel impression he wouldn't have tolerated for a second.

Crossing her arms over the steering wheel, she steeled herself to gaze in at the old homestead, the only real home she'd ever known.

It looked much like it did when she left, but with an unfamiliar air of abandonment hanging over it.

Abandonment, shaping up to be her word of the year after scoring three out of three.

Jesse's coldheartedness toward her – straight out, callous abandonment.

Margot's hard-nosed, so-called 'support' during her crisis – ultimately, abandonment.

What she herself had previously dished up to Uncle Bill – abandonment.

And now, being left alone in the world by the loss of her remaining family member – the worst abandonment of all.

Make that four out of four.

A surge of frustrated anger curdled the misery entrenched in her belly, making bile rise in her throat. She banged her forehead on her arms.

And thanks to my own idiocy, it was left to some lawyer to give me the news about Uncle Bill.

She thumped the steering wheel with a fist.

How could I have been so stupid, to let my prepaid mobile run out so I had to get a new number, and then forget to advise all my contacts?

Her face twisted.

Damn. Damn. DAMN.

Slumping in the car seat, she stared across the house paddock at the aged Queenslander, her home.

After relocating it there from a remote outback station, Bill devoted years to restoring the homestead to its former glory. He completed the painstaking work not long before she and her mother arrived. In the years since, the burning summer sun, savage storms and drenching wet seasons had taken their toll, fading the house's once federation-green roof to a dusty khaki.

As she watched, a willy-willy swirled its gritty way across the front of the house yard, its circular gusts making the grey-green canopy of the ghost gum sway. She recalled insisting the tree be planted close to the house, despite Bill's protests about 'leaf mess in the gutters'. The graceful, silver-barked gum, grown taller in her absence, now dutifully cast welcome shade on the veranda outside her bedroom.

Her gaze travelled to the ground beneath the tree, and LB's grave.

LB.

Her first experience of loving something other than her mother and uncle.

Gero had presented her with the baby sparrow after rescuing the little thing from the floor of the local mechanic's workshop.

'Fell out'the nest, or was kicked out of it,' he'd informed her. 'Saw the nest, way up in the rafters. No way to get 'er back in it.' The plastic ice cream container he handed Abbey, filled with cushioning tissues, held a tiny brown blob. 'Couldn't leave 'er there, it would'a been lights out under some oaf's boot.'

A wistful smile tugged at Abbey's mouth. As a child she'd shared so many adventures, real and imagined, with the little bird. The kind of adventures she would've shared with a sister, if she had one. Her school friends ribbed her, saying she had a 'dirty sprag' or 'flying rodent' for a pet, but she didn't care. To her, LB was her playmate, confidant, and best friend, which was why she was so heartbroken when LB died.

Of old age, Gero assured her. 'She had a good innings for a lil' sparra,' he'd said gruffly, putting a calloused hand on Abbey's shoulder. 'Lived way longer than she would'a done in the wild. You were a good mum to her. Was just her time.'

His niece's despondency at losing her beloved pet had also tugged at Bill's heart, prompting him to suggest they hold a memorial. Gero was invited, naturally, being LB's original saviour, Abbey's quasi-uncle, Bill's best mate, and someone who could be relied upon to be discreet. Bill hoped his down-to-earth cow cocky mates wouldn't get wind of the sparrow's memorial service, or he'd never live it down.

Abbey recalled Gero coming to the memorial dressed in a dark suit, what he called his 'farewellin' dungers'. He had walked sombrely toward the little gathering clutching a loose bouquet of freshly picked native flowers. The bright red bottle-brush and delicate cream-and-gold grevillea blooms bobbed their nectar-filled heads, as though in a mark of respect.

Taking his place beside Abbey in the shade of the tree, he'd put an arm around her heaving shoulders during Bill's slightly off-key rendition of Garfunkel's *Bright Eyes*. After the song ended, the two men watched in respectful silence as a teary Abbey lowered the tiny corpse, wrapped in a handkerchief clumsily embroidered with the initials L and B, into the hole Bill had dug under Abbey's ghost gum.

LB's tree.

Swallowing, Abbey let her glance travel to the front veranda. Beneath it, the Guinea grass – 'damn *Megathyrsus maximus*' Bill called the encroaching growth when in the presence of young ears – had grown waist-high around the stumps. Above the waving blades of grass, peeling white paint on the more exposed veranda railings had bared the old timber to the sun, rain, and dust, weathering it to a silvergrey.

She recalled sitting beside him in paint-daubed dungarees while he sanded and painted the railings. Even when quite young she'd sat in rapt silence as he recited poems by Banjo Patterson, and yarned about the 'old days' of pioneers and early settlers. The memory brought a flood of warmth ... followed an instant later by the familiar tightening in her chest.

When her ears caught a melodious warble from on high, she peered into the canopy of LB's tree, searching for a glimpse of black and white. She spied the magpie as it began another lyrical verse, neck stretched upward to carol its sweet melody into the air.

Her mother's favourite birdsong....

As if of its own volition her gaze slid to the ground on the tree's sunny side, where the small headstone sat within its curved, wrought iron fence.

Leah Miller's final resting place.

The stay on her brother's farm was to be merely a stop-gap for her and Abbey, until Leah found their next bolthole. Instead, *Clearwater Downs* turned out to be the refuge she had longed for during the years of abuse. The loving home she always wanted for her daughter. The one place she never had to leave.

Abbey's breath caught as she glimpsed something new.

Another headstone, beside her mother's grave.

She blinked and lowered her gaze.

At least when I lost Mum I had you, Uncle Bill. Now you're gone too, entrusting me with your beloved farm....

Shame, regret, and a crushing sense of loss squeezed her heart. Biting her lip to keep it from trembling, she dug a set of keys out of the bulging envelope on the passenger's seat beside her. In addition to the keys, the envelope contained a bundle of documentation that bore the ostentatious Dolcher and Dolcher letterhead and brimmed with legalese.

Calling at the lawyer's office on her way to the farm, she had met with Ferris Dolcher, who turned out to be as officious in person as he was on the phone.

After being informed, in his respectful monotone, of the details of Bill's death, Abbey could envisage the house being just how her uncle left it the morning of his last day. She glanced at it again, careful to keep her eyes averted from the grave sites. Still, the knots in her stomach tightened and she took a gulp of air.

I can't do this ... not yet.

Dropping the keys into the console, she threw the ute into gear and reversed in a spray of gravel, ignoring the pangs of self-reproach that rose above the grief.

I need to grab some supplies from town anyway.

6

Rattling into Weerong, Abbey noted with some relief that nothing much had changed in town. Hay from passing trucks littered the streets, and the main noticeboard dripped with the usual assortment of FOR SALE, LOST AND FOUND, and BAITING PROGRAMME notices. The letter P was still missing from the 'Supermarket' sign, perpetuating the long-held 'sewermarket' joke.

The tiny township, pronounced 'We-were-wrong' by its more embittered residents, serviced the smattering of land-holders scattered throughout the district. In addition to the highway roadhouse a few kilometres east of it, the town offered a small supermarket-come-newsagency-come-post office-come-banking agency; a petrol station and mechanic's workshop; hotel; combined produce store, saddlery and western outfitter; and a cute café kept going by the patronage of local womenfolk and occasional tourists. The nearest school and medical facilities were in Miriam Vale, though Weerong boasted its own fire station, manned mostly by volunteers, and a one-cop police station.

Abbey parked outside the supermarket and turned off the ignition. As she sat indulging in nostalgia, her gaze fell on a familiar figure weaving up the street in her direction.

Gerry Alhurst.

As he drew closer she heard him muttering to himself, and glanced at her watch. It was way too early in the day to be under the weather, especially for someone with Gero's history.

Climbing down from the ute, she stood smiling at the old man as he made his laborious way toward her.

Gero, or 'Chook' as he was known around town, was easily recognised by his shuffling gait and the bent-brimmed, stained Akubra hat he wore no matter the weather. To Abbey, the grizzled, blunt, and somewhat charm-challenged Gero was like a grey-muzzled cattle dog, loyal to a fault but inclined to nip at heels. She also knew him to be a warm-hearted, honest, and knowledgeable true man of the land.

Some less tolerant townsfolk, thinking an elderly bloke who lived with only chickens for company had to be more than a little odd, nicknamed him 'Gero the Dero'. It didn't help that a few of them could recall his younger, wilder days.

A time he appeared intent on repeating.

Her smile faltered as his bleary eyes settled on her. One of them sagged to the side as did that corner of his mouth, legacies of a series of strokes.

'Abbey? Lil' Abbey Miller?' He stumbled to a halt and stood swaying in the middle of the road, his customary flannel shirt unbuttoned to reveal a navy singlet over a grey-haired chest. His elastic-waisted cotton pants drooped dangerously to one side, making Abbey's fingers itch to hitch them up.

'Hey, Uncle Gero.' He'd always been like family to her, even though they weren't actually related. 'Yeah, it's me.'

'Lil' Abbey ... well I'll be.' He shook his head and stumbled forward, somehow managing to keep his feet. 'You've – hic! – come 'ome at last. Better late than never I 'spose.' To Abbey's relief, he accompanied the words with a clumsy hitch of his pants, just as a spotlight and antenna-festooned ute roared past with a blast of its horn.

Growling, 'Damn wannabe cowboys,' in the vehicle's general direction, Gero lurched closer to peer into Abbey's face. 'Y'got prettier too,' he slurred. 'Always knew you'd be a looker.'

'Um ... thanks.' Screwing up her nose, she waved a hand in the air to disperse his alcohol-soaked breath.

The wrinkles in his brow deepened as he rambled on. 'Wasted on that loser bloke ... whatshisname? Boyd? Boyce?' When Abbey's gaze slid away he shook his head. 'Never mind, I'll ask me ol'mate Bill. His memory's better than mine.' Gero's puzzled look morphed into one of raw sorrow. His chest heaved and his voice broke as he muttered, 'Don't reckon I'll get an answer though....'

A cattle truck and then another ute passed them with friendly toots, their occupants smiling and waving at Abbey. She rustled up a smile in response.

Well, the word's out now. Abbey Miller is back in town.

Turning to Gero she said gently, 'C'mon old fella, let's get off the road.'

He grinned at her, a fool's grin that revealed stained, gappy teeth. 'Right-o, Girlie, lead the way.'

Taking him by a leathery arm, she guided him to the bench seat in front of the supermarket. Once he was settled she plonked down beside him.

'What's going on with you, Uncle Gero?'

He blinked unfocused, heavy-lidded eyes at her. 'What d'ya mean?'

'It's a bit early to be in the grip of the grape isn't it? Don't tell me you've fallen off the wagon?' She knew better than to use the terms 'drunk' or 'alcoholic' in his hearing. To do so almost guaranteed a shouting match when he was in this condition.

The old man managed a one-sided scowl. 'Sometimes a man – hic! – needs a drink. 'N this here's one-a them times.' A shadow crossed his face and he muttered, 'Lost me best mate, I 'ave. Got nobody now ... nobody.'

'What about the girls? You still have them.'

At the mention of his beloved chickens his face fell further. 'Gonna lose 'em too,' he spat, 'thanks to the bloody *bank*.' He waved a gnarled, unsteady finger at the supermarket-come bank agency building.

'And you have me. The bank can't take that away from you.'

'You, Girlie?' When his mocking snort sent a glob of snot onto the footpath between his booted feet, he had the grace to look contrite. Dragging the back of a shaky hand across his nose, he sniffed. ''N how long are *you* 'ere for, eh? Five minutes? Just long enough to sell the farm 'n head back to the city, I'll bet.'

Abbey opened her mouth, frowned, and closed it again.

'Might take'ya a while t'find a buyer, though. Life on the land's gettin' tougher 'n people are gettin' scareder.' Gero didn't seem to notice her silence. He went on rambling about what he'd like to do to the bank manager, how much he missed his 'old mate', and the two things in life no man can avoid – death and taxes.

She was only half listening when he once more fixed her with watery eyes and slurred, 'Y'know what Weerong means?'

She did, but let him tell her again.

'Abo word, means "place of rest".' He paused, thoughtful. 'Fittin' I guess, considerin' this is your mother's restin' place, and now me ol'mate's as well. Mine too, one day soon.' His face twisted. 'That's if the new owner honours Bill's promise to me a'course. Like as not to renege on the deal 'n leave my remains to rot in a storeroom somewheres.'

Seeing a tear follow the wrinkles to his grizzled chin, Abbey said in a thick voice, 'How about I take you home? After I grab some bread and milk.'

When he gave a glum nod and let his chin fall to his chest, she got to her feet and stood gazing down at him for a long, thoughtful moment, before hurrying into the supermarket.

The moment she stepped through the doors she was greeted with a call of, 'Abbey!' from one of the three checkouts. 'That you, girl?'

'Gidday Marion. Yeah, it's me.' She gave the store manager a smiling wave and kept going, hoping that might satisfy her. When she saw the stocky, sharp-eyed woman sign with an urgent flap of hands for one of the casuals to replace her on the checkout, Abbey steeled herself for what was coming.

Not that she disliked generous, warm-hearted Marion Bolton. The gregarious woman was a pillar of Weerong society, had been like a second mother to her and every kid in town, and could always tell if someone was doing it tough. All the same, Abbey would've liked to settle in before facing up to the obligatory grilling.

No chance of that now.

'Abbey!' As she trotted toward her, Marion spotted Gero

snoozing on the bench outside and frowned. After pulling Abbey into a warm hug followed by the usual good-to-see-you-back-here, it's-been-too-long, you-look-a-bit-thin exchanges, she looked out at Gero and clicked her tongue. 'Poor old Chook, back to 'is old tricks. Dry for decades, now this.' She shook her head.

'Since ... Bill?'

Marion nodded. 'Went on a bender after the service, which is understandable I guess. He *had* just lost his best mate. But then he turned 'round and did it again, and again, 'til now it's every coupl'a days.' The disapproving look settled once more on her round, good-natured face. 'Wish Bob would stop servin' him.' She sighed. 'But I 'spose he's gotta make a crust too, like the rest of us.'

Abbey nodded. Everyone knew that while publican Bob Wellings wasn't a bad man, money rated higher than perhaps it should on his list of priorities. It was a more common failing than she'd realised ... until the Boyces shattered her illusions.

She took care to lighten her expression as Marion once more fixed sympathetic eyes on her. 'So sorry about your uncle, love,' she said gently. 'Bill was a real good'un.'

'Thanks.' Even that one word held a note of bitter regret not lost on the other woman.

She put a comforting hand on Abbey's arm. 'Too bad you had to miss the funeral. Heard you were laid up in hospital.'

Abbey nodded again, not trusting herself to speak.

'You all better now?' Gazing into her face, Marion clucked. 'You're very pale, love. And those dark circles around your eyes....' In the strained silence that followed she blustered, 'A stay in hospital will do that to a person. Fresh country air and sunshine will see you bounce back in no time, and we have plenty of both out here, as you know.' She beamed and gave Abbey's chin a fond tweak. 'You got even prettier while you were away.' Glancing down, she took Abbey's left hand in both hers and tapped the ring finger. 'I'm surprised there's no diamond here yet.'

When Abbey merely blinked, swallowed, and tugged her hand free, consternation flooded Marion's face. 'Sorry, love. Didn't mean to upset you.' She let her arms drop to her sides and charged on. 'How long you home for?'

Abbey cleared her throat. 'Not sure.'

'Heard Bill left the farm to you, and rightly so. You were a daughter to him in every way but one. He also knew you'd do right by the place. A wise old coot, that uncle of yours. He'll be sorely missed around here, that's for certain.' Marion heaved a sigh before saying briskly, 'Anyway, best let you get on. It's good to have you home, love.' She gave Abbey's arm a final squeeze. 'If you need anything, you know where to find us.'

'Thanks Marion.'

Abbey watched her stride back to the checkout calling gidday to other customers along the way. She meant well, but the intrusion in her personal affairs was something Abbey couldn't handle right now.

As she moved down the aisles toward the shelves of bread and the dairy chiller, Abbey suspected that wouldn't be the end of the welcome home greetings. And she was right. It seemed every turn brought a fresh round, leaving her wishing for the big city anonymity that had felt so foreign at first.

Until it became the norm.

7

When she finally stepped out of the store loaded with bags, she found Gero slumped along the bench, head dangling over the end, totally out to it. She dumped her groceries in the ute before rousing him, which took some effort. Thankfully a passer-by helped her load him into the passenger seat.

It was a quiet trip to Gero's place, apart from the engine and road noise, the old man's loud snoring, and the occasional thuds when they hit a bump and his head connected with the window.

Abbey was glad of the break from having to make conversation.

When they arrived at the small parcel of land Gero called his Shangri-La, just over the southern boundary of *Clearwater Downs,* she nosed the ute close to the slab hut. After turning off the engine, she reached across the cabin to give him a gentle shake. 'C'mon Gero, you're home.'

No response.

She shook him again, more vigorously.

'Wha?' He lifted his head, wheezed, and blinked out the window. 'Oh ... right.' He gave a cough and ran his tongue over his dry lips.

Abbey already had her door open. With a cheerful, 'Let's get you inside,' she jumped down from the ute.

When she came around to the passenger side to help him out he waved her away, growling, 'I'm not an invalid,' while fumbling with the door handle. After getting it open, he part-slid, part-tumbled out the door, barely managing to keep his feet when he hit the ground. The jolt seemed to unnerve him, for he accepted her steadying hand and let her lead him to the hut's front door. Rummaging in a shirt pocket for the keys, he grumbled, 'Don't know why I bother lockin' up the joint. Not gonna be mine for much longer.'

He seemed more rational so she risked asking, 'Is the bank foreclosing?' and received a brusque nod in reply. 'Soon?'

Another nod.

Thinking the only remarkable thing was that, all things considered, it had taken the bank so long to act, she followed him into the hut without comment. Once inside she was pleas-antly surprised to find the place as neat and clean as she remembered.

Flourishing potted herbs in metal jam tins lined the kitchen shelves and sat greenly on each window sill. They scented the waft of breeze through the place with their fresh, earthy aromas. A large wicker basket on the counter held a mound of brown eggs, the latest offerings from the well cared-for hens she could hear clucking and scratching around outside.

The basic sink area was clear of dishes and appeared

scrubbed clean, as did the kitchen table with its mismatched chairs. The threadbare sofa near the fireplace sat squarely on three legs and one pile of folded newspapers. On either side of it, two wing chairs sported embroidered antimacassars over their once chintzy, now rubbed-bare, fabric headrests. In front of the chairs, the roughly-made coffee table was stacked high with books on horticulture, herbalism, and permaculture.

Yep, the hut looked the same.

At a sound from outside she went to the lounge room window, to gaze across the spacious and rather grand chook run to the orchard. The rows of citrus, nut, mango, tropical peach, and mulberry trees were all weighed down with blossoms or ripening fruit. The old man had a green thumb, that was for sure. It was a shame he couldn't make enough money selling his produce to meet the mortgage repayments. Of course boozing away a lot of it didn't help....

Frowning, she turned from the window and noticed something fluttering in the dead coals of the fireplace. It was a partially burnt piece of paper, its charred edges catching the breeze. She gave an indulgent head shake.

Knowing Gero, it was probably all that was left of a final notice from the bank.

From in the kitchen she heard him rattling around, muttering about making a pot of tea.

'I'll do it, Gero. Why don't you sit down?' The words were barely out of her mouth when the old man staggered to the side, turning his ankle. His hands flailed helplessly as he crashed to the floor, banging his head against the counter's edge on the way down. With a cry of, 'Gero!' she rushed to kneel by his side. 'Are you okay?'

Pushing himself unsteadily into a sitting position, he

rubbed his temple with a shaking hand. 'I'm alright ... don't fuss. Lost me footin' is all.'

She sat back to stare anxiously at him. He'd have another doozy of a bruise from that tumble, possibly a twisted ankle as well. Peering closer she saw shadows of other bruises, on his cheek and jaw. By the looks of it, he'd taken a few falls in recent days.

No way she could leave him on his own in that condition. She'd just have to put the milk she'd bought in his fridge, and stay the night.

Someone has to keep an eye on the poor old chap 'til he sobers up, and I guess I'm the someone.

A wave of relief washed over her at the thought of not returning to the farm that day.

I'm not putting off going home, she told herself sternly. *I'm not. I just ... couldn't live with myself if I left Gero alone and something bad happened to him.*

Anyway, I'm only doing what Bill would do.

If he were here.

Abbey woke the next morning to the smell of toast and the roll and gurgle of the boiling kettle. A dark figure blocked the early sunlight slanting through the kitchen window and a voice said gruffly, 'Mornin' Girlie.'

She yawned and rubbed her eyes. 'Morning.' Tossing aside the bedclothes, she sat up carefully to perch on the edge of the sofa, stretching her back and combing fingers through her tousled hair.

'I see you found a blanket and pillow for y'self.'

She nodded. Gero crashed almost before she could get him into bed the evening before, leaving her rummaging in an old wardrobe for some bed linen. Although sporting broken threads and smelling strongly of moth balls, the cotton waffle blanket she found felt clean. And while the pillow's lumpy form possessed scant more substance than its equally camphor-imbued pillowcase, she'd been sufficiently weary for none of that to matter.

'Breakfast'll be ready soon.' As he spoke, Gero plonked a bowl on the table and twitched an eyebrow at her. 'There was movement at the station,' he recited, 'for the prunes had passed around.'

Glancing at the dark, glossy fruit in the bowl, Abbey gave an amused snort. 'Still quoting Banjo Patterson I see. You can't be feeling too bad, then.' Greeted with a noncommittal grunt, she watched him moving around the kitchen. 'Looks like your ankle's okay this morning.' She rose to her feet and popped a prune in her mouth. 'What about your head?'

When the kettle began a high-pitched whistle he took it off the stove, saying stiffly, 'My head's fine.' He proceeded to pour the boiling water into a dented metal teapot that looked more geriatric than its owner. 'Thanks for askin'.'

She moved closer to stare into his face and said grimly, 'I thought as much. You have a nice egg there.' When she made to put a finger to the colouring lump on his temple, he jerked his head away.

'Don't fuss.' As though regretting the sharp words, he added more calmly, 'I've 'ad worse.'

'I *bet* you have.' She narrowed her eyes at him. 'Why, Gero? Why go back on the booze after—'

Snarling, 'Don't start,' he rounded on her. 'What would you

67

know about anythin', girl? You haven't been around. Been gone so long it's a wonder you even remembered the way here.'

Stung by the accusation in his eyes and voice, she rocked back on her heels while he scowled at her, his face working. The drawn-out silence was broken only when he turned to lay the table with crockery, cutlery, a slab of butter on a saucer, and a tin of golden syrup.

She took a deep, calming breath and said slowly, 'You're right, I have been away a long time.'

The clatter of crockery stopped as he paused to rest his hands on the counter. Staring out the window, he said in a thick voice, 'When it happened I couldn't get hold of you on the phone. Had to leave it to that lawyer bloke to contact you.'

'That's my fault.' She lowered her gaze to the floor. 'Thanks for trying. As it was, I didn't hear from the lawyer 'til a while later, after Margot gave him my number.'

'Margot Boyce?' Seeing her nod, he gave a derisive sniff. 'Doin' you a solid, was she? Humph!' He turned back to the stove. 'You want eggs? I got some boilin'.'

'No thanks.' She took a seat at the table. 'Just some toast, and then I'd better be going ... home.'

He stiffened. 'To *Clearwater*?' At her nod he announced, 'Right. I'm comin' with you.'

'Don't you want to stay here and ... you know ... recover?'

Lifting a bushy eyebrow at her, he barked, 'What d'you take me for, a nine pound nancy boy? *Recover,* my ass! I'm doin' just *fine,* I'll 'ave you know.' Plonking a slab of golden-brown, thick-cut toast onto the plate in front of her he announced, 'I'm comin' with you, no argument.'

She raised her hands in defeat. 'Okay.' In truth, she was glad. Going home, and entering the house for the first time since losing Bill, wouldn't be easy. Even thinking about it made her heart thump and her stomach clench.

As he watched her spread butter and golden syrup on her toast, Gero muttered, 'Cocky's joy, ya'can't beat it.' Carrying his loaded plate to the table, he took a seat opposite her. 'I'll just 'ave some brekkie and then feed the girls.'

'How are they doing? Looks like you might've gained a few more.'

'Yup, got about two dozen now.'

'Have you named the new ones?' Wiping a drip of buttery syrup off her chin, she threw him a teasing grin.

'Yup.' His expression softened. 'That black hen there,' and he pointed out the window, 'that's Henrietta Three.' His face fell and he said sadly, 'Lost Henrietta Two last winter. Still miss the old girl.'

Abbey assumed an appropriately sorrowful air as he went on. 'And the Rhode Island Red there is Gwen. The others with her are Lauren, Madeleine, and Helen.' He pronounced the names with an 'h' before the final syllable, so that each one ended with 'hen'.

'Hel-hen?'

'Yup.' He grinned. 'Suits 'er down to the ground. If there's trouble in the coop, it's always her that's started it. Even gives the rooster a run for 'is money. Why, the day I got her she flew straight out the pen! A fine pair of wings on 'er, that's for sure. Course I clipped 'em. Can't have me hens flyin' the coop and layin' outside, where I gotta go searchin' for the eggs.' His grin vanished. 'Or stayin' out at night to be torn apart by wild dogs. And there's more of them rotten things around, wanderin' the district lookin' for somethin' to kill. Vicious damn things.'

'Any idea where they're from?'

He pulled the teapot closer and filled their cups with the dark amber brew. 'Strays, I reckon. Stupid people bring 'em to town and then dump'em out here, like they're doin' the mutts some sort of favour.' He lowered the teapot to gaze at her. 'Think one might've made itself at home at *Clearwater.'*

'Oh, great ... Bill would hate that.' Abbey recalled her uncle's unapologetic, 'No dogs, Abs,' to her youthful pleas for a puppy. Her later argument that a dog would be handy for bringing in the cattle received a similarly resolute – and typically pragmatic – response. 'Take too much training before they get useful, and too much looking after altogether. Always running off chasing one thing or another, and scaring away the wildlife.'

He had a point. If there was one thing guaranteed to keep native animals away from the property, it was a dog.

In the absence of resident canine or feline predators, the bandicoots, ring-tailed possums and silvery whiptail wallabies grew used to co-habiting with humans on the farm. At times they ventured quite close to the house, and in the dry season Bill made sure they had access to water in the cattle yards. She remembered the rapture on his craggy face the day he saw a wallaby come for a drink and her tiny joey hopped clumsily around her, finding his feet.

'Yup.' Gero forked the last morsel of soft-boiled egg and buttered toast into his mouth. 'Bill would've given the mutt the short, sharp shrift if he'd been there.' He paused, chewing, to eye Abbey. 'Y'know, an uninvited dog or two might not be all you find different at the old place.'

At her sharp glance he merely shrugged and set aside his cutlery. 'Right. You clear the table and I'll see to the girls. Then we'll go.'

8

Emerging from his swag, Granger tugged on a pair of jeans and went to stand, legs apart, at the entrance to his camp. Yawning, he rolled his head around his shoulders, breathing deeply of the new day's air. Time for his routine of stretches, push-ups, squats, and sit-ups. Exercising was best done in the cool of morning....

Rising from his final sit-up, he blew a long breath and rubbed the puckered scar on his left bicep. The healed wound still gave an occasional twinge, as though to remind him of what he had done, what he had become....

He shook off the thought and busied himself re-starting the camp fire. After a breakfast of fire-toasted bread and fried eggs, he sat back with a pannikin of billy tea.

'For true-blue billy tea, boys,' his father used to say, 'you gotta add a gum leaf or two for flavour. When you're ready to serve it, swing the billy around in a full circle at least three times. That makes the leaves sink to the bottom. Yep,' and he would nod his head sagely, 'that's how a *real* bushy makes a *real* cuppa.'

Granger's lips twitched at the memory, until a rustling movement in a nearby bush had him tensing. He glanced at the hunting knife in the scabbard beside his swag. It was just a lunge away ... if needed.

When the bush gave a vigorous quiver, he dropped to his haunches, eyes fixed on the spot.

A furry figure emerged from the undergrowth. It moved clumsily on all fours, its pouch heavy with joey. Too small and pale-coloured for an eastern grey kangaroo, it was more likely a whip-tailed wallaby. There were plenty of them around.

Granger's expression softened as he watched the little doe make its way out of the undergrowth. At least whip-tails didn't stink like their cousins, the coarser-coated, foul-tasting swamp wallabies.

Once in the clear, the silver-grey marsupial rose onto its back feet and bounced nimbly away, heading for greener pickings. With a grunt Granger uncurled, only to stiffen again when another sound reached his ears. All traces of softness fell from his face, replaced by the customary narrow-eyed intensity.

A vehicle was approaching, along the property's gravel access road.

Abbey tried to avoid the worst patches of bone-jarring corrugation; still the ute bucked, clanged and bumped along the dirt track. She glanced at her passenger. He sat staring out the window, steadying himself with a weathered hand – two for the roughest patches – on the grab handle above the passenger door.

She ached to talk to him about Bill; to hear how her uncle had *really* coped on his own; to picture the gathering at his funeral....

Swallowing, she returned her gaze to the road.

Now was not the time for questions like that. The loss, guilt and regret were still too raw; for Gero too, perhaps.

As they rumbled over a creek crossing, she eyed the tangled remnants of elephant grass in the barbed wire fences, left there during the last wet season. The succulent greenness of the blade-like foliage was long gone, replaced by a sun-crisped brown.

She squinted at the pasture inside the fences. 'It's awfully dry.'

Gero gave a glum nod. 'Driest it's been for a long while. Didn't get a proper rainy season this year.' He sat forward to gaze skyward through the windscreen. 'But judgin' by that mackerel sky and the ants invadin' my pantry, we might be in for a soakin' in the next few days.' He reached down to squeeze a bony knee and winced. 'Yup. My arthur-itus is never wrong, 'n it's tellin' me the rain's comin'.'

'How's the creek level?'

Drought-proof Five Mile Creek, the inspiration for the property's name, formed one of *Clearwater Downs'* boundaries. The precious watercourse snaked through a valley, creating unexpected patches of rainforest where it looped back on itself. Bill had chosen to situate the homestead an easy walk from the most picturesque of these patches. There, the lush vegetation formed a canopy over a deep-ish waterhole in the pebbled riverbed.

An image flashed into Abbey's mind, of floating on her back in the cool water, daydreaming, while sunlight sparkled through the leafy canopy above as if from a golden chandelier.

Roos, wallabies, goannas, bandicoots and echidnas were also regular visitors to the waterhole, along with so much birdlife she'd given up trying to identify all the different species. There were snakes too, 'joe blakes' in Bill-speak. Seen or unseen, they were always around. Same with the spiders. She'd had more than one EEK! moment after walking through an orb-weaving spider's wheel-shaped web strung between trees.

'Level's the same ... at least it was last time I checked.' Gero frowned. 'Was a while ago now though.'

'Who's been looking after the stock since....' Abbey's voice trailed off. A moment later the car lurched over a pothole with a chorus of rattling clunks, making the steering wheel jerk in her hands. She sucked in a sharp breath.

'Flip's been checkin' the water troughs, and throwin' hay to a coupl'a yarded beasts.'

With her back throbbing a protest at all the jarring, Abbey grit her teeth and guided the ute onto the track's smoother centre.

'That's about it, though.'

'Didn't quite catch that, Gero. Who did you say was helping out?'

'Flip.' When she didn't respond, he flicked her a glance. 'You know, Philippa Williamson.'

'Oh ... um ... Flip ... right.' Abbey managed to stop herself using her school friend's nickname, Backflip.

The fiercely competitive Flip had earned the name after taking an unfortunate tumble in front of a packed grandstand at a district show one year. Recalling the incident brought on another painful spasm in Abbey's own back.

She shifted in her seat, balancing her weight more evenly. 'So, she's returned from Brisbane?'

'Yup. Came home 'soon as she finished her TAFE course.'

Abbey gave a thoughtful nod. 'And she's looking after things at the farm?'

'Got a horse on agistment, so she's around most days.'

'Oh.' Abbey's brow creased. 'Why is she agisting when her family has a property?'

'Her father threatened to send this horse to the knackers, apparently. It's a well-bred beast – Anglo-Arab I believe – but a rig. Or as your up-themselves show cronies would say,' and he raised an eyebrow at her, '*Cryptorchid,* as in "short one crown jewel".' Snorting at Abbey's unamused I-know-what-it-means expression, Gero dropped the plum-in-mouth accent. 'Anyway, she bought the horse cheap for that reason, but her dad got fed up with it gettin' his workin' mares in foal. And havin' to mend fences every five minutes. Bill had a ready-made stallion enclosure goin' spare, so he thought someone may as well get the use of it.'

Abbey gave a wry nod. Their first – and last – attempt at a horse breeding programme had left Bill more certain than ever of his preference for raising cattle.

'Was a while after you left.' Gero fixed her with a steely gaze. 'And I think Bill missed havin' someone else around the place.'

Abbey stared straight ahead, tightening her grip on the wheel, until Gero looked away again and the ute's grumbling rattles filled the silence. They subsided a short time later when she turned and idled the car under the familiar, ranch-style log entranceway. Fashioned by Bill from his own timber, it bore the station's hand-carved name in the rough-cut, gnarled and knotted wood.

Bill was so proud of his property's front entrance. So proud of his farm. So proud of *her*....

She blinked, sucked in her bottom lip, and made herself focus on what lay in front of the car's bonnet.

The gate still hung askew but this time she drove through it, stopping on the other side with the motor running.

'Back in a sec.' She climbed down from the ute, sniffing and dragging an impatient arm across her moist eyes. As she jogged back to right the gate, she saw the top hinge was broken clean off the supporting post. That meant she could only rest the gate against the post on the other side and wrap the heavy chain around it.

When she returned to the ute muttering, 'I'll get that fixed,' Gero gave a grunt.

'Reckon you'll find a few things need fixin' 'round the place, Girlie.'

She raised questioning eyebrows at him but when he said nothing more, turned her attention to the homestead. As they drew closer, her mouth dropped open at the sight of scorch marks and the shattered remains of a kerosene lantern on the ground. Then her roving gaze fell on the litter strewn outside what had been the homestead's original semi-detached kitchen, converted to storage by Bill.

Oh no.

Had *squatters* moved in while the place was unoccupied?

She knew that had happened to other farms in the district, after eviction of the owners by their mortgagors. Some farmers didn't wait for the heave-ho. They made the choice to walk away, to wipe their work-hardened hands of the crushing debts and generations-long struggles against bad weather, unsympathetic city-based governments, and capricious markets. Either way, properties ended up vacant. Their weather-beaten, bullet-ridden, often face-down-in-the-dust FOR SALE signs only evidenced the lack of interested buyers, and advertised a target-rich environment for squatters.

Abbey flicked Gero a sideways look. He was in the same boat as other defunct or broken-spirited farmers, but unlike most, he had to face the difficulties alone. As far as she knew, the old man had no children, had never married. She could only recall him mentioning one family member, a sister he referred to as a 'crotchety fuss-budget'. This sister lived 'down south' somewhere, and insisted on yearly visits to give his slab hut a 'good once-over'. No doubt the embroidered antimacassars and moth-balled linen were legacies of those visits.

Abbey's throat tightened. How would Gero cope once he was forced out of his home? Especially now Bill, the next best thing to family he had, was gone? Where would he go, to his sister's? More likely he'd head to the park and drink himself to death....

Glimpsing a dark shape moving on the homestead's veranda, she sat forward in her seat.

'That's 'im,' Gero murmured beside her. 'The mutt I told you about.'

Sure enough, the dark shape morphed into a black and tan dog. It moved to the top step and stood watching them, pink tongue lolling and tail waving a tentative greeting.

Abbey pulled the ute to a stop out the front of the house and turned off the ignition. Sitting back, she eyed the dog. 'It's a good type, a Kelpie maybe. Must belong to someone.'

'All I know is, it moved in not long after....' Gero cleared his throat. ''N it wasn't alone.'

'Squatters?'

'Yup. Flip spotted a couple sniffin' around and came 'n got me. We moved 'em on before they had a chance to break into the house, which was lucky. We kept a closer eye on the place after that 'n there were no more signs of trouble.' Gero's wrinkled brow creased further. 'I'm a bit surprised about that, to be honest. Word gets 'round pretty quick of empty places ripe for squattin'.' He gave a disparaging sniff. 'And the buggers like fresh digs, 'specially ones with stacked pantries 'n clean linen.' Indicating the scorch marks and shattered lantern on the ground, he scowled. 'This here's recent strife. Wasn't like this the other day when I called. Someone wantin' to torch the place by the looks of things.'

Abbey gaped at him. *Torch* the house? But ... why would squatters want to ruin a good squat?'

'Who knows what goes on in their drug and booze-addled —' He broke off, turning away from her loaded glance to squint out the window and gnaw on a thumbnail.

She let the silence do its work before speaking again. 'You saw squatters off on your *own,* from a place that's not even yours? It could've got nasty, Gero, and you might've been hurt ... or worse.' She touched his arm. 'Look, I'm very grateful, but you should've called Jeff and let him handle it.'

Gero gave a snort and lowered his hand to his lap again. 'I did call, 'n he said he'd come out when he could ... but I knew it would've been too late by the time he got here.'

While well liked, local copper Jeff Thompson was considered more affable than effectual. And to be fair, his rural beat covered an extended area of many hundred kilometres. Even doing the rounds kept him busy, without the additional RBT and speeding blitzes he was expected to carry out.

'He's tied up with other things,' Gero went on. 'Been some funny stuff happenin' around the district of late. There's even talk of drug-related activities.' Muttering darkly, 'Newcomers, who needs 'em?' he bent to unclip his seatbelt. 'C'mon, Girlie, stop procrastinatin'.' When he spied the key ring in the console, he grabbed it and shook it at her, making the keys jangle. 'It's time.'

Abbey took the keys from him but remained in her seat, allowing her gaze to rove over the normally well-kept, now dry and neglected-looking, fenced house yard. The only plants that appeared unaffected by the lack of water were the geraniums – pelargoniums, she corrected herself – whose crimson blooms in full sun were so bright they made her squint.

You said they'd make a brilliant show one day, Uncle Bill....

When the breeze caught the leaves of the ribbon-like grass between the pelargoniums, setting them waving, she frowned.

Better get rid of those weeds before they choke out the good plants.

A sense of wholesome purpose followed that thought, along with a glimmer of peace. It was broken a moment later when Gero called, 'You comin', or just gonna sit there all day?'

Her shoulders slumped. She took a deep breath and made herself climb down from the ute.

Gero was gazing upward, watching a fork-tailed spangled drongo chase a moth.

After snapping the unfortunate insect out of mid-air, the glossy black bird darted to a perch in the nearest gum tree.

'Aerial acrobatics. Nicely done.' He chuckled. 'Better than anythin' planes can do.'

Abbey was already heading for the house. On the way she paused to nudge the lantern's remains with a boot, before continuing toward the veranda stairs. On the top step the watching Kelpie's tail-wagging grew more vigorous. It spun like a helicopter blade in fawning, convivial motion.

After climbing the stairs, she bent to scratch the dog's dark head. 'Gidday, cobber. Where are you from?' She eyed the ancient front doormat, now covered in black and tan fur amid the clods of dirt. 'Been here a while, hey?'

Wiping her well-licked hand on the leg of her pants, she straightened and took out the front door key, steeling herself for what lay inside. When she heard Gero's laboured breathing as he came up the stairs behind her, she gathered her courage and slipped the key into the lock. It turned easily with nary a sound.

Bill was a stickler for maintaining the old place. 'Worth having, worth looking after,' he always said.

As she pushed the door open, cool air brushed past her on its way out. It carried a familiar scent, a combination of old toast, leather, fireplace charcoal, and Bill's Old Spice aftershave.

The pot-pourri of home.

On a nearby ridge, Granger crouched amid the undergrowth and took a swig from his water bottle. Wiping the back of a hand across his mouth, he watched as the ute's occupants, a young woman and an elderly man, entered the homestead. When his ears caught a hint of muffled voices on the breeze, his lips tightened.

Was his peaceful solitude about to end?

He swept a glance over the house. There was no evidence it had been broken into, and the people didn't look like no-hopers. Nor had they acted furtively when they arrived. Perhaps they were the property's owners. Probably just as well they'd turned up. It was a shame to have a nice place like this left empty for squatters and vandals to ruin—

His head jerked.

Why should *he* care what happened to it? He was only here because of the convenient, short-term camping spot nearby. Scaring off those vandals was just to protect his own interests.

And because it was the right thing to do; what his father would expect from one of his sons.

With an exasperated grunt, he bent his head to stare unseeingly at the grey-brown grass covering the ground beneath him.

He should've known this would happen, after choosing to camp within cooee of a place he had sworn to never go near again. What the hell was he thinking, breaking his own rule? Now he had risked exposure to save some stranger's homestead from vandals.

And here he was again, watching over the place simply because he'd heard a car.

This wasn't just about ensuring the security of his campsite. It was the old yearning, resurfacing.

He gave a grim snort.

It was a mistake to think time might've healed that wound.

Pushing himself back from the ridge, he got to his feet and slapped the dust off his faded jeans. It was pointless to fret over an unattainable goal, one that was lost to the past. What he needed to focus on was the present and, eventually, the future.

Whirling around, he strode away without a backward glance.

Life is simpler – safer – when all you have to worry about is yourself.

9

The Colonial-style homestead sported the traditional polished timber floorboards, with the lounge room and three bedrooms to the right and left of a central corridor. At the end of the corridor the spacious, eat-in kitchen easily housed a stout timber table and chairs, cast iron slow-combustion wood stove and its electric counterpart, an old-fashioned refrigerator, and a roomy pantry. The open cupboards beneath a clean but worn timber counter top were neatly stacked with well-used pots and pans.

Above the sink, sunlight spilled through the wooden case-ment window that overlooked the vegetable garden. A wilted cherry tomato plant, with bunches of split and insect-eaten fruit dangling from its branches, was all that remained of the latest crop.

Abbey stepped back from the window and her gaze fell to the drainer beside the sink, where a coffee-encrusted mug and Vegemite-smeared plate sat waiting to be washed.

From Bill's last meal.

Her throat tightened and she whirled around, almost bumping into Gero.

He too was staring at the dirty dishes. 'Seems me ol'mate left in a hurry. Left ... expectin' to come back, of course.'

She managed a nod, her face working as she made for the sanctuary of her old room.

It was pretty much as she'd left it; a tad tidier perhaps. Breathing in the room's familiar scent, she wandered around, running a finger over the photos in mismatched frames on the dresser before stopping to gaze at her favourites. In one, a sun-browned man wearing sweat-stained clothes and a determined expression squatted on his haunches beneath a bloodwood tree. He held reins loosely in one hand, the tip of a horse's muzzle visible above his head. The same man was also in the next photo, only older and more familiar. Dressed in a wrinkled chambray shirt, he sat at the kitchen table, frown-smiling into the camera.

Frown-smiling, the term she came up with as a child to describe the way his thick eyebrows remained drawn together over those deep-set, hazel eyes when he smiled.

Uncle Bill.

Her heart swelled in her chest and she hurried on to the next picture. Picking it up, she wiped away the fine layer of dust, and stared into her mother's eyes.

Leah Miller had been a pretty young woman, but her later photos revealed a face deeply etched by poor life choices, ill health, and regrets. In this snapshot, taken just days after their arrival at the farm, her haunted eyes held a deep weariness of spirit. Although she had tried to cover the fading bruises on her chin and temple with makeup, their purple-blue tinge was evident on closer inspection.

And those were just the visible signs of maltreatment she received at the hands of her worst life choice, and biggest regret.

Neil Carter.

Despite never making good on his promise to marry her, Carter had regarded Leah and their daughter Abbey as his property. So when Leah ran away from his alcohol-fuelled abuse, he wasted no time tracking them to Bill's farm. There'd be little opposition to his waltzing in, reclaiming his foolish partner and young daughter, and dragging them back home ... or so he thought.

He hadn't counted on Leah's protective, well-prepared, and highly capable brother.

Abbey had vague memories of a late night argument on the homestead's front veranda, just weeks after she and her mother arrived at the farm. Loud arguments had been a part of her life since infancy, so she easily recognised one of the raised voices; the one bellowing accusations, insults and curses.

Her Daddy was angry again.

She had flinched, dreading her mother's yelps of pain that normally followed a shouting match.

For once, they hadn't come.

Instead she heard meaty thumps and the slide of boots on aged floorboards, punctuated with harsh breathing and pained grunts as hefty blows found their marks.

In her bunk bed in the smallest and cosiest of the homestead's rooms, the little girl clutched the bedclothes tighter beneath her chin. When the door to the room burst open she gave a whimper, but it was her wild-eyed, ashen-faced mother who rushed inside. Shutting the door and propping a chair against it, Leah dashed to the bed, putting a shaking finger to her lips to silence Abbey.

The little girl knew the drill. She waited for her mother to take her into hiding under the bed, as she had many times before. Instead, Leah scooped her up and scurried to the corner of the room beside the doorway, where they would be out of sight if the door opened.

Sinking to the floor and huddling there with Abbey tucked under her quivering chin, Leah whispered over and over, 'We'll be alright. Bill will take care of us. We'll be alright.'

Morning found them still huddled there. When sunlight slanted through the window onto her face, Leah had woken with a start, making Abbey stir in her sleep. Uncurling her stiff limbs with care, Leah rose to her feet and tucked her drowsy daughter back into bed, before creeping to the door. After moving the chair away, she paused to gather her courage. Wincing at the tiniest of creaking sounds, she opened the door a crack to listen.

All quiet.

Taking a deep breath, she slipped out, closing the door behind her with a click.

It was enough to rouse Abbey, who blinked, rubbed her eyes with her fists, and yawned. When her drowsy, 'M-mum?' went unanswered, she sat up. After an anxious peep under the bed, she climbed down and padded to the door. Opening it carefully, she stuck her head out and saw her mother tiptoe to the end of the corridor.

Pressing her back against the wall, Leah peeked around the corner, before rushing into the kitchen.

Abbey hurried after her. Her small, bare feet made barely a

sound on the worn carpet runner. Peeking around the corner as her mother had done, she saw her uncle seated at the kitchen table, head in his hands.

At his side, Leah whispered harshly, 'Are you alright? Where's Neil?'

With a low groan, Bill slowly raised his head. One of his eyes was half-closed with a shadow of bruising developing around it, and beneath his nose a trickle of dried blood was visible against his skin. He ran his tongue over the welling split in his lower lip and rasped, 'Gone. With his tail between his legs like the mongrel he is.'

'He l-left? But Bill, he'll come back.' Leah's shaky voice rose a notch. 'He won't give up. He'll be back—'

'No he won't. He knows what's waiting for him if he comes here again.'

Leah followed her brother's gaze to his prized 1894 silver lever-action Winchester rifle, resting against the wall.

Abbey remained out of sight, her young eyes widening as fear and bewilderment coursed through her.

Why did Uncle Bill have blood on his face, and how come he sounded so different, so ... scary? And what had happened to her Daddy? Was he hurt too? Had he hurt Uncle Bill?

And her mother. Why was she staring at the gun like it was a monster? And what was it doing in the kitchen instead of where it lived, high on the wall above the fireplace?

When Gero became aware of the silence pressing in on him, he shuffled to the bedroom door and poked his head around it. Abbey stood with her back to him, staring at a photo. Unwilling to break the quiet moment of reflection, the old man backed away and returned to the kitchen.

Catching the sound of his shuffling footsteps and the creak of floorboards, Abbey swallowed the lump in her throat and set down the photo of her mother. After glancing at the empty doorway, she let her gaze travel the room. It fell on the sheaf of blue, red, and green ribbons hanging from one wall. They represented years' worth of awards won at district shows and gymkhanas, mostly for sporting events and six-bar jumping. Comanche's feisty temperament and compact confirmation had made him spot-on for tests of speed and agility, not so much the controlled etiquette required for rider class or dressage.

If she hadn't known that before the disastrous Gretna Green incident, she certainly did after it.

Her thoughts flicked to her old Pony Club buddy, Rosalie. They'd lost touch years ago. Where was she now? Had she taken up riding again after recovering from the accident?

When the girls decided to enter the two-up Gretna Green race at a club rally day, an eager Rosalie had climbed behind Abbey to settle herself on Comanche's rump. The instant she wrapped her legs around him, the startled gelding dropped his head, bunched his lithe body, and bucked his way down the club's gravel driveway. He only stopped after tossing a screaming Rosalie high into the air, leaving Abbey clinging to his neck.

After regaining her seat, she rode back to where Rosalie had fallen. What a shock it was, seeing her friend, the hardy survivor of many a previous fall, lying white-faced and whimpering on the ground. Rosalie's mother came running over to kneel beside her, murmuring anxious words as she assessed her daughter's injuries.

Abbey recalled the wail of the ambulance siren, and her

friend's bawling as the paramedics loaded her in the vehicle. While she stared anxiously after the departing ambulance, Bill's words had rung in Abbey's ears, from the day they first inspected Comanche.

'One white foot buy him, two white feet try him,' he'd cautioned. 'Three white feet be on the sly, *four* white feet pass him by.'

It was a common saying in horsey circles, and she would normally take her uncle's advice on all things horse. But Abbey had fallen in love with the blood-red bay galloway with four white socks and clever – Bill said cunning – look in his eyes. So she had countered with the alternate saying: 'One white foot keep him not a day, two white feet send him far away, three white feet sell him to a friend, four white feet keep him 'til the end.'

Of course Bill was proven right. While he was her prettiest and most spirited horse, Comanche also had a hard mouth, would shy at anything, and was inclined to bolt.

In the aftermath of the Gretna Green incident, Bill suggested Abbey consider trading the gelding for a taller mount. He thought she should have an all-rounder, one that would do well in other events like dressage and show-jumping. He also made Abbey visit Rosalie at least once every week during her recuperation, as a lesson in accepting responsibility.

Despite those regular visits, the girls' friendship never regained the same footing. And if her memory served her correctly, it was Backflip, Philippa Williamson, who had gone on to win the event that sparked the mishap....

'Hello?'

Startled, Abbey hurried out to the corridor. A sinewy figure stood in the front doorway silhouetted against the daylight, which made a halo of her wispy, pixie-cut blonde hair.

The two women stared at each other until Gero stuck his head around the corner of the kitchen and called, 'Gidday Flip.'

'Gero.' Flip dipped her head at him and returned her gaze to Abbey, who was quietly taking her in.

Her elfin face hadn't changed, and still belied Flip's strength of character. A tough competitor at Pony Club meets and district gymkhanas, she even managed to pip Abbey to a blue ribbon or two in the bending, flag, and barrel races. And what made her wins more impressive was that she'd scored them not on a purpose-bred sporting pony, but on a retired pacer, a hand-me-down Standard-bred she'd retrained herself.

'Good to see you back, Abs.'

'Good to be back, Flip.'

They shared a tentative smile.

Later, as the three of them chatted over cups of tea – Abbey had mixed feelings when she first opened Bill's well-stocked pantry – she made two important discoveries. The first was that the company of other people dispelled the house's hollow emptiness, the feeling a crucial element was missing. And the second was that Gero and Flip shared a disturbing conviction.

That Bill's death was no accident.

'Doesn't make sense, his being out on the ridge at that time.' Gero shook his head. 'He knew the dangers. Not only that, he hated the place. Hated what had happened there, hated that he felt sort'a guilty 'bout that poor young fella who died ... which I always told 'im was crazy. He wasn't even here when it happened ... was on the other side of the world, near enough. And what could he've done even if he *was* here? Not like he could keep watch over that spot like some sort'a sentry.'

Flip nodded. 'Bill used to nag me to stay right away from that ridge, never ride anywhere near it. He was so grouchy about it, I reckon he would've evicted us if I'd even tried! So why would he turn around and do exactly what he'd warned me not to?' She paused to glance at her watch. 'Ooh ... I'd better get cracking if I wanna get a ride in. Gotta meet Banjo in a coupl'a hours.'

Banjo Patterson, whose long-suffering mother was alone in calling him by his real first name, Will.

'You and Banjo still...?'

Flip gave a wry snort. 'On-again, off-again while he follows the rodeo circuit. Still doing, y'know, the bull riding. Gets another scar each ride; starting to have more scars than skin.' She sighed. 'Keeps telling me this'll be his last season, but then the new posters come out and I get the old "just one more circuit" spiel. Lucky for me, I stopped believing his promises a long time ago.' Rising to her feet, she smiled down at Abbey. 'Thanks for the tea.'

'You're welcome.' Abbey rose too. 'It's been great catching up on the local goss.' They shared a smile, and as Flip headed for the door Abbey called, 'And thanks for keeping an eye on the place, while....'

Flip raised a hand as she walked. 'Don't mention it. I was coming to feed Onesie anyway.'

'Onesie?'

Flip stopped and half-turned. 'My latest horse.' She grinned. 'His real name, Master and Commander, is too much of a mouthful for everyday use. I like Onesie better and it suits him, seeing as how he's a rig. Though the way he behaves sometimes you'd swear he's an entire.' She gave a roguish wink and then sobered. 'You okay with him staying on here? Bill said I could use the enclosure as long as I liked.'

'Sure. That's fine by me.'

Flip dipped her head in thanks. 'Let me know when you're ready to ride again, Abs. You'll need an update on the horses in Bill's mob. Some of the beggars haven't had a saddle near them for ages, and are likely to dump you 'soon as look at you. Oh, and the Agnes Active Riders would love it if you gave us a trick riding demo one day ... when you feel up to it, of course. We've got some keen kids in the group now.' With a final wave and a jaunty, 'Catch'ya later,' she strode out. The heels of her riding boots thudded on the wooden veranda and stairs, before crunching across the gravel toward the stallion enclosure.

'Onesie?' Gero scowled. 'That's a bit harsh.'

Abbey gave an amused, 'Humph,' and turned to find him eyeing her.

'You doin' okay, Girlie?'

'Yep.'

'Gonna be alright here on your own?'

Her stomach lurched. She swept a glance around the house's familiar dimensions, contents, and aura. How could she feel anything *but* safe and at home here?

With a firm, 'I'll be fine,' she watched Gero massage his pasty forehead with unsteady fingers. Clearly yesterday's bender was taking its toll.

He ran his tongue over his dry lips. 'I've had a captain cook around the house and didn't see anythin' out of place. There's the scorch marks 'n broken lamp outside, but it looks like some Samaritan chased off the firebugs. Was probably just good-for-nothin' kids makin' trouble. Doubt they'll come again now the place is occupied. You'll be fine, I reckon.'

'Of course I will. You don't need to worry about me.'

'Right then, I'm off home. Got stuff to do.' Seeing Abbey reach for her car keys he barked, 'Don't bother, I'll walk.'

'It's a bit far—'

Not wanting to hear the words, 'in your condition,' he didn't let her finish. 'Not far when you go cross-country. You know that.'

'It's no trouble to drive—'

'Said I'll *walk*.' He inhaled, adding more calmly, 'Need to clear my head.'

She raised her hands in surrender. 'Okay then, if you're sure.'

'I'm sure.'

Going to the sink, she filled a tumbler from the rainwater tank and handed it to him. 'Have this before you go, it'll help the head.'

He grouched, 'Stop fussin', Girlie,' but took the glass from her. After sculling the contents he handed it back with a curt, 'Seeya. Y'know where I am if you need me.'

10

The birds raised the alarm before Granger heard the sounds for himself. Keeping low, he made his way through the waist-high seedy grass until he could see the stock track. A short distance south of his campsite, the dry, hoof-compacted track snaked through the paddocks between the creek and the property's cattle yards.

Dropping to his haunches, Granger watched from his vantage point as the man shuffled past. It was the old bloke who'd been at the homestead earlier. Despite the lumbering gait he moved confidently, as though familiar with the route.

There was something vaguely familiar about him too ... something from the past. But Granger had no time for reminiscing, even if he wanted to indulge the impulse. There was game to hunt so he'd have fresh meat for dinner.

He waited until the old man moved out of sight, before rising and heading back to camp.

. . .

After clearing away the dishes that evening he sat on his swag, one knee hugged to his chest, and listened to the soft calls of roosting birds and the chorus of crickets in the trees. He found the solitude of living rough under the stars calming. It helped him regain a sense of control over his destiny.

When his gaze fell on the slim-bodied Martin Backpacker travel guitar lying on top of his duffel, he picked up the instrument and strummed a progression of chords. The travel-worn guitar managed to stay in tune despite living a rough life. He stared down at it, musing on all the places they had been together, and the diverse audiences their music had drawn.

An image flashed across his mind, of an olive-skinned boy in a white turban and loincloth who bounded up to him, beaming. The little chap had laughed, twirled, and danced to the music, making everyone around him smile and laugh too, until....

Thrusting aside the memory, Granger finger-picked another sequence of chords. The combination of notes had the usual effect, of quieting the inner voice that persisted in dredging up painful or guilt-ridden memories.

The same voice that urged him to keep moving, and rebuked him for staying on here despite the risks.

Abbey rolled onto her side for the umpteenth time. Her eyes no longer blinked in unison they were so tired, but their lids just wouldn't stay closed. After dragging a hand over her face, she dropped her arm and thumped the mattress with a fist. Here, in the cool darkness of her own room, her own bed, why was sleep eluding her? The answer, of course, lay in the emptiness of the room up the hallway from hers.

Bill's room.

It felt like a vacuum, tugging at her.

Tossing aside the bedclothes, she padded to the window and opened it wider, letting more of the cool night air drift in.

LB's tree was a dark silhouette against the glow of the half moon.

LB ... whose loss had left her devastated and heartsick. Yet the passage of time applied a scab over the wound, healing – hardening perhaps? – her heart, so she could cherish the memories of her little brown friend with fondness instead of pain.

Would time do the same now, with Bill's loss? Or would the aching hollowness remain forever, reducing her to tears at every nostalgic turn?

This is why I can't sleep. I have to stop fretting, make myself think about something else.

She blew a frustrated breath and climbed back into bed.

I could start with this: how the hell am I going to manage the farm on my own?

It had taken a force of will to leaf through the legal documentation for the monetary details of Bill's legacy; a heart-rending task she could no longer avoid. Ferris Dolcher had stressed, with a meaningful lift of eyebrows, the importance of gaining a complete picture of her new situation. And he was right.

I'm hugely grateful you trusted me with Clearwater, Uncle Bill. And it was noble of you to bequeath some of your cash reserves to The Royal Flying Doctors and other charities. Unfortunately, your philanthropy has left me limited funds for the farm's upkeep. With little scope to earn more in my current condition, I hope I can prove worthy of your trust.

She once more punched the mattress.

There I go, fretting again.

Dragging up the bedclothes, she made herself lie still. She heard the click of a dog's nails on the veranda outside. The Kelpie was still hanging around.

I should probably give him a name. Can't keep calling him 'the dog'.

When her ears picked up a slithering sound in the ceiling above her head, she smiled into the darkness. It was bound to be the carpet snake Bill called 'Old Mate'. Bill reckoned Old Mate was better than any man-made mouse trap. And since the snake took up residence in the ceiling, there hadn't been a single rodent sighting in the house.

When the overhead slithering stopped, her ears caught other, muffled sounds carried on the breeze from a distance away.

She cocked her head to listen, glad of what Bill called her 'cat-like hearing'.

Yes, definitely a guitar, and snatches of a man singing.

She frowned.

Gero was her closest neighbour but he was no songbird, and didn't listen to music as far as she knew. His radio was for hearing marketing reports and emergency alerts, nothing more. Besides, his hut was down-wind and too far away for sounds to carry. Anyway, the deep voice didn't sound like an old man's, nor a professional singer's.

So who was the amateur songster? Someone camping nearby? A squatter maybe?

The sounds came and went with the movement of night air through her window. She closed her eyes and strained to hear better.

Was it wishful thinking, or was that Bill's favourite Garth Brooks song, *The River?* She recalled him struggling to learn that piece, kicking back in a squatter's chair on the veranda strumming away on his beat-up, nylon-stringed acoustic guitar. At her teasing about his fumbling fingers and off-key chords, he had stuck out his tongue at her, and then went on to explain the song's message.

'It's about the importance of pursuing our dreams.'

How he must've regretted saying that to me, when not long after I left to chase my own dream, turning my back on him and the farm.

She ran a hand over her face.

I can't disappoint him like that again, or betray his trust in leaving me the farm, his most precious possession. I have to make this work ... somehow.

Have to do right by him and the farm.

Have to make up for past disloyalty.

She heaved a sigh as the notes of the song continued drifting through the window.

Music like that held such healing qualities....

Thrusting aside the other, disturbing thoughts, she yawned and snuggled under the bedclothes.

I don't care where the music is coming from, I'm going to take it as a gift. I can look for signs of a new squat tomorrow.

She closed her eyes and focused on the music. Her breathing slowed, and in her final waking moments she imagined Bill sitting on the veranda outside her room, quietly singing to the gentle strumming of his guitar.

As the glow of morning crept in through the open window, Abbey rolled onto her back and lay staring at the ceiling, arms behind her head. The dream was still fresh in her mind. A replay of scenes from her childhood, it evoked sensory memories, like the musty, papery scent of her mother's shoebox of 'precious things'.

The smell had greeted her the day she scampered into Leah's room after school and leaped up beside her mother, who had the open box in front of her....

'See this?' Leah held up a pink-ribboned locket of baby hair. 'That's yours, my darling, from when you were tiny. Such a beautiful baby....' She gave a tender smile and tweaked her daughter's already pink cheek. 'Now a pretty little girl.' Still smiling, she handed the locket to five year-old Abbey, who gave a pleased gasp.

'And this.' Leah took out a tarnished brooch. Its paste jewels still sparkled in the light. 'This was my mother's, along with these clip-on earrings.' She passed them to her daughter who sucked in an awed breath. Watching Abbey turn the costume jewellery over in her small hands so that the 'gems' glinted, Leah's indulgent smile widened.

A newfound peace had settled on the farm after weeks went by with no further sign of Carter. It appeared his one and only violent 'visit' was a one-off. Even Leah started to believe he was gone from their lives for good.

Idly flipping through the assortment of faded photos and letters in the shoebox on her lap, she stopped when her fingers flicked over a sepia-coloured envelope. She stared at it, her expression sombre, before taking the letter out of the box and waving it at her distracted daughter.

'I want you to read this, Abbey. When you're older.'

11

The letter.

Tossing aside the bedclothes, Abbey padded to the dresser and dug out her mother's precious shoebox. Taking it back to bed with her, she sat cross-legged on the rumpled sheet and lifted the lid, closing her eyes while breathing in the scent.

Still the same.

Opening her eyes again, she flipped through the contents until she found the envelope. Its sepia surface was now spotted with age, the slit in the flap crumbling and ragged as though having been roughly torn open all those years ago.

She put it to her nose and breathed of its dusty, old paper smell.

Had her mother hesitated before opening the letter, worried about what it might contain; what it might mean for the two of them?

Lowering the envelope, she carefully extracted the single

flimsy sheet of writing paper. The words on it were still clear, written in an elegant, if unsteady, hand.

Dear Leah,

I regret that I cannot give you this news in person, but it was with great reluctance that Neil gave me your mailing address, and only after exacting a promise that I not attempt to visit you, in respect of your wishes. While this saddens me I can understand your reasons, my son's having confessed all to me in his final lucid moments.

As you have no doubt gleaned, Neil has lost his battle with the liver disease that plagued him for years. While you may not share my sorrow at his passing, I want you to know that toward the end he was wracked with guilt over the hurt he caused you, and others. He hated the monster he had become, and mourned the loss of what should have been the best years of his life, as a loving husband and father to his little family.

Despite his shortcomings I will always consider my son a good man made bad by circumstances, and choose to remember him as the kind and clever boy my wife and I raised. How we regretted encouraging him to enlist in the Army after leaving school. We thought military service would be the making of him. Instead it produced an angry, violent man, a stranger to us and everyone he knew.

I believe what is now called post-traumatic stress disorder was at the root of his problems. Had Neil received treatment for that condition, things may have been very different for us all. We might even have had the monster ousted and our real son returned. I continue to blame this deficiency and the military machine that failed him for the unhappiness that followed, especially that suffered by you and our darling granddaughter. If only we could have met her, that would have given my dear wife something to live for. I am convinced that the shocking transformation of our only child hastened her departure from this life. I too have not escaped its toxic influence, and don't expect to outlive my son for long.

I know it would mean a lot to Neil, and to me also, to have you and his precious daughter attend his funeral, the details of which I include below. But I will certainly understand if you cannot be there. I can only hope you will find it in your hearts to forgive our family for failing to provide the loving care you both deserved.

Sincerely,

Harold Carter

Slowly folding the page again and slipping it back into the envelope, Abbey sat tapping the letter against her chin, recalling the first time she'd read her grandfather's words. It was on her thirteenth birthday, when she felt old enough – and strong enough – to revisit her mother's shoebox.

After reading the letter, she had sprinted to the yards where Bill was working a chestnut filly. Climbing onto the top rail, she waved the envelope at him.

'Did you know about this?' She hadn't meant to sound so accusatory.

While the horse maintained a collected canter at the end of the lunge rope, Bill shaded his eyes with one hand and squinted at his niece. After seeing what she held aloft, he returned his gaze to the filly, slowing it to a walk and bringing it to a halt in front of him.

'Did you hear what I said?'

'I heard you.' He patted the horse's neck. 'And yeah, I knew about that letter.' After leading the filly to the fence, he tied the halter rope to the knotted loop of twine secured around a post. If the youngster should pull back, the twine would break before the tack did. Tack cost a whole lot more to replace.

'So ... you know what's in it, Uncle Bill?'

He bent to pick up a grooming brush. 'Read it the day it arrived.' As he ran the brush over its body, the filly fidgeted at first before quietening under his steadying hand. 'Your mother showed it to me.'

Abbey turned the letter over in her hands. 'I don't remember going to his ... my father's ... funeral.' She frowned at her uncle's back as he ran the brush from the horse's shoulder to its rump in firm, rhythmic strokes. 'Did Mum reply to him ... to Grandad?'

He paused to tug a wad of hairs out of the brush. 'No.'

Abbey's frown deepened. 'Why not? He's family.'

'*Was* family.' Bill glanced at her over one shoulder. 'Died not long after writing that,' and he tilted his chin at the letter in her hand. 'Lasted just long enough to put his son into the ground.'

'Oh.'

Bill slipped under the horse's neck to brush the other side. 'Wasn't that your mother didn't care. She felt mean-spirited for ignoring the old man's plea, and for shunning Neil's funeral for that matter. But she said you were born a Miller and must stay a Miller.'

'I don't understand.'

'Y'see....' Bill leaned against the filly's side, resting his arms across its now shiny back. 'Your mother was terrified the Carters might try to lay claim to you, so she kept them at arms' length.'

'Lay claim to me? You mean, take me away? Why would they do that?'

'Might've thought they had cause to, once you'd become an orphan. That goes some way to explainin' your mother's wariness of everyone 'cept you and me. I used to wonder about that.' He blew a long breath and took up brushing again. 'Remember how she'd take you to the swimming hole whenever strangers called here, even after your father was ... out of the picture?'

Abbey gave a silent nod and watched him finish brushing down the horse and remove its halter. Giving it a final pat on the neck, he walked away. After a short pause the youngster followed him to the fence. When he lifted the feed bin onto the middle railing, the filly buried its velvety muzzle into the bin's contents.

As the chaff's grassy fragrance rose into the air, Abbey took a deep breath. 'Uncle Bill?'

'Yeah?'

'Can you tell me about Mum's ... last days? I was away at school so much, and ... I think, maybe ... she put on a brave face for me.'

Bill bent his head and tugged the last strands of horsehair out of the brush, before coming to stand in front of Abbey. Rubbing the brush against a dirt-smudged palm, he fixed her with a firm gaze. 'Your mother's last years were blessed with the peace and contentment she'd longed for all her adult life. Though she didn't speak of 'em often I knew something of her troubles, and was always at her to come here, to the farm, to live. When she finally arrived with you in tow, she told me this was the home she'd always wanted for the two of you.'

He gazed across at the house, a faraway look in his eyes. 'Got the perfumed garden she'd dreamed of having too. Had me set up a swing seat among the plants so she could smell the rose and other blossoms. Spent hours out there, listening to the birds, knitting and embroidering, watching you ride your ponies.' His eyes refocused and he raised a work-hardened hand to cover one of Abbey's. 'Here, she was surrounded by the people and things she loved. And more than anyone or anything else, she loved you. It gave her comfort knowing that even after she was gone you had a forever home. Here, with her kin.'

Abbey stared at him without speaking. It had never occurred to her that she might be anything *but* a Miller. While her mother's brother was always 'Uncle' Bill, he'd been more like a father to her. She was pleased – proud – when people assumed she was his daughter. Neil Carter was nothing more than a blurry memory, one tainted with fear and confusion; someone from the past she had no desire to learn more about. It was enough knowing he'd been a military man.

And a terrible choice of life partner.

Later, after a simple breakfast, Abbey strode to the yard through a shroud of early morning mist, the heels of her riding boots crunching on the dew-dampened gravel and the dog padding silently behind her. Taking care to avoid straining her back, she slipped the western saddle Bill had called his 'leather armchair' over the round middle rail, and headed for the tack shed.

Sensing action, the Kelpie jogged closer, ears pricked and dark eyes following her every move.

With Dr Hughes' stern warnings ringing in her head, Abbey glanced at the dog. 'Even *you* know it's impossible to "ride" the boundaries on foot, don't you, Dopey? That's your name, by the way. Hope you like it.'

Dopey gave an enthusiastic tail wag, eyes staying on her as

she entered the shed. His ears twitched at the sounds of move-ment from within and then her voice floated out. 'I *am* going to be careful, and I'm not riding just *any* horse.' She emerged, bridle and saddle cloth over one arm, and a large white bucket part-filled with lucerne chaff in her other hand. 'Nor do I need Flip to tell me who'd be the safest and smoothest ride, or the easiest to yard.' Moving to the fence, she raised her voice in the well-known call. 'C'mon Cooper, c'mon.'

The dark bay, part-Clydesdale gelding, Bill's 'bomb-proof rocking horse', had an appetite that made him an easy catch in the largest of paddocks. What was it Bill used to say? 'The best horse is the one you can grab any time and do anythin' with. Can't be bothered with "show ponies" that lead you on a merry chase every time you wanna catch 'em. Give me a strong, quiet horse over a high-bred, spirited type any day.'

She slapped the side of the bucket. 'C'mon, Coop.' Her voice cut through the humid morning air. 'C'mon boy.' Pausing, she caught the thuds of heavy, feathered hooves trotting toward her, and felt matching vibrations through the ground.

The countryside's quiet was broken by birdsong, the clop of Cooper's hooves on the compacted dirt track, and Dopey's panting as he loped by the horse's side, pink tongue lolling. Grabbing a leaf from a sapling they passed, Abbey scrunched it in her fingers and buried her nose in it. The sweet eucalyptus scent transported her to happier times ... out riding with Bill, the two of them watching for birdlife above and wildlife around them. With the reassuring warm strength of the horse beneath her, she would throw back her head and breathe deeply of the air cleaned and scented by the trees.

She let the crushed leaf drop to the ground and gingerly leaned forward to pat her mount's stout neck. At a twinge in her back, she eased herself upright again and felt the discomfort fade.

She was grateful for the comfortable saddle and the gelding's smooth gaits. Although fresh at first, jogging instead of walking and shaking his head when she checked him, making the snaffle bit jingle, he'd soon settled into the long-legged, rolling stride she found easy to sit.

Think I'll hang on to you, old fella. Might have to offload some of the others though, especially the unbroken youngsters.

She leaned back, stretching her muscles as Dr Hughes had advised.

Let's face it, my horse-breaking days are probably over.

It pained her to think of selling off Bill's animals, although he'd always been a staunch pragmatist, and there *was* no point keeping horses that weren't being used. Even when turned out they needed drenching, supplementary feeding, hoof trimming and teeth rasping, among other – equally costly – things.

Being good types they'd fetch decent prices, and she could use the money for the farm's upkeep. Bill would approve of that.

She sighed and sat straighter, guiding Cooper off the track to follow the fence line. Her ears caught rustlings in the forest canopy above her head and she glanced up, to see a Rainbow Bee-eater take flight. Admiring the bird's brilliant colours as it darted toward an ill-fated, airborne insect, she turned her face toward the morning sun and heard her uncle's voice in her head.

'Wanna know the best remedy for the blues? Count your blessings and keep busy. Works every time.'

Okay, Bill.

She closed her eyes and filled her lungs with air, savouring its grassy earthiness.

I'll start with this: I'm home, and there's nowhere in the world I'd rather be right now.

Tomorrow can take care of itself.

12

Granger swore under his breath and let the foliage spring closed in front of him. He sat back on his haunches, shaking his head and squeezing the bridge of his nose between thumb and forefinger. If she kept to that same bearing, the horse rider might stumble across his campsite. And that wouldn't do.

It wouldn't do at all.

Abbey heard Dopey give a muffled bark at the same time as Cooper's gait changed. Focusing her gaze ahead, she gave a start when a man emerged from the scrub. A tall, well-built man with a stern face and unblinking, smoky blue eyes.

Their gazes locked and she stiffened and reined in Cooper. The abrupt movement brought on a warning stab of back pain.

Seeing her wince, the stranger's brows drew together. He raised a hand and called, 'Gidday.'

The amiable note in his deep voice eased her apprehension into annoyance, which only intensified when Dopey raced up to him, tail a blur of happy welcome. The man crouched to rub the dog's head and took one of its front paws in a firm grip. After feeling around it, he plucked out a burr.

Abbey frowned.

Had Dopey been limping?

Her frown deepened.

She hadn't noticed, was too busy indulging in nostalgic self-pity.

Damn it.

A tug on the reins jerked her forward and she sucked in a pained breath. She loosened her hold as Cooper gave a couple more tugs and then dropped his head to sample the green pick under the trees' dense shade.

Not wanting to have to dismount to pick up the reins, she leaned forward to grab the buckle as it slid down the horse's neck. The fresh scent of crushed grass filled her nose, bolstering her courage.

She straightened to fix the man with an accusing glare. 'You know you're trespassing?'

He met her gaze. 'I thought this area was national park.'

This earned him a raised eyebrow and a tart, 'National parks aren't normally fenced with barbed wire, and full of cattle.'

He gave a wry grunt. 'True. Though I can't say I've seen any cattle.'

When he bent to give the wriggling dog at his feet another pat, she noted the sweat-stained brim and crown of his Akubra hat. At that angle only his dark sideburns were visible. There were no rats-tails, dreadlocks, nor effeminate 'man bun' that might indicate a city slicker, or a bogan. And judging by his sensible clothes and boots, the bloke was an outdoorsy type.

No sign of a backpack though.

Her eyes narrowed.

The object of her critical assessment gave Dopey's silken ears a final rub before uncurling and fixing her with a steady gaze.

'I did come across a fence, come to think of it. A whole section of it was down.'

'Down?' Her brow furrowed. Broken fencing was bad news. 'Where?'

When he tilted his head to indicate the direction, she noticed his left eye's tendency to squint more than the right. He also had a scar running from the corner of his mouth to the middle of his stubbled chin. It was a lot like the scar a loony Angus poddy, the first and last of their 'pity buys' from the cattle sales, had given Bill.

'Not far. Where the fence line runs closest to the river.' He eyed her. 'I take it this is your property?'

She lifted her chin. 'It is.'

He continued gazing at her. 'I could mend that fallen fence if you like? Have done my share of fencing in the past.'

Her glance flicked to his hands. They were certainly work-manlike. And there was something quintessentially man-on-the-land about his strong physique and wide-legged, ready-for-action stance. It'd take more than appearances for her to consider employing a blow-in trespasser, though. More ready funds, for one thing.

Her lips tightened. 'You think because I'm a woman I can't mend a fence on my own?'

Apart from a crinkling in the corners of his eyes, his face

remained expressionless. 'Not at all. It's just that I've got time on my hands, and could use a quid or two 'til I can next get to the bank.'

'I see.' She tilted her head to the side. 'So you're not just passing through?'

The intensity in his thickly lashed eyes had her fighting an urge to look away.

His gravelly drawl broke the stalemate. 'Followed the river here and found an ideal camping spot.'

'Oh yeah. Where?'

Another vague chin tilt toward the general area behind him.

'Well,' she said crisply, 'camping *anywhere* here,' and she waved an expansive arm, 'is trespassing.'

'So you said.'

She pursed her lips, unsure what to say next. How could she force a man like him to move on if he chose not to? It would be foolish to even try; would probably only amuse and then antagonise him. And if she came back with a posse to evict him – assuming she could raise a posse – he might retaliate. Perhaps set fire to the bush as other expelled squatters in the district had done ... although he didn't have the belligerent stray-dog appearance of someone callous enough to start a bushfire. He was also way too strong and healthy to be a druggo, and maintained a courteous distance from her the whole time they'd been talking.

All the same....

Gathering the reins, she hauled up Cooper's head. The gelding resisted at first, snatching a final mouthful of grass and clanking the bit against his teeth as he chewed.

To her surprise, the man stepped forward to run a large hand down the horse's broad face and neck. Startled by his sudden proximity, she tightened her grip on the reins. His expression changed and he backed away, head bent, looking annoyed with himself.

She stared at him. 'What's your name, anyway?'

He raised his eyes, his expression impassive once more. 'Jackson. You?'

'Miller. Where do you live, Mr Jackson?'

Was that a flicker of amusement on his face?

He cleared his throat. 'Here.'

'I mean, where do you live normally?'

'Normally?'

She nodded.

'Here.'

She rolled her eyes. 'Okay ... so where are you from?'

'Originally?'

'That's what I said.'

'Up this way ... but not for a while.'

'I see.' Arching an eyebrow, she gave an affected sigh. 'Well, can you tell me what you live on, or is that a state secret too?'

'The land.'

'Does that include my uncle's ... that is ... *my* cattle?'

His eyes narrowed. 'I'm no cattle rustler, if that's what you're thinking.'

'So you haven't been tempted to kill and eat one of my beasts?' At the curt dip of his head in reply, she bristled. 'What do you live on, then? Fresh air?'

'I have rations, and there are plenty of rabbits around the place.' He gave a wry snort. 'They grow fat 'n tender on your pasture.'

'Humph.' She frowned when the flicker of a grin tugged at his firm mouth. 'And how did you get here, Mr Jackson?'

'On foot ... Mrs Miller.'

'It's *Miss.*' At his offhand nod she felt a renewed flash of irritation, mostly at herself. What did it matter to either of them if she were married or single? 'So,' she said tartly, 'you're on a hike. Well then, it won't take you long to *hike* your way off my property.'

'So that's a no to my mending the fence?'

'Yes, that's a no.' To her annoyance he arched a dark brow and dipped his head at her, before turning and melting into the scrub, robbing her of the indignant exit.

Clicking Cooper into a spritely walk, she stuck out her chin and muttered, 'Damn squatters, thinking they can just lob on private property and set up camp.' She glanced back at Dopey, who stood staring after the man. 'And you were no help, wagging your tail at that stranger the whole time. Guess I can't count on *you* for protection.'

'Well, he *was* my mate before you arrived,' came that same deep voice from the bush, with a teasing ring to it. 'Guess he's opted for the soft life now.'

'Oh!' Her head flew up and she scowled. With a click of her tongue she urged Cooper into a jog.

The cheek of the man! Lucky for him her priority right now was to find and fix that broken fencing.

It was fortunate she had chosen to make checking the property's – *her* property's – boundaries the first priority. She dropped a hand to the leather saddlebag by her right leg and fingered the bulges made by the pliers and chain strainer. Just as well she brought them along. If she followed the river she should find the break fairly easily, assuming 'Mr Jackson' was correct.

Behind her Dopey gave a whimper, and turned his attention

from the spot where the man had disappeared to gaze after her. His white-pawed front feet darted uncertainly first one way and then the other until, with a final longing glance at the empty spot, he loped after her.

Cut.

All three strands, and all in the same spot.

Abbey eyed the breaks.

Intentional vandalism or stock theft?

By who? The squatter? Apart from the fact he didn't seem the type, why would he bother to cut a fence he could easily climb over? Her expression tightened.

Unless he wanted to remove stock.

But if that were the case, why would he *tell* her about the break? He'd want it to stay undiscovered as long as possible, to give him time to get away with the stolen cattle.

Her forehead creased further as she stared at the mix of tracks in the dirt. Cattle, horse, marsupial, and even the odd bird print, all gleefully traversing the unauthorised gateway.

Great. Now I'll have to go next door to reclaim any stock that wandered, and check my herds for any extraneous beasts.

After Cooper ambled through the gap, Abbey dismounted and left him ground-tied while she took out the pliers and strainer and went to work on the breaks. Dopey flopped to the ground in a patch of nearby shade, panting and watching her. He only sprang to his feet again when she set down her tools with a drawn-out groan and rose from her squatting position. Putting a hand on both sides of her waist, she leaned back slowly to stretch, screwing up her face as the knotted muscles loosened.

Dr Hughes would NOT be happy if he could see me now, but what else can I do? Leave this gaping hole in the fence? I don't think so.

She gave a wry huff.

Maybe I should've accepted the squatter's offer, he certainly looked capable enough. But can he be trusted?

While waiting for the spasms in her back to ease, she re-packed her tools and then idly watched Cooper graze. His munching and the swish of his tail at the odd fly added to the chorus of country sounds. After some more gentle stretching, she climbed gingerly into the saddle and urged him onward. As they set off, she leaned forward to eye the tracks. They led onto a well-trodden path that headed to the cattle yards of the neighbouring *Weerong Station.*

'A well-heeled man with big plans,' was how Bill had described the station's new owner. He'd said something else too, something less complimentary, but she'd been only half listening while mastering a tricky new movement. She did recall him chuckling, 'A "pretty boy", that's what he is. Don't get me wrong, he works hard ... on projecting the cattle baron image. That takes a lot of effort, y'know.'

With a sigh she urged Cooper into a loping canter.

Guess it's time I met Mr Pretty Boy Cattle Baron.

Her knock on the door was answered promptly.

'Hello there.' The man standing inside the doorway, sporting a fashionable stubble and combed-up hairstyle, flashed Abbey a white-toothed grin. He looked to be in his thirties, and very sure of himself. Spotless cream moleskins hugged his well-built lower body, and not a single crease marred his chambray shirt. He wore its long sleeves rolled up to his elbows, exposing the ropey muscles of his lean forearms. She caught a waft of cloying aftershave and resisted the impulse to screw up her nose.

Pretty boy indeed. And gym junkie if I'm any judge.

'I'm sorry to bother you—'

'Having such an attractive visitor is never a bother.'

Attractive?

She glanced down at herself.

Grubby and sweat-stained more like it. And...

Putting her nose to her upper arm she took a quick sniff.

Oh dear.

When she raised her eyes again, she found him grinning lazily at her. She cleared her throat. 'I'm from *Clearwater Downs* next door. My name's Abbey Miller, and—'

'Ah.' He gave a knowing nod. 'Bill's daughter.'

After a weighty pause she said, 'Niece, actually.'

'Niece, of course.'

Was that a note of condescension in his voice?

'You've been away a while, I believe?' His smile widened and he held out a pale hand. 'Vince Pearson. Pleased to meet you, Abbey Miller.'

Seeing his trimmed, pearly-white nails she glanced down at her own hand, grimaced, and hastened to wipe it against her pants before shaking his. 'You're the station owner here, Mr Pearson?'

'Vince. And yes, I'm the owner.' He stood to one side. 'Won't you come in?'

'Um ... thanks ... but I'd better stay out here, I'm a bit grubby.' She flicked him an apologetic glance. 'I'd like a quick word, though, if you have a moment?'

Pearson ran his eyes over her and shrugged. 'Okay.' Crossing his arms over his chest, he leaned against the door jamb to stare down at her with an arch expression.

She took a breath. 'It's about our boundary fence.'

Pearson straightened. 'Oh yes?'

'A section over by the river has been broken ... cut, actually ... and it looks like some stock might've strayed.'

A chill crept into his pale blue eyes. 'You think the fence was deliberately cut?'

'I know it was. Each of the wire strands was cleanly "broken" in the same place.' She saw his expression darken and hurried on. 'I fixed the hole.' When he remained tight-lipped, she prompted, 'So now I just need to check for strays.' She flashed him a wry grin. 'More likely *into* your place than out of it. Okay with you if I take a look around your bottom paddock?'

'My own stock are down there. How will you tell yours from mine?'

She stared at him, trying to judge if he was being funny or deliberately obtuse, before saying, 'You run Brahmans and Herefords, don't you?'

'Mostly.'

'And they're branded?'

'Of course.'

'Ours are too, and they're all first-cross Nguni so they're quite different to other breeds. And their speckled grey colour makes them easy to spot in a herd.'

'Nguni ... yeah.' Pearson rubbed his chin. 'Your uncle approached me a while back about some new breeding programme he was trialling. Wanted to know if he could use my polled Hereford bull to breed out horns and increase body mass in his next batch of calves. I told him I'd be happy to talk stud fees, though we never got to that point. He may have been hoping for free services, but....' He flashed another toothy grin. 'That bull's a prize-winner and his stud fees are worth a quid, that's why I bought him. Scored me a champion ribbon from last years' Ekka.'

At his mention of the Brisbane Exhibition, Abbey's eyes clouded. She lowered her head and scuffed the toe of a boot in the dirt.

Pearson eyed her with interest. 'A conversation for another time, perhaps.' The smarmy note to his voice was replaced by a professional edginess. 'Anyway, you go ahead and check that paddock. Of course I'll need to run my eyes over any beasts you find before you remove them. Not that I don't trust you,' he added with an oily smile, 'I'd just like to see these Nguni for myself.'

'I understand.' Her own voice hardened. 'I'll yard any I find,' and she waved a hand toward the station's recently expanded metal stock yards, 'so you can check them, before I take them home.'

'Are you doing this on your own?'

'Seems likely.'

'I could lend you one of my boys if you like?'

Although having extra hands to cut out strays would be useful, especially considering her under-par physical condition, something made her baulk at the idea. 'Thanks for the offer, but I don't want to put you to any bother.'

'It wouldn't be any—' At the chime of a phone from inside, Pearson cocked his head. With a curt, 'I'd better answer that,' he stepped back from the doorway.

'Of course.' Abbey moved down a step and raised a hand. 'Thanks—'

He was already closing the door.

Nice manners you have there, Mr Pearson.

Turning on her heel, she strode to where Cooper stood at the rail with his head down, eyes partly closed, and one back foot resting on a toe. He roused at her approach, ears flicking when she murmured, 'C'mon, boy,' as she untied him. After climbing into the saddle, she cast a final, pensive glance over the freshly painted and gleaming station homestead. 'Let's go. We've got a paddock to check.'

None.

Not a single Nguni beast in Pearson's bottom paddock.

It didn't make sense. All the one-way cattle tracks headed in this direction.

Abbey rode one final circuit, checking the few stands of shrubbery in case they hid beasts from view. All she found were Pearson's fat Herefords. Some stared and snorted at the human intruder on the large, dark horse, while others pranced away, tails tossed high over their glossy backs. Abbey had to give it to him, his stock were in top condition.

The man might project more the city slicker than cattleman image, but he appeared to understand the importance of animal husbandry and effective farm management, which all cost money. And from what she'd seen, he didn't skimp on anything.

Unlike most cash-strapped farmers in the district, including his nearest neighbour.

She sighed and guided Cooper into the shade of an iron-bark near the inner fence line. Loosening the reins so the gelding could graze, she gave a drawn-out groan and leaned forward to cross her arms over the saddle's pommel, stretching her throbbing back. When she caught a glimpse of speckled grey amid the Brahmans in the next paddock along, she sat up with a frown.

How did they get into *that* paddock? Surely not through another broken fence?

Unlikely. Pearson's internal fences were in as-new condition, like everything else on the property.

Damn.

She was going to have to tackle him again. Sitting low in the saddle, she considered her options.

It would pay to arm herself with figures before approaching Pearson again. If she was right and he had a keen business head, it would make their discussions easier if she quoted accurate figures to him. Thankfully Bill had been a stickler for keeping the farm's books up to date, she should be able to easily download a report of current stock numbers.

Gathering her reins, she turned Cooper for home.

Her back let her know she'd been sitting too long, staring at the computer screen.

Time for another tea break and stretch.

Coming up to speed on the farm records had taken longer than expected, despite their being fairly up to date.

Efficient as ever, Uncle Bill.

Abbey pushed back the chair and rose gingerly to her feet. As she made her way to the kitchen her footsteps echoed on the cypress pine floorboards in the otherwise quiet house. Passing the kitchen dresser, she flicked on the radio and country music from Bill's favourite station filled the silence. She swallowed the lump in her throat and busied herself filling the kettle.

Can't afford to brood. Just have to get over it and move on.

She stared out the window.

Easier said than done.

When the kettle overflowed she gave an annoyed huff and wrenched off the tap. She remained standing at the sink holding the dripping kettle, her gaze fixed on a patch of disturbed ground near her mother's grave.

Her stomach twisted into a familiar knot.

What was it the grief management website advised? 'Face your feelings.' 'Acknowledge your pain.'

I should pay my respects....

She turned away from the window and its gut-wrenching view.

One day, Uncle Bill ... but not today.

13

Abbey poured boiling water over the teabag and jiggled it in the cup as she made her way back to the computer. Questions tumbled over themselves in her mind, along with the image of scorched ground outside.

Had squatters really tried to torch the house?

Would they return for another try?

Gero mentioned someone seeing them off. What someone?

And what about the boundary fence being cut on purpose. Why, and by whom?

Gero reckoned there'd been funny things happening lately....

A chill crept up her spine.

He also harboured suspicions about Bill's death ... suspicions shared by level-headed Flip.

When fear blossomed in her chest, Abbey thrust the questions aside. She couldn't afford to dwell on whys and what-ifs, had to stay focused on the job at hand.

Putting her steaming cup on the desk, she settled herself in the chair.

'Day at a time, girl,' Bill used to say when she was stressed about exams or upcoming shows. 'Take things a day at a time and she'll be right.'

She blinked her mind clear and woke the computer. A satellite photo of the twelve hundred acre farm materialised on screen. It showed the property stretching back some three kilometres from its two kilometre main road frontage, to the national park boundary. Five Mile creek snaked through the property like an Eastern Brown, and to the ongoing frustration of neighbouring farmers, disappeared below ground just shy of the north-western boundary.

Clearwater Downs had always enjoyed the best access to the precious water source. When it came to landholding selection, Bill had chosen well.

Abbey opened the farm management database and perused the stock records, last updated just days before he....

Swallowing, she made herself focus on the screen, scrolling through the report's fields.

Ninety-two Nguni cows and forty-three heifers. Of the cows, seventy-five were in calf to a poll Hereford, Cassanova, owned by David Graham.

Abbey wrapped both hands around her cup and sat back to sip her tea. The Grahams' spread, *Oakey Creek Station,* was on the other side of Miriam Vale. Why would Bill have gone to the trouble of transporting a bull from so far away? He could've just paid Pearson stud fees for what was supposedly a top-notch bull, situated just next door. Seeing a link to a footnote, Abbey clicked on it and read the entry. It noted the length of Cassanova's agistment on *Clearwater Downs,* along with agreed remuneration arrangements. The Grahams were to have the pick of one of the Hereford-Nguni bull calves.

Abbey closed the laptop and sighed. *Clearwater* cattle had strayed onto Pearson's property, for sure, but until she did a head count she couldn't be certain exactly how many were missing. And Pearson struck her as the type to be anal about details. To have the situation resolved to her satisfaction, she had to go to him with accurate information.

Sitting straighter, she arched her back to ease the dull ache. While Cooper offered the smoothest gait of all the horses, she wasn't getting back on him today. She drained her cup, rose and rinsed it in the sink, keeping her eyes averted from the window and the view of recently disturbed ground.

Picking up the car keys from off the dresser, she headed outside, taking care to lock the front door behind her. She climbed into the four-wheel-drive, settled herself squarely in the bucket seat, and slipped the key in the ignition. The diesel engine started easily enough, but ran rough until it warmed up.

Keep going, old mate. Can't afford to replace you. Not in the near future, or the distant for that matter.

With financial figures bouncing around her head, she made for Miriam Vale.

Granger heard the ute motoring along the property's access road.

Miss Miller perhaps, going out in a car this time.

He went back to toasting a slice of bread over the open fire, but in his mind's eye he saw a pair of grey eyes sparking with indignation, slender hands grasping reins, and a suppressed wince of pain on a girl-next-door face.

A face with a cute dusting of freckles across the nose....

Trundling through the white post-and-rail fence at the entrance to *Oakey Creek Station,* Abbey followed the winding track to the Graham residence. Though she took it slow to keep the dust down, clouds of it still billowed in her wake. On approach to the Queenslander-styled homestead, she slowed to a crawl and pulled in next to the house.

Rhonda Graham emerged through the open front door to stand on the veranda, drying her hands on her frill-edged and flour-dusted apron while squinting at the car. She wore her long hair pulled back and coiled at her neck. Her figure was still trim beneath the floral-patterned cotton shift, but her weathered face was more lined than Abbey remembered.

'Abbey!' Rhonda smiled as she watched her climb down from the ute. 'We were hoping we might see you.'

'Gidday, Rhonda.' Abbey returned the smile. 'Hope this isn't a bad time?'

'Not at all. Come on in, I'll make us a cuppa.'

'Thanks.' Abbey climbed the stairs and followed Rhonda inside.

As they entered the expansive, country-style kitchen smelling of stewed apple, cinnamon, and a hint of vanilla, Rhonda flicked her a glance. 'We were so sorry to hear about your uncle.'

'Yeah ... I really....' Abbey's voice grew breathy. She swallowed. 'Really miss him.'

Rhonda turned to put a warm hand on Abbey's arm and gave it a squeeze. The compassion in her gaze was almost Abbey's undoing. She was relieved when Rhonda gave her arm a final pat and withdrew her hand.

'I'll put the kettle on, and let Dave know you're h—' She was interrupted by a squelch from the two-way.

'Oakey Creek One to Oakey Creek Base. You there, Ronny? Over.'

Rhonda smiled. 'That's him now.' Striding to the small desk beneath the window, she picked up the two-way radio's handset.

'I'm here, darl, and we have a visitor. Abbey from *Clearwater Downs*. Over.'

'Abbey Miller?'

'Yep. How far away are you?'

'About ten minutes. I'll head in. Put the billy on.'

'Already done. Seeya in ten.'

'Right-o.'

The two women were sitting on the veranda in white cane chairs at a matching table, sipping tea from the delicate china cups Rhonda kept for 'special', when a wiry dun stockhorse appeared. It loped through the paddock gate and up to the homestead's fence.

Slipping his worn riding boots out of the stock saddle's stirrups, the rider climbed down from the horse and flicked the reins over the rail. He took a moment to dust off his stained moleskins before striding bow-legged to the front steps. Removing his sweat and dirt-stained hat as he climbed the stairs, the tall man fixed his gaze on Abbey, who rose to her feet.

'Hello, young lady.' His weathered face split in a wide grin. 'Pleased to see you back here.' He extended a large, work-roughened hand to grasp hers firmly.

Abbey gave a smiling nod. 'Thanks Dave.' As she resumed her seat, she steeled herself for what she knew would come next. Beside her, Rhonda was busy pouring another tea, a sugary straight black, in a plain-coloured mug.

Dave pulled out a chair and sank into it with a grunt, pushing his sweat-dampened fringe back from his forehead. 'Sorry about Bill. He was a top bloke, and well liked.' To Abbey's relief Dave didn't appear to expect an answer, was busy taking the mug of tea Rhonda held out to him.

When Rhonda indicated the plate in the centre of the table, he wiped his hands on his pants. Taking a piece of still-warm apple teacake, he popped the whole thing in his mouth. 'Mmm ... this is great, love. You should enter one in this year's show. Reckon you'd come home with another first prize for baking.' After a fond glance at his wife, he turned back to Abbey. 'There was quite a crowd at the funeral, lotsa folk wantin' to pay their respects.'

She pressed her lips together and nodded.

'So,' Rhonda said brightly, 'tell us what you've been up to down south?' She glanced at Abbey's left hand. 'Didn't get married or engaged while you were away?'

When Abbey merely shook her head and stared into her cup, the Grahams shared a glance.

'Say,' Dave piped up, 'we heard you'd become a famous trick rider. You always did sit a horse well.'

'Thanks.' Abbey took a breath and lifted her chin. 'Though I was hardly *famous*.'

'But you rode in some high-profile shows,' Rhonda said with a fond smile. 'We even saw you on TV once.'

Abbey gave a coy grin. 'My fifteen minutes of fame.'

They made small talk for a while and then Dave said, 'I'd like to stay chatting but I'd better be gettin' back. I've left Dean pushing the mob.' He threw them a wry grin. 'Hopefully they're still in the state.'

'Oh Dave,' Rhonda chided with a laugh. 'You know he's getting better at mustering.'

It had come as a shock when their youngest was born with an intellectual disability, especially after their other children were all-round fit and healthy from birth. After recovering from the blow, Dave and Rhonda resolved to make sure Dean was given the same opportunities as his siblings. They arranged for him to attend a special school in Bundaberg, and taught him how to ride a horse, and help around the farm. It took a lot of time and patience, but they regarded it as worth all the effort.

'Yeah, the lad's doing alright.' Dave fixed Abbey with a level gaze. 'Before I go, do you mind me askin' what's happening to *Clearwater?*'

'Uncle Bill left it to me.' A ripple of apprehension crossed her face.

'Right.'

Both Grahams smiled their approval.

'If I'd known that....' Dave blew a breath. 'Anyway, I was at your place the other day, gettin' Cassanova back. That's my poll Hereford bull. Your uncle had him servicing his cows. After Bill ... um ... well....' Dave cleared his throat. 'I wasn't sure what'd be happening with the property, so thought it prudent to bring my bull home.'

'Completely understandable, Dave.' Abbey met his steady gaze. 'Cassanova was on loan for the last three months?'

'Yeah ... that's about right.' Dave looked thoughtful. 'Bill came to me after first approaching Pearson, who wanted an arm and a leg for stud fees, apparently. Not real neighbourly of the selfish sod, considering all the help Bill gave him when he first took over *Weerong Station*. Pearson keeps spruiking how his bull won a blue ribbon at the Ekka, which I have my doubts about. Don't get me wrong it's not a bad animal, just not worth the fees he's askin' ... and which nobody around here is prepared to pay.'

Abbey dipped her head as Dave went on. 'Anyway, when I got to your place I couldn't see my bull in any of the paddocks. Eventually spotted him next door.' He paused to swallow another mouthful of cake. 'I went straight over there and informed Pearson, who wasn't happy, but let me go get Cassanova. He couldn't really say no. The bull is branded and well known in the district. On top of that, he might've got the benefit of some services, although I doubt he'd say they were a benefit.'

'You don't trust Pearson?'

Rhonda answered first. 'There's just something about him that doesn't sit right. He's all-round too ... smooth ... for my liking.'

Dave put a hand on her shoulder. 'I don't really know the man, but I recall Bill mentioning squabbles they'd had over straying stock. And that wasn't the only dispute between them.'

'Oh?'

'For a while there Pearson was pestering Bill to sell him *Clearwater*. Not that your uncle would consider selling the property in any case, but Pearson wasn't even offering what it's worth. Then, when Bill discovered someone was syphoning water from his section of the creek, Pearson was the obvious culprit. Who else could afford the shiny new pump and lengths of pipework that were in place.' Dave's eyebrows twitched. 'Bill confronted him about it and they almost came to blows.'

When Abbey's eyes widened, Dave gave a chuckle. 'Although I always regarded your uncle as a pacifist, he could be quite the force to be reckoned with at times. And handy in a fight if provoked.'

'Yes.' Abbey's thoughts darted to the night her father came to the farm. After a reflective pause she said, 'I'm sorry for the trouble you had getting your bull back, Dave.'

'Not your fault. If you ask me, Pearson's to blame, for not looking after his fences better. When I couldn't find my bull on your spread I rode the fence line, and discovered a break. That's how I tracked down Cassanova. After I moved him back through, I fixed the fence.'

Abbey frowned. 'You fixed the break?'

'Well, I thought it possible Cassanova was responsible.' Dave gave a wry huff. 'He can be toey when there are cows on heat within cooee.'

'Did it look like the wires had been cut?'

'Deliberately?' Dave pursed his lips. 'It's possible, though I didn't take an awful lot of notice at the time. Why do you ask?'

'Because it's happened again.'

'Another break?'

'Cut, all three strands.'

Dave crinkled his chin and shook his head.

'Yeah. So like you, *I* have stock to retrieve from next door.'

He eyed her gravely. 'If you need a hand, just say so. Dean

and I can head over there. He could use some more cutting and mustering practice.'

'And you might want someone with you,' Rhonda cut in, 'when you go to see Pearson.'

Abbey smiled at them. 'Thanks, but judging from Bill's records I think there are only about ten strays. I should be okay to collect them on my own.'

'Well, the offer stands, so keep it in mind.' Rising, Dave slapped his hat against his leg before donning it again. 'I best get goin', Dean'll be wondering where I've got to.' He tipped his hat at them and grinned. 'Better not tell him I've been here sippin' tea and scoffin' cake with you ladies.'

'A step ahead of you, darl.' Rhonda held out a bulging paper bag. 'And you better make sure he gets it.' She winked at her husband. 'You know he'll give me a full report when he gets home.'

Dave's grin widened and he rolled his eyes. 'You spoil that boy.'

'I spoil you both.'

After planting a kiss on his wife's waiting cheek, he straightened and turned to their guest. 'See you, Abbey. Don't be a stranger now, you hear?'

The sun was blazing from high in the sky by the time Abbey returned home. Dopey bounded to meet the car, his tail in full circular wag motion. As she climbed out of the ute, wiping the sweat from under her eyes, she gave the nearest tyre a kick.

'Damn busted air con. Why can't you just rise from the dead?'

When Dopey gave a happy whine and put his front paws on

her thighs, she bent to rub the dog's ears, keeping her hands free of his licking tongue.

'Got some things to do around here this 'arve, boy, and we've got a big day tomorrow. You any good at working stock?'

Dopey gazed adoringly at her and wriggled closer.

She gave an amused snort. 'Somehow I doubt it.'

14

Abbey woke before the alarm the following morning and lay on her back in the Queen-sized bed Bill had suggested she buy, '... with an eye to the future.' He had no doubt expected her to bring home someone to share it one day.

I imagined that day was near, but I was wrong.

As her thoughts strayed to Jesse for the first time in a while, she was pleased to feel only a vague sting.

It seems you're easier to get over than expected.

Though having someone like him to lend a hand around the farm would've been a huge help. To share the workload and the worry; provide a comforting shoulder when things got tough. Even better if that someone was able to boost the coffers and ease the financial burden.

She gave a wry huff.

That wouldn't be you, Jesse Boyce. Money only flowed one way around you – inwards. Your mother schooled you well.

Her face clouded.

I refuse to be like her, always on the look-out for the next financier. I'll manage on my own, one way or another.

If only my back was fully healed. I could get paid work around the district to help with a few bills....

Refusing to brood further, she pulled her knees in to her chest in a bear hug, an exercise the physiotherapist had recommended for stretching her back. After holding the pose she released her knees, rolled to the side, and carefully climbed out of bed.

Padding to the kitchen in her shorty pyjamas, she put the kettle on the range and a slice of bread in the toaster. While waiting, she packed a few Anzac biscuits and an apple into a sandwich bag. Morning tea.

Important she keep up her strength.

Raising her hands toward the ceiling she stretched her body right up to her fingertips, pleased to feel no twinges. Hopefully her back would handle another stint in the saddle. Going to her room she pulled on a pair of jodhpurs and a long-sleeved cotton shirt, both worn soft by years of wear.

After breakfast she donned riding boots, grabbed her helmet, pocketed a pencil and the notepad containing handwritten figures, and headed to the door. Dopey leaped up from his mat as she stepped onto the veranda, and followed her into the tack shed. She had shut Cooper in the house yard the day before so he'd be there, ready to go. When he saw her coming he gave a soft whinny and left his now empty hay net to saunter to the fence.

By five-thirty she was in the saddle and on the move.

Cooper didn't take much urging to settle into a steady, ground-eating gait. With Dopey jogging by their side, they made good time assessing the stocked paddocks, with Abbey noting the head count in each.

After arriving at a total figure and calculating the number of missing stock, she tucked the notepad into her pocket. Finding a shady tree to sit under, she stretched out and ate her morning tea. When her eyelids drooped, she rested her head against the tree's broad trunk, closed her eyes, and listened to Cooper grazing nearby.

The swish of his muzzle across the grass, followed by the crunch, tug and chew when he found a tasty clump, made a contented, comforting sound. It was accompanied by the whisper of breeze through the tree's canopy high above, and the melodic trill and warble of bird calls.

Nowhere else I'd rather be....

Back in the saddle after the short break, and pleased to have found no sign of the pesky squatter, she turned the gelding's head toward Pearson's property and clicked him into a spritely canter.

'Time to get our strays back, Coop.'

On *Weerong Station,* she counted nine Nguni cattle amid the stock in the lower paddock nearest *Clearwater's* boundary.

Nine of the ten she was missing.

Not a bad result for a morning's work.

Working her way along the tree line, Abbey cut the speckled beasts from the herd and assembled them in a group. Cooper arched his neck and jogged like a keen cow pony as they pushed the mob forward, until Dopey ran in front of him with a growling bark. As the gelding gave a snort and jerked to a stop, Abbey peered ahead and saw four riders galloping toward her.

Dopey's bark intensified, and she waved a hushing hand at him. 'Alright, Dopey, alright.'

He glanced at her, whimpered, and slinked into the underbrush.

She shook her head.

My hero.

When the four riders drew closer she recognised Pearson on a flashy palomino stallion. The other three with him rode dark-coloured stockhorses. Whips and other implements dangled from their stock saddles. They circled the mob, making the cattle shift and bellow. Pearson pushed his stallion right up to Cooper, who took a step back before Abbey checked him.

Cocking an eyebrow, Pearson let his eyes rove over her. 'May I ask what you're doing on my property, Miss Miller?'

Her hackles rose at his condescending demeanour. 'Retrieving my cattle, as we discussed previously.' Her tone was starchy and she eyed him steadily. 'I did a complete stock count and discovered ten of my stock were missing.' She swept a hand over the shuffling mob. 'Found these nine in your bottom paddock. Was going to yard them for you to check, as agreed, but you can see for yourself now that they're not part of your herd.'

He gave a cool, assured smile. 'You'll still need to come to the house, to pay the stud fees you owe.'

'What stud fees?' She noticed the three stockmen share a smirk, and her ire rose.

'Your stock have been "cohabiting" with my bull, therefore you owe me stud fees.'

She frowned. 'These cattle were already in calf, to David Graham's bull.'

Pearson paused to eye her. 'I take it you have proof of this?'

'I do.'

At her confident reply, his eyes narrowed. Leaning forward in the saddle, he rubbed a hand over his chin. 'Of course there's also the agistment cost to consider.'

'Agistment?' Her frown deepened. 'You know the fence had been cut, I told you that myself. And it's not like I would *choose* to have my cattle stray onto your property.' She glanced around. 'Especially as the feed here isn't as good as mine, I have to say.'

'Not as good?' He jerked upright and swept a glance over the surrounding paddock. Turning back to her with a stony expression he growled, 'In your opinion.'

She shrugged.

A low note of warning crept into his voice. 'Correct me if I'm wrong, but I get the impression you think someone *intended* for your stock to stray onto my property.' He paused to fix her with a challenging gaze. 'I do hope you're not accusing *me*, Miss Miller.'

'Of course not. I'm just saying—'

'Cattle rustling is a serious charge, even these days.'

'I never said anything about—'

'Then again....' Pearson nodded to his stockmen, who closed ranks around the mob cutting her off from them. 'Perhaps you aren't aware of such things.' His eyes flashed and he gave a loud, affected sigh. 'A young lady on her own out here in the sticks with a sizeable property to manage.' He shook his head. 'It would be awful if you went under. I don't know why your uncle would want to burden you so.'

She grit her teeth as he went on in the same smarmy voice.

'City life offers so much more. I'm sure a pretty girl like yourself would prefer living back there to being stuck out here.' Tipping his head at a thoughtful angle, he tapped his chin. 'You know, it just occurred to me that I might be able to help you out.' One side of his upper lip twitched. 'There'd be benefits to amalgamating our two properties. As you mentioned, your paddocks offer better year-round feed. So I might be interested in taking the place off your hands.'

She stared at him, wide-eyed at his gall. 'You're offering to buy *Clearwater Downs?*'

'I'm offering to help you out of a difficult situation.'

Anger glittered in her eyes. 'Well, unlike you, I don't see running a well-managed property as a "difficult" situation, *Mr* Pearson.'

'It may have been well managed in the past, but things can change quickly on the land.'

'Perhaps, but I *am* my uncle's niece.'

He went on as though she hadn't spoken. 'And the more run-down a property becomes, the more it devalues, and the harder it is to sell.'

Her nostrils flared.

'And while that may not concern you now, you need to think about the future.'

Lifting her chin she said through tight lips, 'Thank you for the lesson in rural economics, Mr Pearson. If you're quite done, I'll take my cattle and go.'

'You're free to go, of course, Miss Miller. But I'm sure you'll understand why I can't let you take these cattle.'

She stared at him. 'You know they're not yours.'

'That may be so but there's still the question of agistment fees, which I hate to say, are now in arrears.'

'You're kidding, right?'

His expression hardened. 'I never "kid" about money or business, Miss Miller. And these cattle have been grazing on my apparently *inferior* pasture for some time now.'

They glared at each other, and then Abbey ground out, 'I'm not leaving without my stock.'

'Oh, but I think you *are.*' Pearson's sneer faltered when a deep voice rumbled from the nearby scrub.

'And *I* think you should let the lady take her cattle.'

Abbey's eyes widened as she turned toward the voice.

Beside her, the palomino snorted and threw up its head, coiling its pale-gold body as the rider's legs tightened around its girth.

Struggling to keep his wild-eyed mount in check, Pearson puffed, 'Who the hell are *you?*' as a large, stern-faced man materialised from the tree line. 'And where did you come from?' After sweeping a glance around the bush as if expecting a whole regiment to appear, he fixed his pale eyes on the interloper.

Granger crossed his arms over his broad chest and stared coolly back at him. 'We met the other night. At least your *thugs* and I did.' He waved a hand at the stockmen and noticed one of them hastily reposition his leg against a saddle flap, as if to hide something.

Sauntering over to him, Granger pushed the man's leg aside, to stare at a crossbow bolt tucked into a fold in the flap. 'This is mine.' Plucking the bolt from the flap, he ran a hand up and down the shaft, checking its condition. He arched an eyebrow up at the man. 'Thanks for returning it.'

At the sarcasm in his tone the stockman scowled and made to reach for something on his horse's off-side. When Granger tapped the bolt against the hunting knife strapped to his leg, the man froze.

Barking, 'Leave it,' Pearson raked his gaze over Granger, taking in the man's size and physique. 'That was you?'

Granger dipped his head and moved to Cooper's side. Flicking Abbey a 'trust me' glance, he took hold of the gelding's bridle and led the horse closer to the milling mob of Nguni. 'And unless you want to get into the details of that *encounter* here and now,' he said smoothly, 'the lady and I will take our leave. *With* her cattle.'

A flush crept up Pearson's neck and into his face. He glanced sideways at Abbey as his horse began dancing again, half-rearing when he checked it.

Growling, 'This isn't over,' he spun the stallion around. 'Come on, boys.' When he dug his gleaming spurs against its quivering side, the palomino gave a squeal and leaped into a gallop, throwing up clods of dirt in its wake.

Doing their best to shower Granger and Abbey with more tufts of grass and dirt, the three stockmen sped after their boss.

Shielding their faces from flying clods, Granger and Abbey watched until the four disappeared over a rise.

Neither spoke for a long moment.

Granger let go of Cooper's bridle and looked up, to find Abbey gazing down at him.

'I thought you were moving on, Mr Jackson?'

He gave an amused huff though his expression remained stern. 'If that's meant to be a thank-you, Miss Miller, it falls a bit shy of the mark.'

Abbey frowned, unsure whether to be grateful or annoyed at his assumption she needed 'saving'. She continued staring at him, assessing him. 'What did you mean when you said you'd met those "thugs" before? It didn't look like they recognised you?'

He shrugged. 'It was dark,' and then pointed at the Nguni. 'They're a bit stirred-up. I could give you a hand to herd them back if you like?'

She chewed her bottom lip, wanting to repeat the order for him to move on. But the confrontation with Pearson had rattled her, and she felt safer in the company of the big man standing at Cooper's head. 'You won't be much help without a horse.'

'Just take it slow, the dog and I will keep up. We could take a shortcut, over the western boundary where the gully drains into Five Mile.'

This squatter certainly knew his way around the place.

Abbey's brow creased. 'There's no gate there.'

'So we do what they did.' He pointed to her saddlebag. 'Cut the fence and push the mob through. Only we'll close it up again behind us.'

Abbey eyed him. It was actually a smart plan. Taking that route would cut a fair chunk of time off the trip, and keep them well away from *Weerong's* homestead.

Lifting her chin, she gathered her reins. 'Right, let's do it.'

15

The saw-back of the tactical knife's ten-inch blade easily severed the barbed wire strands. Abbey eyed the wicked-looking weapon with some trepidation as Granger tucked it back into its scabbard.

A furrow formed in her brow.

How much did she know about this Jackson character?

Know? Almost nothing. But she *felt* he could be trusted. Was certain of it, for some inexplicable reason.

After folding the cut strands out of the way, he stepped back for her to push the mob through the newly created gap. When she followed the last beast past him, he put out a hand. 'I'll need the chain strainer.'

She reined in Cooper, fished the tool out of her saddlebag, and handed it to him. 'I assume you've used one of these before?'

With a curt nod, he took it from her and tilted his head toward the dispersing cattle. 'Keep 'em moving. I'll catch up when I've finished here.' Seeing her sceptical expression, he added, 'And I'll drop the strainer back to you, and be on my way.' With a wave of a hand, he turned his attention to the fence. Pushing his rolled-up sleeves higher on his arms, he went to work.

She couldn't help admiring the way his impressive bicep and tricep muscles rippled as he worked, and the breadth and depth of his chest....

Annoyed at herself, she shook away the wayward thoughts and clicked Cooper into a walk. When she gave in to the impulse and glanced back at him, Granger caught her looking. Whipping her head around, she urged Cooper faster, while behind them Granger turned back to the job with a twitch of firm lips.

While pushing the cattle forward, Abbey thought about the two men. Pearson was not a friend, that was clear. And while she wasn't sure about Granger, it was clear he was no friend of Pearson's either. The ancient proverb, *the enemy of my enemy is my friend,* sprang to mind, followed by a question.

Was Pearson really the enemy?

He had offered to buy *Clearwater,* and selling the property *would* free her from the burden of responsibility....

Her eyes narrowed.

Could Pearson prove to be her unwitting saviour?

The bloke might be shifty, but she could arm herself with professional help from the likes of the officious and pedantic Ferris Dolcher....

Hang on! What the hell?

Surely she wasn't considering *offloading* the farm Bill had entrusted to her care? Land he'd poured so much of himself into? Where he now lay, along with her mother?

Then again, if she didn't sell, could she manage the property on her own? Even Bill, an experienced and capable man of the land, had struggled at times to make ends meet.

In addition to being alone, she was also in reduced physical condition. Lots of tasks she could normally handle herself were out of reach, for now at least.

Would selling the farm be the sensible move, or betrayal disguised as a solution?

Bill had been nothing if not sensible, but it didn't matter which way she looked at it. Selling his beloved farm would mean letting him down ... again.

Granger noted her grim, brooding expression when he jogged up beside her a while later. As she pulled Cooper to a stop he held up the strainer. 'All done.' He was breathing hard from the run.

She stared distractedly down at him, before blinking her eyes into focus and reaching for the tool.

Was a short term solution standing right there in front of her, puffing? One that would give her time to properly consider her options and make the right decision?

As he bent to put his hands on his taut thighs and suck in some breaths, she cleared her throat. 'Thank you, Mr Jackson.'

He straightened and tilted his hat at her. 'You're welcome, Miss Miller. Now, if that's all, I'll be on my way.'

As he made to move off she said in a rush, 'Are you still looking for work?'

He stopped to raise questioning eyes at her.

'I can't *pay* you,' she went on, trying not to sound apologetic, 'but I can offer you board and lodging.' Marvelling at her own boldness, she added quickly, 'You'd be sleeping in the stable building, above the stalls. It's not luxurious but is quite spacious, and weather-proof.'

His chin crinkled as he gazed thoughtfully at her.

Rabbit most nights *was* getting a bit old, and the thought of showering in a real bathroom again was tempting. And there was something about this young woman that made him feel ... what? Protective, maybe?

Finally he said, 'Food and lodging will be fine for now. I'll go collect my gear.'

'So, you can start straight away?'

He nodded.

'Do you know where to come?'

He was already striding off.

At his back-handed wave in reply, she shook her head and mumbled, 'I guess that's a yes.' Looking down for Dopey she spied him trotting after Granger, tail doing a relaxed wag. 'Here, boy!'

At her call, the Kelpie stopped in his tracks and glanced back at her.

'Come on, Dopey.' When she patted her saddle the dog jogged back to Cooper's side. 'Good boy.' Raising her eyes to see Granger melt into the scrub, she murmured, 'He's not your master, you know. Just a blow-in, so don't get too used to having him around.'

The stable building at *Clearwater Downs* contained spacious stalls down one side and an enclosed storage room for tack and tools. As he strolled up to the narrow building, Granger noticed Abbeys' mount in the house yard. Picking at a hay net, the heavy horse appeared to have had a hose and a rub-down to remove under-saddle sweat. Inside the building, Abbey's saddle sat astride a stall rail, a thick saddle cloth spread over it to dry.

At the far end of the building a sturdy timber ladder led to a hayloft. When Granger climbed the ladder to survey the area, he found hay bales stacked to head height in rows to the right and left of a central walkway. It would be easy to shift the bales around to make room for his gear, and a mattress to sleep on. He got straight to it. On moving the end bales, he uncovered a timber-framed double casement window in the wall. It opened easily on oiled hinges and let in the easterly breeze. It also offered a panoramic view of the homestead, paddocks, and eucalyptus-blue mountain range beyond.

A handy vantage point.

He stood taking in the view, feeling the breeze evaporate the sweat from his arms and back.

As far as 'Aussie sheds' went, this one *was* luxurious, despite what she'd said.

He turned back to his gear. After unloading what he'd need, he flattened a bed of hay and spread his swag on top of it. Testing it with a hand, he gave a satisfied grunt. It was a definite improvement on hard ground.

When he caught the crunch of approaching footsteps on gravel he peered down toward the open doorway.

Dawdling to an uncertain stop just outside, Abbey called, 'Um ... Mr ... Jackson?'

'Up here.'

She stepped inside and found him gazing down at her. 'Oh, you *are* here. I wasn't sure....'

'Arrived a short while ago.' His steady gaze didn't waver.

She nodded, quashing the urge to fidget. 'Is ... um ... everything okay? Will you be comfortable in here? I have spare blankets in the house if you need any. And pillows ... if....'

When he shook his head she caught the glimmer of a smile, as though he were amused by her bluster. She felt a flash of irritation at him and herself. Something else, too. Like an electrical current zapping her nervous system....

Refusing to examine the cause, she took a breath and stood straighter. 'It's a bit late for lunch but I've made sandwiches, and will be brewing a pot of tea. They're up at the house if you'd like some.'

'Thanks.'

Abbey watched him descend the ladder, his movements fluid and effortless.

One day mine will be like that again.

'Right. Well ... follow me.' Turning on her heel, she strode out of the stables, telling herself to get a damn grip and stop blustering. The bloke was just a temporary worker. Why get all het-up over him being there with her?

Maybe because it was just the two of them ... here, alone. And despite the trust he engendered in her, he was a complete stranger.

Had this been a really bad idea?

Granger followed her out, shortening his stride to stay a respectful distance behind. He didn't want to add to her discomfort. It was clear she felt awkward about his being at the farm, and there was something physical going on with her too. Her movements appeared stiff, unnatural. And he'd caught her giving more than one pained wince.

After removing his boots he followed her inside the homestead. When his eyes adjusted to the lower light, they fell on an assortment of D'Arcy Doyle prints, hanging from picture rails along the corridor. He read the plaques on the frame of each print as he passed. *The Budding Socceroos, Match Practice,* and *Sunday Morning,* all reflected the artist's appreciation of flowering jacaranda trees. The fourth in the collection, *The Old Stockman,* offered the quintessentially Aussie image of a silver-haired horseman on a chestnut making his way through knee-high grass, a windmill in the background.

Abbey led Granger into the kitchen at the back of the house, where a platter of freshly-cut sandwiches sat under plastic wrap in the centre of the table. She motioned for him to take a seat while she set the kettle on the range. While waiting for the water to boil, she cast him a quick sideways glance.

'I can't keep calling you "Mr Jackson". What's your first name?'

'Jackson.'

'Your name is Jackson *Jackson?*'

This time he actually laughed. It was a deep, rumbling sound that wrapped around her like a hug. Despite its warmth, she shivered.

'Jackson *Granger.*' He moved closer, hand extended.

She hesitated, feeling foolish. 'You let me call you "Mr Jackson" all this time?'

'Sorry. The subject just ... never came up.' He had the grace to look chagrined. 'Most people call me Jack.' Taking her slender hand in his large paw, he gave it a brief shake before letting go and stepping back.

'Abbey ... Miller....' Her voice trailed off. Seconds ticked by while she stared, perplexed, at her tingling hand. Hastily dropping it to her side, she gushed, 'Right ... well ... um ... pleased to meet you properly, Jack Granger.'

'And you, Abbey Miller.' He stood watching her, curiosity in his eyes.

'Please, take a seat.' She indicated the table with a lift of her chin. 'And help yourself to a sandwich.'

And stop staring at me.

When he turned away, she blinked hard and blew a silent breath through pursed lips. A moment later the kettle gave a whistle and she lifted it off the range. After pouring the steaming water into the brown ceramic teapot that lived on the tray beside the stove, she slipped a knitted cosy over the pot and carried the tray to the table.

Granger looked up, his mouth full of ham and salad.

'Tea?'

Setting down the sandwich, he slapped the crumbs from his hands and nodded.

'How do you take it?'

After swallowing the mouthful, he said thickly, 'Black.'

She began pouring, inclining her head at the bowl on the tray. 'Help yourself to sugar.'

'Thanks.' He picked up the sandwich again. It appeared tiny in his hand.

'You know, your surname rings a bell.' Setting down the teapot after pouring their drinks, she tapped her lips with a finger. 'Say ... would you have any connection with Granger Farm, out Lowmead way?'

The atmosphere in the room changed.

Became highly charged.

16

'It's a big spread, near Lowmead.' Abbey gazed at him, wondering at the sudden change in his demeanour. 'Has a dam right beside the road, and in the centre, a sprawling Queenslander homestead perched on a rise.'

A Queenslander with sweeping verandas, decorative cream railings, and walls painted a colour his mother called peppermint green; a colour he and Johnno had fun describing in gross, schoolboy terms when they were kids. Out of Melanie's hearing, of course.

A look akin to pain crossed Granger's face. Opening his fingers, he let his half-eaten sandwich fall to the plate. 'I know the place,' he said stiffly.

She continued eyeing him. 'And ... do you know the owners?'

His expression darkened. 'Not any more.'

'But you knew them before, the Grangers who owned the place?'

Grabbing his mug of tea, he put it to his lips and mumbled, 'I knew them.'

She watched him sip the steaming brew. Why was he being so cagey?

About to press him, she noted the tightening line of his mouth. 'I don't mean to pry,' she said cautiously, 'I'm just—'

'Look.' His eyes flashed. 'I'm not one for small talk, okay?'

Her voice hardened. 'Since when is interviewing a new employee "small talk"?'

'Is that what this is, a job interview?'

'Of a sort.'

'If I'd known that....'

She tilted her head to the side. 'You would've had more to say, or even less?'

Despite acknowledging she had a right to be curious, he glowered at her. That he was having to field tricky questions was his own fault. He had failed to keep his distance, had ventured too close to where the past waited to torment him.

He blew a resigned breath. 'I had family connections around here ... years ago.' When he saw her open her mouth, he said sharply, 'Can we leave it at that?'

'Well ... okay.' Abbey sat back to study him. It appeared she'd made a dent in his rugged, self-reliant persona.

Time for a change of subject.

'I want to thank you for your help with Pearson this morning.' She frowned. 'I couldn't tell if he was serious or just trying to rattle me. He certainly rattled Coop, and that's saying something.'

'Coop?'

'The gelding I was riding, Cooper. He's a cold blood, so not easy to upset.'

With a nod, Granger drained his cup and set it down, keeping his hands wrapped around it. Staring into the dregs he said slowly, 'I'd steer well clear of that Pearson bloke if I were you.' Before she could say anything more, he pushed his chair back and rose to his feet. 'Thanks for lunch. Now, what would you like me to start working on? Reckon the wood pile could use some attention.'

'You can take the rest of the day to settle in if you like?'

He shook his head. 'I'm ready to start work.'

'Alright then.' She shrugged. 'You can start by chopping some wood. Tomorrow we'll do a boundary ride and check the fences. You *can* ride can't you, horses that is?'

'It's been a while, but yeah, I can ride.' He took his plate to the sink and rolled up his sleeves.

'Don't worry about that. I'll let you off dishwashing duty this time.' Seeing him head for the door, she raised a hand. 'Oh, and just so you know, most days dinner will be at six pm and breakfast at six am.'

'Right-o.'

As the flyscreen door clattered closed behind him, she rested her hands on her hips and arched her back to ease the knot of muscles.

Not one for small talk is something of an understatement.

Granger paused for a breather after stacking a pile of firewood near the kitchen's outer wall. Glancing over at the gelding – Cooper – now dozing in the house yard, he noticed a newly-cut post lying at the base of an existing fence post. When he sauntered over to inspect it, he spotted evidence of rot on the existing post.

Old man Miller had obviously intended to replace it.

He was still bent over the post when something nudged the top of his head. Stepping back, he saw Cooper on the other side of the fence, nodding at him.

'Gidday, big fella. Got nothing for you, I'm afraid.' He rubbed the gelding's face and ears and then headed to the stable building.

A short time later he emerged carrying a rope halter, a shovel and pinch bar, and a biscuit of lucerne hay tucked under one arm. Returning to the yard, he slipped through the railings and put the halter on Cooper, who was already snatching mouthfuls of hay from the biscuit.

Granger gave an indulgent snort. 'Lucky you're a guts, old son, so you won't take it as an insult when I tie you up over there. Don't want you in the way and maybe getting hurt.' He led the horse to the other end of the yard, stuffed the hay into the hay net, and hitched him to a nearby rail.

By the time the post was in place, dusk was setting in. Cooper pawed the ground with a plate-sized front hoof, protesting at being tied up for so long with only an empty hay net for company.

After gathering the tools and tossing them outside the fence, Granger went to the gelding and took off the halter. 'There you go, boy.' He slapped the horse's solid neck.

'That looks good.'

Granger glanced over a shoulder, to see Abbey walking toward him eyeing the newly installed post.

'It was down the to-do list a bit,' she went on, 'but I'm glad you took the initiative. I can cross it off now.' She raised her eyes to meet his. 'I meant to say earlier, you can shower at the house.

And if you have any clothes that need washing, just dump them in the laundry basket.'

Not a move women's libbers would applaud, she knew, but there was something heart-warming about once more having a hard-working farming man's clothes to launder.

He tipped his hat at her. 'Appreciate the offer, ma'am.'

'You're welcome. Don't expect me to do your ironing, though.' They shared the light moment and then she sobered. 'Dinner's almost ready, so don't take too long.'

He surprised her by snapping a salute. 'I won't, ma'am.'

She dipped her head at him and grinned.

When he knocked on the homestead's front door a short time later, Abbey called from the kitchen, 'You don't need to knock, Jack. Just come on in.'

He obeyed and found her laying out cutlery. A large glass vase, filled with an assortment of bright geranium flowers amid native blossoms and greenery, sat in the centre of the white-clothed dining table. The spicy scent of geranium was barely discernable over the other, mouth-watering aromas in the room.

Abbey glanced at the toiletries bag and bundle of clothes in his hands. 'The bathroom's down the hall, second door on your right. Don't be long, I'm about to dish up.' When she caught him eyeing the third table setting she straightened, wiping her hands down the legs of her pants. 'Oh, and Gerry Alhurst is joining us for dinner. Gero's a neighbour and long-time family friend.'

'Granger, you say?' Gero stared at the taciturn man seated across the table from him, while at the kitchen counter Abbey tensed.

After pensive mutters of, 'Granger ... Granger,' Gero took a loud intake of breath and slapped his thigh. *'That's* who you remind me of. *Jim* Granger from over Lowmead way.'

Abbey swallowed a wince and bent her head over the hot tray of roast vegetables.

'He was a bear of a man too, with them same steely eyes and pointy nose you got there.' Gero waved a gnarled finger at Granger. 'You're his youngest lad, I bet.' It was a statement rather than a question. 'But ... what did Abbey say your first name is?'

Granger exhaled audibly. 'Jackson.'

'Yeah.' Gero nodded, his gaze fixed on the past. A drawn-out moment later his eyes cleared and he fixed them on the younger man. 'Been away from here a while, have ya son?'

'Yep.'

Pleased Granger was being just as guarded with Gero as he had been with her, Abbey began forking the golden-brown vegetables onto a platter.

Gero, however, was more determined. Ignoring Granger's increasingly stony countenance, he charged on. 'As I recall, your family farmed here for decades.'

Granger stared at him without speaking.

Oblivious to the increasingly charged atmosphere, Gero continued. 'If I remember right ... your older brother – Jonathon is it? – inherited the farm.'

Abbey couldn't help herself. 'You're talking about Granger Farm?'

The old man nodded, while Granger lowered his gaze to the plate in front of him.

With a hoarse chuckle, Gero turned to Abbey. 'You're right, Girlie, he doesn't say much! Let's see if a beer will loosen those lips.'

She watched, concerned, as he took two stubbies from the esky he'd brought along and handed one to Granger.

Without looking at her he snapped, 'Don't worry, I only brought two.' He twisted off the cap and raised his bottle. 'Cheers, son.'

After a brief hesitation, Granger tapped his ice-cold bottle against Gero's. He joined the old man in taking a long pull of beer, and then glanced at Abbey. 'Not drinking?'

'Way ahead of you.' She reached for a stemmed, three-quarters full glass and raised it in an air-toast, making the white wine sparkle under the overhead lights. 'Cheers.' After taking a sip, she turned back to the wood stove and opened the door of the burner compartment.

'That's an oldie,' Granger said. 'The original?'

With a nod, Abbey closed the cast iron door and wiped an arm across her brow. 'This trusty old girl just keeps on working, cooking our food, and heating our water.'

'More reliable and useful than any modern stove,' Gero muttered. 'And will outlive 'em all, no doubt.'

'We had the same type,' Granger mused aloud. 'Mum loved it in winter but said it made the kitchen unbearably hot in summer.'

Gero flicked Abbey a glance. 'See, it's workin',' and he indicated Granger's half finished beer with a lift of his grizzled chin. 'He's startin' to open up.'

He ignored the younger man's sharp glance. 'You a hard worker like your old man, boy?' Eyeing Granger's tall, muscular build, he said, 'Reckon y'might be, judgin' by appearances.' After raising bushy grey eyebrows at Abbey, he turned back to Granger.

'Y'know, it was a sad day when your father passed. I recall him bein' well liked around these parts.' A sing-song lilt crept into Gero's voice as he once more delved into his memory bank. 'Melanie took his passin' hard. A real lady, that mother of yours. She still alive?'

At Granger's nod, Gero gave a slow, reverent shake of his head. 'Was another sad day when she left the district ... the end of a good era.'

Granger stared into his beer while Gero continued. 'Have t'say, I was glad they weren't around to see what happened to the farm. Would'a broken Jim's heart to see them power lines cuttin' a swathe through his paddocks, 'specially after all the trouble and expense he went to, establishin' improved pasture.' He raised a defensive hand. 'Not that I blame your brother, mind. We all know what a struggle it can be these days, keepin' a farm afloat. And after the power company put that new substation in at Takilberan, what could affected landholders do but take the compensation bein' offered. Progress can't be held back, so they tell us.'

He didn't notice Granger's back stiffen and his expression harden.

Abbey did. It shattered the air of camaraderie in the room, the feeling of family she'd been relishing.

'Sure made it hard to sell them properties though, when the time came.' Gero gave a sad headshake. 'Always a shame to see quality grazing land sold off cheap.' He fixed Granger with an intense gaze. 'Don't suppose you had much of a say in the sale of the farm, bein' the younger of the two boys.'

'No say at all.' At the bitter edge in Granger's voice, Gero and Abbey shared a glance.

In the heavy silence that fell she said brightly, 'Right, I need a volunteer to carve the roast.'

17

Granger's internal clock, as reliable as any Swiss-made timepiece, roused him at five AM. Early rising, ingrained in him from youth, was part of who he was. While other aspects of his life had been taken from him, at least the integral elements remained.

Rising with a yawn, he stretched to his full six foot three. Going to the window, he stood rolling his head around his broad shoulders. Outside, morning light glinted from dewdrops caught in spider webs spun overnight on the yards and fences below. The sunlight brushed gentle fingers across the dewy ground and paddocks as it made for the grey-blue mountain range to the west.

Standing there, he was hit by a sensation of ... being home? Belonging? Or was it just that same pig-headed yearning refusing to stay buried?

Thrusting those thoughts aside, he took a deep breath of the new day. His ears caught the chorus of morning bird calls as he bent to rest his hands on the window sill. Out here it was hard to imagine waking to a sea of tightly-packed roofs; breathing in exhaust fumes peppered with last night's curry and this morning's burnt toast; and hearing the drowsy, petulant cries of humans and animals amid the rumble of garbage trucks and school buses.

While unsure what future lay ahead for him, one thing he *did* know was that a suburban lifestyle would not be part of it. Better to spend the rest of his life camping out and living off the land as he had been these past months.

A light flickered on in the homestead, drawing his gaze and bringing an image of Abbey to mind. The image brought with it another pleasant sensation, one he hadn't yet analysed....

She'd said breakfast would be served at six. If it was anything like last night's roast pork dinner, he didn't want to miss it. The crackle alone had made the meal memorable, not to mention the golden-brown roast veges, steamed greens, and pan-made gravy. When his stomach growled at the memory he put a hand to it and heard his father's voice in his head.

'Can't beat a roast meal, Mel.' It was his standard compliment to his wife every Sunday lunchtime.

Melanie Granger would beam first at her husband and then at their two young sons. 'You men eat up, now,' she'd say, knowing how much her boys enjoyed being called men.

Granger blew a long breath.

Those were happier times, back when he and Johnno were close; when it was assumed they'd spend their lives on the farm, bring up their own kids there. How quickly things can change....

A waft of frying bacon drifted across from the house, making his stomach growl once more. Rousing himself, he moved to the tank water-filled basin he'd set on a hay table the night before, and splashed his face. When he'd finished shaving, he dug jeans and a long-sleeved cotton shirt out of his duffel and slipped them on. It wasn't yet six, and he wasn't comfortable lobbing at the house unannounced. He'd wait for her to call him to breakfast.

By the time Abbey stepped onto the homestead's veranda and waved to him, Granger had caught a black colt and yarded him with Cooper.

As he strode to the house he caught her eyeing the colt, and glanced back at the animal. Its three white socks flashed as it did the rounds of the yard, high-stepping and carrying its tail flag-like. Turning, he met Abbey's curious gaze as he continued to the house.

'See you've grabbed yourself a mount.'

'Yep.'

'Flashy ... part-Arab maybe. That why you chose it?'

'Nah.' He shrugged one shoulder. 'It kind of volunteered.'

'Oh?'

'Was the first to run up and stick its head in the feed bucket.' At her doubtful expression, he frowned. 'Should I be worried?'

Her left eyebrow twitched. 'Can't say. I'm not even sure if that's one of ours. Bill....' An emotion flitted across her face before being firmly quashed. 'My uncle, Bill Miller. This is ... *was* ... his farm.' She paused to stare at the veranda floorboards while Granger watched her without speaking. After a moment she lifted her head to eye him. 'Anyway, I know some of the horses here but not the new ones like that colt. Couldn't even tell you if he's broken-in.'

'Well, he's definitely halter-broke, and shod.'

'Promising signs I guess, though with those white feet Bill would've shod him regardless.'

'Only one way to know if he's saddle-broke.'

'Yeah, but it won't be me that finds out. Hope you're feeling lucky.' At his wry glance, a smile tugged at the corner of her mouth. 'C'mon, breakfast is on the table. Can't have you starting your first day on an empty stomach.'

Granger leaned his arms on the yard's top rail, rested a booted toe on the bottom rail, and eyed the colt. 'If he doesn't already have a name, can I suggest one?'

Abbey saw the horse prick its ears at the sound of his voice. 'Sure.'

'Gordon.'

'Um ... *Gordon?*'

Granger's lips twitched. 'Lightfoot.'

'Oh, right.' She gave an amused huff and nodded. 'The way he moves on those three white feet, *Lightfoot* suits him. I can imagine it being his show name if he were in a trick riding outfit.'

'I prefer plain old Gordon.'

'And I'm sure he couldn't care less either way.' Slapping the rail with both hands, she pushed herself back from the fence. 'I'll take Coop out of the way so you can mount up in here.'

'Good idea.' Granger climbed through the fence to where Gordon stood halter-tied to a circle of twine around a post. The colt nuzzled him as he took the saddle cloth off the rail and slipped it over the horse's freshly brushed back.

Next came the saddle. Gordon merely swished his long tail as Granger cinched the girth strap firmly around his belly. Once unhitched from the post, the colt followed him meekly in a turn around the yard.

So far, so good.

After slipping on the snaffle bridle, Granger threw the watching Abbey a 'right, here we go' glance.

Gordon stood quietly enough, bobbing his head and mouthing the bit, making it jangle. Gathering up the reins to steady the horse and stop him dropping his head, Granger grabbed a handful of dark mane, slipped a foot into the stirrup, and took an exploratory hop. When the horse's only reaction was to shift its feet in the dirt, Granger swung himself into the saddle in one smooth movement and settled into a firm seat.

Seeing him put his legs against the horse's side and give a gentle squeeze, Abbey called, 'Don't let him put his head down.'

The words were barely out when the young horse gave a startled snort, opened its mouth wide, tucked its chin into its chest, and launched forward with a flying pig-root.

Granger's long legs clamped around the horse's barrel as it bucked left and right, tail and hooves flying.

Abbey covered her grin with a hand, but when he raised an arm in rodeo fashion, she clapped and yelled, 'Yeeha! Ride-em cowboy!'

'Not bad. He in training for the next rodeo?'

Abbey whirled around to see Flip striding up to join her.

'Hey, Flip.'

'Abs.' Flip rested her arms along a rail. 'I'm here to feed Onesie. Didn't expect to catch a show this early in the day.' She grinned and lifted her chin at the action inside the yard.

Granger's face was a picture of concentration as he rode out Gordon's flagging bucks. After the colt's final half-hearted pigroot, Granger gathered him into a fast trot around the small enclosure. Once the horse settled, he sat deeper in the saddle and urged him into a controlled canter.

Flip's eyes followed him. 'Not bad.' She gave a slow nod. 'Not bad at *all*.'

Something in her friend's voice made Abbey turn to eye her. 'You haven't seen this colt before?'

Flip licked her lips. 'Wasn't talking about the horse.' When Abbey didn't respond, she glanced at her sideways. 'Where did you find him?'

Abbey refused to bite. 'The colt was in with the others. Jack said he was easy to catch.'

'And what about him ... Jack is it?' Flip arched a provocative eyebrow. 'Was *he* an easy catch?'

Abbey gave a dry laugh and shook her head. 'Same old Flip.' The comment earned her an impish chuckle.

'I calls it as I sees it.' She leaned in to nudge Abbey with an elbow. 'And from what I'm seeing, you've got yourself a fine specimen there, Abs. And just to be clear, I'm not talking about the horse ... although I've always liked the look of that colt. Anglo-Arab, I think.'

Abbey fixed her with a stern gaze. 'Jack and I have a *working* relationship, Flip, nothing more.'

'Oh. So you didn't hogtie him down in the big smoke 'n bring him back here?'

The question raised the spectre of Jesse Boyce.

At Abbey's sharp, 'No,' Flip arched questioning eyebrows.

Forcing the image of Jesse from her mind, Abbey swallowed and said more calmly, 'Jack's starting work today as general farm hand.' She hoped that would satisfy her friend; didn't want to go into details about how she and Granger had met.

'Oh? So I take it he's not spoken for....' Flip's eyes followed

Granger as he leaned down from the horse's back to open the timber gate to the yard. 'That *is* interesting.'

Abbey eyed her sternly. 'What about Banjo?'

'What about him?' Flip scowled. 'Most of the time Banjo wouldn't know if I was around or not. Only thing he stresses 'bout is being given another shot at the next damn bull ride.' She thumped the rail with her hands and pushed herself back from the fence. Seeing Granger about to ride out of the yard, she ran fingers through her untameable blonde hair and dusted off her shirt. 'You gonna introduce us?'

Abbey sighed and raised a hand to signal Granger. When he rode over to them, she said, 'Jackson Granger, this is Flip ... er ... Philippa Williamson. She agists her horse here. It's the rig,' and she lifted her chin to indicate the dark head hanging over the half door of the stallion enclosure.

Granger nodded at the visitor, who stepped forward and raised a hand.

'Gidday, Jackson.'

'Jack.' When he leaned down to shake her hand, the colt snorted and danced beneath him. He quieted it with a hand on its neck and a gravelly, 'Steady.'

'Granger, hey?' Flip eyed him. 'Any connection to Granger Farm over Lowmead way?'

That same question.

Abbey couldn't look at Granger, but guessed his tightened-leg reaction by the colt's sudden head toss and on-the-spot jig.

'Once,' came the reluctant, drawled reply. 'A long time ago.'

'Oh yeah?' Seconds ticked by as Flip waited. Finally, when he didn't elaborate, she smiled and said, 'Well, pleased to meet you, Jack. And that was some impressive riding. I know who to call on when Onesie gets above himself. Oh! And on the subject of riding....' She dug a hand into a jeans pocket, pulled out a folded page torn from a newspaper, and handed it to Abbey. 'You see this in the Courier Mail?'

Unfolding the page, Abbey read the headline.

QUEENSLAND TRICK RIDING TROUPE REPLACED AS OPENING ACT

Equestriennes manager Margot Boyce 'crestfallen' by troupe's failure to impress during the *Australiana Extravaganza* show's first season.

Flip studied her friend's face as she read the article. 'That was your troupe, wasn't it?' At Abbey's distracted nod she said, 'Well, they're not doing so great by the sounds of things.' Grinning, she nudged Abbey with a shoulder. 'Must be missing their star performer.' When this received no response, she stepped back and said breezily, 'Now I'd better grab some feed for that horse of mine, before he starts eating his stall.' She dipped her head at them. 'I'll catch'ya later.'

Granger returned the nod as Abbey called absently, 'Yeah ... seeya Flip.'

From her perch on Cooper, Abbey pointed to the bottom of the front paddock. 'We'll start from there and make our way around the fence line.' She looked across at Granger. Their heads were on the same level thanks to the different heights of their mounts. The colt was no slouch at sixteen hands, but seventeen-hands Cooper towered over it. 'How's Lightfoot going?'

'Gordon's doing okay.' He threw her a teasing half-grin.

'He's a pretty animal by any name, and moves well. I think Flip might be right about him being an Anglo-Arab.'

Granger kept his gaze ahead. 'Pretty horse or not, riding beats walking.'

'True.'

They didn't speak again for a while, busy working their way along the boundary checking for and fixing defects in the barbed-wire fence. Abbey would often let the reins drop to Cooper's withers while she scribbled notes in the pad she kept in her shirt pocket. Once, Granger saw her go to cross a leg over the front of the saddle, only to wince and gingerly return her leg to its original position. Beneath her, Cooper continued his laid-back, lumbering amble.

'Have you been injured?'

Her head jerked up at the question. 'What?'

Granger's steady gaze didn't waver. 'I've noticed you favouring your back.'

'I ... had a bad fall recently.'

'How bad?'

Bitterness crept into her voice. 'Bad enough to end my career.'

And my relationship.

She pressed her lips together.

'You're a trick rider?'

'*Was* a trick rider.' It was only something she used to do, something from her past. 'Now a full time grazier.'

'Ah.' He nodded and said nothing more, for which she was grateful.

As they headed down the western boundary toward Five Mile Creek, Abbey threw over her shoulder, 'The creek's over this next rise,' and clicked Cooper into a trot. 'I want to check something out.'

As they neared the waterline she could hear a chorus of bird calls above the gurgle of flowing water. With Granger close behind she urged Cooper through the thick foliage, pushing aside any branches that came too close with her hands.

The bush opened to reveal a deep, slow-running creek. When Cooper made his way to the water's edge and dropped his head for a drink, Abbey leaned back in the saddle. Resting both hands on the horse's broad rump, she scanned the area as Granger emerged from the foliage behind her.

'What are we looking for?' He loosened his reins so Gordon could take a drink.

When the colt pawed at the water with a front hoof, Cooper shook his head at the younger horse as if to reprimand it. A smile tugged at Granger's lips, but Abbey's focus was on a spot up the creek.

'There!'

Granger peered in the direction of her pointing finger. Something long and black lay across the bank and disappeared into the water. 'You mean that poly pipe?'

'Yeah.' Abbey scowled. 'Dave Graham was right, someone's been syphoning water. I'll give you three guesses as to who might be the likely culprit.'

Urging the colt into a jog, Granger headed along the bank toward the pipe.

The horse's ears flicked back and forth as its hooves squished in the mud along the water's edge. As they drew nearer the pipe, Granger could see it ran all the way up the bank and across to the boundary fence.

He reined in Gordon and glanced over his shoulder, as

Abbey ambled up on a wet-whiskered Cooper. 'It's a wonder we didn't notice this yesterday when we pushed the cattle through.'

Her expression remained tight. 'We weren't looking for it yesterday.'

Dismounting, he passed her Gordon's reins. She held the horse back when it made to follow him.

After wading through a shallow section of the creek and squeezing between the strands of barbed wire, Granger disappeared into the thick scrub.

Emerging a short time later brushing grass seeds off his pants, he announced, 'The pipe leads to a pump hidden back in those trees.'

'On Pearson's land,' Abbey muttered darkly. 'No surprise there.'

'The pump's not running at the moment,' he went on, 'but it's fuelled up, and looks almost new.' When she continued staring into the distance he prompted, 'So, what do you want to do about it?'

She blinked and pushed the brim of her Akubra back from her forehead. After wiping away the circle of sweat-dampened dust with her forearm, she repositioned the hat, leaned forward, and crossed her arms over Cooper's withers. 'Well, although I'm prepared to share water with those in need, I'm not happy to have it stolen from me.'

'Fair enough.' Granger eyed the pipe and shook his head. 'The water table can't be too far below the surface. Pearson could've simply installed another windmill and more tanks on his own land. From the looks of things, he has the means.'

'He certainly does. And in the rainy season this whole area floods, so there's plenty of water available from other sources. But he clearly saw *this*,' and she flicked a disgusted hand toward the pipe, 'as the easy solution.' They were quiet for a long moment before she said resignedly, 'I'm open to suggestions about what to do here.'

Granger pointed to the spot where the pipe emerged from the scrub. 'We could cut out this whole section and drag it away. It'll take them a while to find out why the pump's sucking air, and another while to make repairs. They'll need to bring in a whole new piece. Maybe you could use a bit of pipe on the farm? This section *is* on your land.'

Abbey nodded and reached into a saddlebag. Drawing out a compact hacksaw, she said, 'We can use this.'

As he took it and the colt's reins from her, Granger gave an amused grunt. 'You came prepared.'

'One never knows what tool one might need on a ride around the farm.'

They shared a grin as Granger swung himself, the bottoms of his jeans dripping, into the saddle.

By late afternoon they were back at the homestead. Abbey halted Cooper beside the mounting block in the yard, unhitched the length of pipe from her saddle, and let it drop to the ground. Dismounting took some effort, even with the block's help. She sucked in a breath and winced as she climbed down from the tall horse.

Granger was already on the ground, watching her. 'I'll see to the horses, boss.' He stepped up to Cooper's head. 'And find somewhere to stash the pipe.'

'Thanks, but call me Abbey. "Boss" makes me feel like I'm in an episode of *Bonanza*.'

One of the few TV shows Bill liked to watch.

Throwing Granger a tired smile, she handed him her reins. 'My back has seized up a bit, I'm afraid.' At his concerned frown, she added, 'It should come good after a few stretches.' She put her words into action while he hitched the horses to the fence.

After unsaddling them, he proceeded to rub them down using firm, sweeping strokes of rubber curry comb and body brush.

She almost envied the horses their mini-massage....

Whirling around, and immediately regretting the hasty move, she called, 'Dinner at six,' over a shoulder as she made for the house.

This arrangement with Granger was working out well, but she mustn't lose sight of the fact it was a short-term business arrangement.

Nothing more.

18

The four-wheel-drive Toyota inched its way in the darkness, headlights on high beam and roof-mounted spotlight probing the track ahead. Bringing the vehicle to a stop next to a patch of thick scrub, the driver trained the light down low.

Bits of chrome metal glinted in the undergrowth.

The passenger door opened and a man jumped down to hurry to the Toyota's back tray. Grabbing a jerry can, he lugged it into the scrub and kneeled beside the irrigation pump.

In the car the driver checked his watch.

Two minutes past midnight.

At the glugs of fuel being poured into a tank, and the astringent whiff of petrol fumes, he climbed out of the vehicle and joined the other man.

After dropping the emptied jerry can at his feet, the man turned the key on the pump.

The starter motor engaged with a clunk and the engine gave a cough before settling into a steady drone.

Putting a hand on the outlet pipe, the driver frowned. 'Doesn't feel like it's pumping.' He lifted his chin at the man beside him. 'Go check the other end. Tell me if anything's comin' out.'

The man switched on his torch and followed the outlet pipe for a distance from the pump. He returned shaking his head. 'Nothin'.'

Swearing under his breath, the driver switched off the pump. 'C'mon.' Together they followed the inlet pipe through the barbed wire fence until it entered a thick patch of scrub. When they skirted the vegetation to the creek side, their torches found only bare bank where the inlet pipe should have lain. Shining their torches around, they saw only churned mud.

The driver scowled. 'A whole section's gone.' He waved his torch at the surrounding undergrowth. 'Check the scrub.'

Returning a few minutes later, the man fixed him with an anxious gaze. 'It's not here.'

'That's just *great*.' The driver let go a string of curses. 'He's not gonna be happy about this.'

Dressed in clean tee shirt and jeans, short spikes of damp fringe clinging to his forehead, Granger took a seat after Abbey refused his offer of help with breakfast.

She pointed to an open ledger on the table. 'I found some details on Lightfoot's origins, thought you might be interested. His birth name was Rhapsody in Black, but my uncle christened him Raven when he bought him a year ago.'

'Raven is an okay name, but Gordon's kind of grown on him now.'

Seeing Granger bend over the ledger and run a finger down the entries, Abbey smiled and finished laying out the plates and cutlery.

When he murmured, 'Sired by Aswad Amyr, a purebred Arab, and out of quarter horse mare Tessamia Baytarma,' she glanced at him. He had shaven off his stubble, revealing the scar's line from the corner of his mouth to the middle of his chin. From beneath the sleeve of his tee shirt another deep, puckered indentation ran the full length of his left bicep.

Judging by appearances, the bloke had been in the wars....

For some reason that thought niggled at her, reminding her how little she knew about the man seated at her kitchen table.

She took a breath and asked breezily, 'Was it you I heard playing guitar last night?'

He raised his eyes from the ledger to meet hers. 'Hope it didn't keep you awake?'

'Not at all, in fact I found it relaxing. You have a good singing voice too.'

'Thanks. I find music helps me wind down and sleep better.'

'You have trouble sleeping?'

He shrugged a brawny shoulder. 'Sometimes.'

'Any particular reason?'

The shrug was slower coming this time. 'Just ghosts from the past.'

'Oh?' She threw him a sideways glance. 'If you don't mind me saying ... the past is something you seem reticent to talk about.'

His expression stiffened. 'Like I said before, I'm not one for small talk.'

'I get that, but surely you can understand my wanting to know more about a new employee.'

He sat back in his chair, arms crossed, eyes hooded. 'Like what?'

'Like ... you're not a criminal are you? On the run from someone, or the police?'

'The Police?' He gave a snort. 'Of course not. There's just ... stuff ... from my past I prefer to leave there, in the past.'

Staring at him, she murmured, 'You're not on your own there.' Taking a slip of paper from a pocket, she held it out. 'Okay, then. Here are some jobs I'd like you to start on.'

He scanned the list and nodded. 'Gordon can certainly use the exercise.' He glanced at her. 'Want me to saddle Cooper for you?'

'I won't be doing any riding today.' Her tone was sharper than intended.

Eyeing her, he said warily, 'Back playing up?'

At her peeved nod, he rose to his feet, tucking the jobs list in his pocket. 'I'll do the dishes—'

'No need.' She carried their plates to the sink. 'I'd rather you made a start on those jobs,' and she tilted her chin toward the outside.

'Right. Well, thanks for breakfast.' As he strode out to the front veranda, Granger saw the Kelpie rise from the top step with a glad wag of its tail. Bending, he scratched the dog's ears. 'Someone's having an off day, mate, so for now it's just you, me, and Gordon.'

At his approach the grazing colt lifted its head, gave a whinny, and sauntered through the open gateway into the yard.

'Gidday, mate. You expecting a feed?' Granger rubbed the horse's face with both hands. 'A bit of hay should keep you going 'til we get back.' When he made for the shed the colt followed close behind. It stood by the door until Granger emerged, carrying a biscuit of lucerne hay and with a saddle, cloth, and bridle slung over one muscular arm, a rope halter dangling from the other. He slipped the halter over the horse's head and let it snatch a mouthful of hay. 'How about you return the favour and forego the pig-rooting this time?'

From the kitchen window Abbey watched the colt quietly follow Granger to the fence. He looped the halter rope over the railing, leaving it long enough for the horse to finish the rest of the hay. He then proceeded to brush down and saddle the colt with the same competence Abbey had witnessed before.

She returned her gaze to the filling sink.

When she raised her eyes to the window again, she saw him clip a water bag to the saddle and tuck tools into the saddle-bags. Moving to the horse's near side, he gathered the reins. She could tell he half expected another bout of equine defiance when he swung into the saddle. This time the colt merely tossed its head when urged into a spritely walk, and was rewarded with a pat on its dark neck.

Granger rose to the trot as they gained speed. After settling into a canter, horse and rider disappeared over the nearest ridge, heading toward the first job on the list – fixing the front gate.

Bending her head, Abbey absently drew figure-eights in the detergent froth with the tip of a finger.

Would her back eventually heal, or would she always have to rely on others for help to run the farm? That was assuming she didn't accept Pearson's offer, of course. And if she did sell, where would she go, and what would happen to Gero? Then again, if she hung on to the place, could she cope on her own after Granger left?

When her stomach sank at the thought of him leaving, she frowned and stilled her hand.

Was she becoming too reliant on the – admittedly capable – blow-in? Was that reliance influencing her decisions about the future? Worse still, was she *attracted* to Granger? Had Flip's radar been right?

I wouldn't be that pathetic, surely.

Then again ... Jesse.

Her shoulders slumped. Resting both hands on the edge of the sink, she stared into the froth.

Just by looking at her Jesse must've sensed her naïvety about the opposite sex. All she'd seen in him, through rose-coloured glasses tinted even rosier by relief and gratitude, was a country bloke keen on her. One handy with horses and gear and making do, like Uncle Bill, and – more importantly – nothing like her soldier father.

The perfect match for her.

Or so she'd thought.

Now she knew Jesse had been right in his assessment of her. She *had* been a naïve fool.

Snatching up a tea towel sporting the obligatory farmyard scene of scratching chooks and crowing rooster, she began vigorously drying the dishes.

Men, apart from Uncle Bill of course, had always been something of a mystery to her. The gross, potty-mouthed – not to mention bad-smelling – boys at school were to be avoided rather than admired. Even her teenaged hero worship of champion rider Shane Kelly proved short-lived, overshadowed by her admiration of his *way* more talented steed.

As a girl, she found horses *so* much easier to like than boys....

By the time she began seeing men in a different light, all the blokes she might've looked at twice were either married or spoken for. Whenever young jackaroos lending a hand with a muster cast hopeful glances her way, Bill kept them too busy and weary to make any moves on his niece. When she realised what he was doing she confronted him.

'Those roughnuts aren't worthy of a second glance from a nice girl like you,' he told her gruffly, 'and they know it. Foot-loose fly-by-nighters, most of 'em. Here today, dust trail tomorrow.'

And so the male of the species remained something of a mystery until Jesse entered her life, only to exit again as soon as the going got tough.

At least Granger was doing things the other way around....

She sucked in a breath.

Enough of that!

There were big decisions to make and important things to do.

And the first item on the list was to check in on Gero.

19

The old man sat on the front step of his hut, arms crossed and head bowed, a dismal picture of defeat.

After hurriedly parking the ute, Abbey jogged over to him. As she drew near, she glimpsed the bulging cartons and tea chests stacked haphazardly around the side of the house.

'Gero?' At her gentle enquiry he raised bloodshot eyes, shook his head, and let his chin sag back to his chest. In that brief glimpse she saw loss, anger, and despair. She touched a hand to his shoulder. 'What's happened, Gero?'

After a long moment he growled, 'The damn bank, that's what's happened.' Running the back of a hand across his nose and mouth, he swallowed.

The bank had foreclosed.

Knowing that was always going to happen didn't make the situation any easier to accept.

Abbey leaned in to sniff the air. No smell of alcohol on him. *That's a relief.*

She drew back quickly when he sat straighter.

'Thrown me outta me own home they have,' he said tersely, 'the *mongrels.*'

Searching his eyes, she found a glimmer of the old spark.

A promising sign.

When she sat beside him on the step, he put his head in his hands and moaned, 'What am I 'sposed to do now, hey? Where am I 'sposed to go? This is my home, *damn it!* And what about my girls? What's gonna happen to th-them?' His outburst ended in what sounded suspiciously like a sob.

Tears stung Abbey's eyes but this was no time to get all emotional. The old man needed practical help.

Help he was going to get.

'C'mon,' she said brightly, getting to her feet and holding out a hand. 'You're coming home with me.'

'With you? To the farm?'

'That's right.'

'But....'

She could see the doubt in his welling eyes. 'You're as close to family as I have now, Gero.'

The truth of that, along with the realisation she would be abandoning him too if she sold the farm, made the breath catch in her throat. Swallowing, she said firmly, 'You can think of it as a temporary arrangement if you like, until you work out what you want to do.'

He gazed at her for a long time before saying gruffly, 'What about the girls?' His wobbling chin was almost her undoing.

'W-we....' She cleared her throat. 'We'll sort something out for them, don't you worry. Now, let's get your boxes loaded up.' Turning, she eyed the stack. 'Won't be able to take them all this trip. Which ones do you need first?'

He sniffed, rose to his feet beside her, and brushed off his clothes. 'I'll show you.'

A few days later they sat on the homestead's front veranda, enjoying after-dinner iced teas and listening as Granger finger-picked a country ballad on his guitar. Abbey glanced beside her at Gero. The old man was leaning back in the cane chair and gazing into the night sky with an air of contentment.

Contentment.

Something Abbey could feel descending on her too.

She was pleased to see the old man settling in to life on *Clearwater*. Unable to face disturbing her uncle's room, she had installed Gero in what Bill used to call the 'freeloaders' or guest room. Although he wasn't one for 'gettin' all gushy', Gero made it clear he was grateful for his new accommodations. He was back on the wagon too, evidenced by his brighter eyes and the increasing steadiness of his old hands. To help him stay on track, she stopped drinking wine in his company. Even Granger took to having ginger beer with dinner instead of the alcoholic variety.

All-in-all this was turning out to be a good, if possibly short-term, arrangement.

In a break between songs Abbey eyed the trumpet-shaped, steel-stringed instrument and smiled. 'You play well, Jack, but I have to say, that's a weird looking guitar.'

Beside her Gero muttered, 'Who cares what the thing looks like.' He continued staring skyward. 'It's what it sounds like and what it does for your soul that's important. Same goes for people.' His words carried a ring of gratitude not only intended for her. Abbey knew it extended to the self-contained man sitting across from them, head bent over his guitar as he checked the tuning.

In the process of making storage space in the shed for Gero's furniture and sealed tea chests, Granger had discovered rolls of chicken wire buried under other gear. Without letting on to anyone, he used the wire to rig up a spacious chook run with access into a wired-off, covered calf pen at the back of the barn. The first Abbey knew of the project was when Granger asked to borrow her ute. When he eventually admitted the reason for the request, she insisted on helping him collect Gero's squawking brood from the hut's run. After they were settled in their new home, their clucks and squawks soon brought Gero hobbling over.

Recalling his joy at having his 'girls' close again, a lump rose in Abbey's throat. Along with it came the swell of gratitude for Granger's kindness toward the old man. Gero had said something about one of the Granger boys having done military service, and she was glad that boy wasn't Jack. Clearly a man of the land, he had no doubt expected to stay on the farm. It was sad his brother had failed as a farmer, bringing about the loss of Jack's future as well.

That's soldiers for you....

The velvety hush of evening, broken by the nightly chorus of crickets and the far-off, eerie calls of curlews, closed around the three on the veranda. Abbey joined Gero in star-gazing while Granger took up playing again. When she recognised one of the songs as *Heaven was Needing a Hero,* Abbey closed her eyes and sang along in a soft, low voice.

Granger looked up from his guitar and caught a bevy of emotions crossing her face.

Appreciation.

Nostalgia.

Regret.

She opened her eyes as the song came to an end and found the two men gazing at her. Turning her face away she mumbled through quivering lips, 'That song makes me think of *my* hero, Uncle Bill.'

Gero put a craggy hand on her shoulder. 'Have you said your farewells, Girlie? Properly, I mean.'

She shook her head without looking at him.

He dropped his hand. 'Well, you need to. What about we gather at the graveside later this week, just the three of us. Jackson here can do the honours with his guitar. It'd be like when we farewelled that bird of yours all them years ago, remember?'

Granger gave a slow dip of his head in encouragement, his eyes on Abbey.

She was shifting her gaze from him to Gero and back again. 'Gather at ... the graveside?' Her voice was little more than a whisper.

'Yeah.' Gero nodded. 'You know, lay some flowers, say a few words ... that sort'a thing. You weren't at the funeral, so this'd be your chance to say your piece, get it off your chest.' When Granger raised questioning eyebrows at him, the old man huffed and glanced at Abbey.

She wouldn't meet his eyes.

Turning back to Granger, Gero said, 'They had a fallin' out, see, over her chasin' the trick ridin' dream with them *Boyces*.' His Adam's apple bobbed angrily in his throat. He swallowed and went on. 'Anyway, they never got 'round to fixin' things between 'em, before Bill—'

With a harsh scrape of chair legs on floorboards, Abbey jumped up and dashed inside, banging the screen door and leaving the men staring after her.

Murmuring, 'Guess it's still a painful subject,' Gero linked his hands across his stomach and went back to gazing at the star-littered blackness above.

Granger stared at him a while longer before rising to his feet. 'I'm going to call it a night too.'

'I've been thinking.' Pausing to take another mouthful of scrambled eggs on toast, Granger gazed thoughtfully ahead while chewing.

'Oh yeah?'

'That old shack down the bottom of the house paddock. What's the story with it?'

'The shack? It's been there since pioneering days. When Uncle Bill bought the property he lived in it for a while, 'til this house was finished.' Abbey dropped two more pieces of bread into the toaster. 'Why?'

'I checked it out yesterday. Reckon it wouldn't take much to make it liveable.'

She grew still and glanced sideways at him. 'Liveable? For who?'

'Your old mate, Gero. There's even the remnants of a chook run right beside the shack.' Granger tapped his dark-stubbled chin with a finger. 'Being close to the creek, it has easy access to water. Probably good soil too if he wanted to start a garden....'

Turning, she fixed him with a disbelieving gaze. 'You're suggesting I do up the shack for Gero to *live* in?' At his nod, she threw both hands in the air. 'I can't even afford to pay you a wage! Where am I supposed to find the money to renovate a derelict old dump?'

After swallowing another mouthful, Granger said calmly, 'It's actually not that bad. Reckon I could do most of the work, using materials lying around the farm. I even discovered a stash of house paint in the storeroom.'

'*You* would do the renovations?'

'Yep. I've done a bit of building work in the past. Know my way around a drop-saw.'

'I'm sure you're quite capable.' She stared at him. 'But why would you be prepared to do that?'

He frowned as if unsure how to answer, and didn't for a long moment. Finally he said slowly, 'Because I know what it feels like to have your home taken from you.'

20

'She gonna join us, d'you reckon?' Waving away a fly with the wilting bunch of native flowers he was clutching, Gero glanced at the man standing beside him in the shade of LB's tree. Smartly dressed in cream moleskins and a fresh shirt, Granger stood waiting with an air of quiet composure.

Blowing an impatient breath, Gero tugged his jacket down with his free hand. 'It took hard work from both of us just gettin' her to agree to have this ... what'd you call it? Memorial? I hope it wasn't a waste of time, blowin' all that hot air. Not to mention huntin' down flowers and stuffin' myself into these damn farewellin' dungers again.'

Raising his eyes, he scanned the yard once more. 'Worth it though, I guess. The girl needs to say her goodbyes. No point hangin' on to the past, unless you're an old crock like me that is.' He flicked Granger a wily glance. 'You young'uns got a whole lotta livin' ahead of you.'

Half expecting the old man to ask what his future plans

might be, Granger stiffened. Then Abbey appeared on the homestead's veranda and he forgot all else.

She stood silhouetted against the afternoon sun, the skirt of her sun dress fluttering around her legs like a kaleidoscope of white and yellow butterflies. As she descended the stairs and walked toward them, sunlight winked off the gilt straps of her sandals and gleamed from her dark hair. She wore it up, tied with a satin ribbon the same colour as her dress. Another bow bobbed from Dopey's collar as the dog loped beside her.

Gero gave an audible sigh and murmured, 'That's one pretty picture, ain't it?'

The only response was a silent, reverent nod.

Leaning closer, he muttered, 'Y'know that bugger from next door rang earlier today?'

Whipping around to stare at the old man, Granger snarled, 'Pearson?' At Gero's nod, he said tightly, 'What did *he* want?'

'Smooth-talkin' as usual, probably hopin' to convince Girlie to sell him the farm. Tried the same ploy with her uncle. 'Course Bill wouldn't have a bar of it; gave the bugger the short, sharp shrift.'

When Gero paused for breath, Granger waved an impatient hand. 'And?'

'That's all I can tell'ya.' The old man scuffed the ground with the toe of his boot. 'Didn't hear the rest of the conversation. She took the phone off speaker and went into her bedroom.'

Granger gave an irritated grunt.

'Of course I'm hopin' she knocked Pearson back, for a whole bunch of reasons. But you know, she'd be foolish not to give that option some thought.' Gero raised world-weary eyes to find Granger scowling down at him. 'Not sayin' she *should* sell up,' he went on hastily, 'which'd be a bugger of a call for her to make in any case. Bill loved this farm 'n shed a lot of blood, sweat, and tears here. Sellin' it would be like betrayin' his trust.'

Gero pensively sucked his teeth before continuing. 'She probably hasn't said anythin' 'bout this to you, but....' He shrugged. 'You're no fool either. Look, *Clearwater* is sailin' close to the wind, finances-wise, like most properties around the place. Sellin' can be a real attractive option to those doin' it tough. And Girlie's doin' it tough in more ways than one.'

Granger gave a slow nod. 'I got the impression money was tight.'

'That's always been the case, even when her uncle ran the farm. 'N he was a clever bloke.' As Abbey drew near, Gero nudged Granger with an elbow. 'Better get playin' that thing.' He indicated the guitar leaning against Granger's leg. 'Don't want her changin' her mind at the last minute and bolting.'

Taking up the instrument, Granger slipped the strap over his head and began finger-picking the intro of *Heaven was Needing a Hero*. He didn't look up when Abbey joined them under the shade, until a fragrant waft of soap and citrus had him raising his head. He found her gazing at him with an unreadable expression. She had gone to some trouble with her appearance, as a mark of respect for her uncle no doubt. The light application of makeup she wore highlighted her outwardly-upturned eyes, high cheek bones, and full lips.

When his fingers fumbled on the strings, Granger made himself look down again and concentrate on the song. After a few more bars of the intro, Abbey gave a dip of her head and turned toward her uncle's final resting place.

As Granger strummed the first verse, she began to sing. Her voice was breathy, a sweet whisper amid the silvery warble of butcher birds and the rustle of gum leaves above. When she reached the chorus he sang along with her, and was rewarded with a strengthening of her voice and the ghost of a grateful smile.

By the time the song ended tears were trembling on her lashes, running down her cheeks, and dripping from her chin. As she turned on unsteady feet Granger glimpsed her face and flicked a glance at Gero. The old man wore a pained expression but made no move to comfort her. Thrusting his guitar at him, Granger stepped forward and wrapped Abbey in his arms.

Enveloped in a soothing stillness, and with the strong beating of his heart under her ear, she allowed her body to sag and gave in to the grief, the regret, the sorrow. As she sobbed into his chest he stood firm without speaking, chin resting on her silken head, arms holding her firm against him.

And for the first time in a long while, Abbey felt safe.

Gero looked on in silence before blowing a long breath and moving to stand by the graveside. After bending to lay the loose bouquet on the mound of dark soil, he straightened with a grunt and bowed his head. Clasping his hands in front of him, he said gruffly, 'Well, Bill me old mate, here we are again. Me chin-waggin' and you listenin', as usual.' He gave a wry huff. 'Seems you're gettin' more send-offs than I've had hot dinners. Anyway, this gatherin' is for the benefit of others, but I want you to know Girlie's home now and she'll do you proud, just you wait 'n see.' He raised his head. 'Right, I've said my piece.' Shuffling to one side, he threw Abbey a significant glance.

She drew away from Granger to mop her face with a tissue and gather her courage. Gero's words had rekindled the ache of guilt and obligation, making her wish she could turn and flee.

Instead, she scrunched the tissue into a ball and stepped up beside the old man.

'Uncle Bill, I....' The rehearsed statement withered on her tongue as she finally let her gaze drop to the recently turned ground. The small headstone bore the engraved words *William Wallace Miller. 1 April 1943 – 3 October 2019. A damn fine mate, a damn good bloke.*

In that hasty glance Abbey missed the slouch hat decal etched at a jaunty angle above the last two letters. Pointing at the headstone she turned to Gero with a question in her eyes.

He shrugged. 'Couldn't reach you, Girlie, so it fell to me to organise it.'

'I'll reimburse you—'

'You'll do no such thing. That there was the somethin' special I could do for my best mate....' His voice broke and he swallowed. Still his words sounded choked when he said, 'So don't go takin' that from me.'

She gave his arm a squeeze. 'Thank you, Gero. From me *and* Uncle Bill.'

He dipped his head and stepped back to join Granger, leaving Abbey standing by the graveside.

She cleared her throat. 'Uncle Bill, I ... wish you were ... standing here beside me, so I could tell you in person ... how much I miss you and ... how sorry I am for ... everything, especially for leaving the way I did ... for turning my back on you and the farm.' Her voice thickened and she glanced behind at the two men, who nodded their encouragement.

Clasping and unclasping her hands, she took a deep breath and turned back to the headstone. 'Thank you for having faith in me despite....' Another throat clearing. 'I love you, Uncle Bill. You'll always be the man I thought of as Dad.' She took a shuddering breath and lifted her chin. 'I ... I miss you, and ... I'll try to do right by you, and not let you down ... again.'

When she stopped speaking, Granger took up finger-picking a melody, its gentle notes surrounding them as they stood immersed in their memories. When Abbey moved to his side, Granger played a soft outro and then lowered the instrument. He offered her his arm and she slipped her hand into the crook of his elbow with a faint, grateful smile.

As they walked back to the homestead, she murmured, 'Thank you, Jack.'

'I didn't do anything.'

'You were there, and played that lovely music.' Her voice held the croakiness of recently shed tears. 'Uncle Bill would've been chuffed.' They walked on in silence and then she glanced up at him. 'What did you mean when you said you know what it feels like to have your home taken from you?' Though his expression didn't change she felt him stiffen. 'You don't have to answer that—'

'It's okay, just....'

She saw his chest rise and fall. 'Yes?'

'It's a long story.'

'You could just give me the gist?'

'The gist?' He gave a wry snort and dragged his free hand over his close-cropped hair. 'The gist is....' His chest rose and fell again. 'My brother sold the family farm, the one he and I were supposed to co-own after Dad died.'

'Granger Farm?'

'Yep.'

'How could he do that without your agreement?'

'You have to understand ... our father was a true-blue, dyed-in-the-wool traditionalist. Despite being aware of Johnno's preference for paper-pushing and the city life, Dad left him the farm because he's the eldest son. I suspect he was also hoping to mould Johnno into the farmer he always wanted him to be.'

Abbey screwed up her face. 'Oh.'

'Yeah, bad idea. But Dad had a contingency plan. He knew farming was all I ever wanted to do, so he intended for me and Johnno to run the farm jointly. He even built a second residence under the house so we could both live on the property with our families.' Granger turned his face away, squeezing a large hand into a fist and then releasing it. 'I'm glad he didn't have to witness how things turned out....'

'Did your father note that joint arrangement in his will?'

Granger shook his head. 'Didn't think he needed to, I 'spose.'

'So was your brother aware of his wishes?'

'Dad made sure we *all* knew in advance what he wanted for us *and* the farm.'

'So ... what happened?'

He took his time answering, as if weighing up whether or not to do so.

Finally he said in a monotone, 'Long story short, my brother made a mess of things and took what he thought was the only way out.'

Abbey's brow creased. 'Why didn't you step in?'

'I was away, making good on another promise to Dad. Was gone a few years. A few years too long as it turned out.'

'And your brother didn't tell you what was going on at home?'

Granger shook his head.

'So ... he sold the farm and left you in the lurch.'

'And betrayed our father, and evicted our mother. She

should've been free to stay on at the farm as long as she liked instead of being shunted off to a retirement home.'

Abbey eyed the bitter twist of his mouth. After a drawn-out moment she said in a low voice, 'And ... you've never forgiven your brother?'

He gave another curt headshake. 'When he signed the contract of sale, he not only betrayed our family, he ground my future into the dirt.'

Abbey stared out the kitchen window to where Granger squatted beside the water pump that fed the stock troughs, Gero at his side. They were fixing a slow leak in one of the joins ... at least Granger was. Gero was 'supervising', leaning on a post and chatting his head off by the looks of things. His prattling and hovering didn't appear to bother Granger, who now and then asked the old man to pass him a tool, or handed him one to return to the toolbox.

Abbey felt warm stirrings of gratitude and lowered her gaze to the sink.

You'd be pleased if you could see this, Uncle Bill. A healthier, more contented – even happy – Gero.

She was doing it again, talking to her uncle in her head. He felt somehow closer since the memorial, and she felt more at peace with his absence. Was she experiencing a sort of closure?

Perhaps....

And then Granger's earlier words echoed in her mind. 'When he signed the contract of sale ... he ground my future into the dirt.'

She could've been in the same situation if Bill had sold *Clearwater*. But he'd hung in there, riding out the rough times if the farm's books were anything to go by, keeping her future safe.

And bequeathing the farm to her.

Trusting the farm to her.

She thought about Pearson's offer.

Could she betray Bill like Granger's brother had his family? Or would she prove Gero right and do her uncle proud, by holding on to his precious legacy no matter what?

'Penny for 'em.'

She gave a start and whipped around to see Gero standing in the corridor behind her.

'What?'

'Penny for your thoughts. You were miles away, Girlie.'

She gave an amused huff and went back to the dishes.

He came further into the kitchen. 'Say, um ... me 'n Jack were talkin'.'

She grinned, aware who'd done most of the talking.

'He reckons I should start a market garden, over by the creek. Thinks the soil there'd be pretty good for growin' veges, maybe a fruit tree or two.'

'Oh yeah? And what do *you* think?'

He grinned. 'I reckon he might be on to somethin'.'

'Good. So you're going to do it?'

'Think so. Jack offered to give me a hand gettin' the garden beds ready. One thing we got plenty of 'round here is nature's fertiliser, good ol' manure, so it shouldn't be hard gettin' things growin'.' Sobering, he went on. 'The girls are startin' to lay well again now they're settled in their new home. Jack reckons I could make some dosh sellin' eggs and produce at the local markets.'

Abbey glanced at the three overflowing egg baskets on the

counter. 'Your "girls" supply way more than the three of us could ever eat, so you have plenty to sell. And home-grown produce is becoming more popular all the time.'

Gero's face clouded. 'No wonder, now people know what them damn battery hen places are like. Purgatory for chickens is what they are. Poor critters.'

Abbey wiped her hands on a tea towel and turned to face him, resting her back against the counter edge. 'Gero?'

'Yeah?'

'Did Jack mention anything about the old pioneer shack?'

'What about it?'

'He didn't tell you his idea?'

'What idea?'

'He's offered to fix it up, make it into liveable quarters.'

With an absent, 'Oh yeah?' Gero was about to head to the bathroom when Abbey's next words brought him to an abrupt standstill.

'They'd be *your* quarters, Gero. Your forever home. If you want them to be, of course.'

The word 'forever' was out of her mouth before she realised the implications.

Guess there's no selling the place now.

I'll just have to make this work....

The knowledge she'd made a decision, albeit subconsciously, brought on a swell of virtuous liberation.

Anyway, selling up would've meant betraying Uncle Bill's trust, and I couldn't live with myself if I did that.

Gero's eyes widened further. '*My* home ... *forever*? Here, on *Clearwater*?'

Abbey nodded and watched the bevy of emotions cross his face.

'I thought this was a temporary arrangement,' he rasped, 'just 'til I found somethin' permanent.'

'You're family, Gero, and family takes care of its own. Uncle Bill felt that strongly, and so do I.'

His Adam's apple working in his throat, the old man came to stand in front of her.

Giving her arm a squeeze with a sun-spotted hand, he croaked, 'Can't tell you how downright ... *honoured* ... that makes me feel, Girlie.' He sniffed, swallowed, and lifted his chin. 'Jack, the bugger, never mentioned this plan of his. 'Spose he didn't want to get my hopes up, or somethin'.'

'So should I give him the go-ahead, or would you like to think about it some? It goes without saying that we won't proceed if you're not interested in staying on here.'

'Not interested? Hah! You *kiddin'* Girlie? Of *course* I want to stay on! This has always been my second home, now it'll be my *home* home.'

'I do have one condition.'

'Yeah? What's that?'

'I want you to carry on having dinner with us most nights here, in the homestead.'

So I can check you're staying on the wagon.

'Won't get no complaint from me 'bout that, 'specially as you rustle up better tucker than anything I can throw together.' They shared a smile and then a deeper crease formed in his wrinkled forehead. 'These renovations ... will they cost a lot?'

'Won't know for sure 'til we start work, but Jack said there are some building materials lying around the farm he can use.' She put a cautionary hand on Gero's arm. 'When finished it'll be liveable, but won't be a palace.'

'Who wants a palace? I'll just be glad to have a home of my own again.'

She saw the old man's eyes water before he sniffed and turned away.

'Why is Jack doin' this?' he said gruffly. 'What's in it for him?'

'Nothing that I can tell.' She gazed thoughtfully out the window again. Granger was still hard at work on the pump, sweat making his shirt cling to the ridges of his well-muscled upper body. When she'd asked if he was serious about the project, his response had been a firm, 'Wouldn't have mentioned it if I wasn't dinkum.'

Turning back to Gero she murmured, 'Says he knows what it's like to lose your home. I guess he can empathise with what you're going through.'

Gero nodded. 'Knew he'd be a good'un, comin' from that family. Just didn't realise *how* good, 'til now.'

21

Abbey came inside whistling, her shirt and worn-thin cargo pants stained with white paint from working on Gero's quarters.

In between sessions of scraping and sanding, patching and sugar-soaping, while Granger measured, cut, and hammered nearby, she took care to stretch and rest her back. It was twinging less and less often, making her increasingly confident of a full recovery.

She was also more confident about working with Granger. He wasted no time standing around chatting, was skilled with tools, and inventive when it came to finding solutions. Working alongside she found his strong, quiet presence reassuring ... easy ... and very agreeable.

Not wanting to dwell on that, she got busy cutting sandwiches.

At a rap on the flyscreen door, she gave a frustrated huff. 'I told you, Jack,' she called, 'you don't have to knock.' When silence followed and Granger failed to appear, she cut the last sandwich in half, set down the knife, and moved to where she could see down the corridor.

A figure in smart western clothing stood outside the front door, one hand shielding his eyes as he peered in through the flyscreen. In his other hand he held a cellophane-wrapped bouquet of flowers.

Her jaw dropped and she ducked back into the kitchen.

'Abs?' His voice was so familiar, once so dear.... 'You there?'

She stood in the centre of the kitchen, hands pressed to her cheeks, eyes fixed on the past.

Jesse Boyce.

The man who'd helped forge her trick riding career; who ran to her side when she had the accident; who she'd lain waiting and longing for in her hospital bed. Here, now ... when she rarely thought of him any more, having relegated his callous rejection to the past.

Still, his voice, his presence, sent her foolish heart racing.

My first love....

He knocked again. 'Hello?'

Her mouth tightened.

My fair-weather boyfriend.

Blinking hard, she smoothed her hair and clothes and stepped into the corridor again.

He flashed his trademark grin on seeing her. 'Hey Abs.'

'Jesse.' Peeved by the waver in her voice, she cleared her throat. 'What are you doing here?'

'I ... came to see you.' After an uncomfortable pause, he said tentatively, 'Are ... you gonna let me in?'

She gazed at him for a long moment before moving to the

door and opening it, slowly. When he leaned in to kiss her, she twitched her face to the side.

Smothering a quick frown, he held out the flowers. 'These are for you.'

She took the bouquet from him, dangling it face-down at her side like a bag of rubbish.

The crease reappeared in his forehead. 'Don't you like 'em?'

Ignoring the question, she said in a low voice, 'What are you doing here, Jesse?'

'I told you,' he said jauntily, 'I came to see you ... to see how you're doing.'

'Because you care about me?'

'Well ... yeah. Of course.'

Jesse could always put on the sincere act, even when blatantly lying. She stared at him, stony-faced. 'Like you did when I was in hospital?'

He exhaled and dropped the jaunty attitude. 'Look, Abs....'

Catching sight of Granger squinting over at them from beside the recently repaired pump, she stepped aside and inclined her head. 'Let's talk inside.' For some reason she didn't want Granger knowing their history, hers and Jesse's.

'Okay.'

She led him down the corridor to the kitchen, where she turned to face him, arms crossed over her chest. 'Why now?'

'What?'

'Why are you here *now?*'

'Like I said—'

Her hand shot up. 'No. I want to know why you've suddenly remembered you care about me.'

'I haven't just sudd—'

'Which seemed to have slipped your mind right when I

needed you the *most*. Where were you then, apart from chasing after someone else?'

His gaze slid away from hers.

She continued eyeing him. 'You and Stacey became quite the item, I believe.'

'Well, I—'

'Right after she became the troupe's star performer.' Abbey uncrossed her arms to tap her lips with a finger. 'Am I seeing a pattern here?'

His shoulders slumped and he bent his head.

'You shouldn't have come here, Jesse.' She heaved a sigh. 'It's too late. I needed you *months* ago when you were nowhere to be found, at least not by me.'

Something akin to desperation flickered in his eyes. 'Look, Abs, you know what this business is like.' Moving closer, he wrapped a hand around her arm, rubbing his thumb against her tanned, satiny skin.

Instead of being heartened by the gesture, she flinched and frowned at his hand as if it were a bothersome sunspot. Struck by the sharp contrast with her reaction to Jack's touch, her breath quickened at the memory of his arms enfolding her at the graveside memorial....

'We have to go where the shows take us,' Jesse was saying, unaware of her emotional upheaval. 'You know that, Abs. And with you down for the count....'

Snapping out of her nerve-tingling reverie she said sharply, 'Spare me the post-mortem. I've heard all this before.'

When she tugged at her arm only to have him firm his grip, she glared into his eyes. 'Let ... go ... of ... me.'

He ignored her warning tone. 'Let me explain—'

'Take your hand *off* me. Now.'

'But—'

She wrenched her arm up and back, and out of his grip. Taking a step away she pointed toward the front door. 'Get out.'

'But I've come all this way to see you.'

'So you have.' Her eyes narrowed and she stared at him thoughtfully for a long moment. 'Tell me again why you're here?'

He gave a bemused frown, as if she were being childish or a bit dense. 'Because I wanted to apologise for being a total pratt. Tell you how much I've missed you. Patch things up between us.'

Outrage bubbled hotly within her, rising in a flush of colour up her throat and into her face. Muttering through tight lips, 'You thought you'd patch things up … with a lame apology and *these*,' she shoved the flowers into his chest, crushing and bruising the unfortunate blossoms. 'You have some *gall*, Jesse Boyce, rocking up here after the way you treated me. How could you leave me lying seriously injured in a hospital bed, pining for you? Not only did you ignore all my calls and never visit me once, you – and this is the *pièce de résistance* – got your new girl-friend to phone and tell me to get lost. And why? Because you were too *gutless* to do it yourself.'

Grabbing at the falling bouquet, he puffed, 'It wasn't like that—'

'Sure smelled like it to me.'

'—Stacey and me, we didn't … it wasn't … 'til much later—'

'I don't *care* how long it took for you to make all Stacey's dreams come true.' Abbey's words dripped sarcasm. 'The fact is, if you'd ever truly cared about me you wouldn't be here, trying to win me back. You would never have left my side, no matter what.'

'I did wrong by you, I realise that now. That's why I'm here, Abs, to ask you to forgive me.' Hope shone in his eyes and he once more held out the ruined bouquet. 'I want us to be together. I mean it.'

Something about his wheedling manner gave her pause. Always the strong one in their relationship, he was acting more like a cap-in-hand beggar. Why? There had to be more to it than just remorse; he *was* his mother's son after all....

She arched an eyebrow at him. 'You can drop the act, Jesse. And tell me the *real* reason you're here.'

His lips compressed and she noticed for the first time how thin they were. An image sprang to mind of Granger's firm, well-rounded mouth.

How would it feel pressed against her own?

What the?

Her eyes widened.

Where did THAT come from?

'... because,' Jesse was saying, 'I ... love you, Abs.' His gaze slid away from her and he scuffed the toe of his shoe against the floorboards.

Jolted back to reality by his words she blinked hard, twice, and then coughed to clear her throat. 'I don't think you know what love *is,* Jesse. Try again.'

When he once more met her eyes, something in their flinty grey depths told him his was a lost cause. Dropping the contrite act he said sullenly, 'I thought you might need someone to help run the farm.'

'Finally, we're coming to the truth.' She fixed him with a penetrating gaze. 'I already have someone helping me, two in fact.'

'I mean someone you can *trust.*'

Her mouth fell open. 'And you think I'd trust *you,* after what you did?'

In the mulish silence that followed she suddenly recalled the Courier Mail article. 'Oh, of course!' She clicked her fingers. '*The Equestriennes* are down on their luck.' With a shrewd nod, she crossed her arms again. 'Let me guess ... the bookings have dried up.'

His surly expression changed into something like a wince.

'You thought I wouldn't hear the troupe has fallen on hard times?' She shook her head at him. 'We live in a rural area, Jesse, not on another planet.' When he remained mute she stared at him for a long time, before asking in a hard, flat voice, 'How did you know about the farm?'

He exhaled audibly through pursed lips before muttering, 'Some old busybody cornered Mum at the Bundaberg rodeo. Said she knew you.'

'What "old busybody"?'

He frowned. 'Think her name was ... Bolton ... or somethin' like that.'

Abbey rolled her eyes.

That'd be right. Marion and her flapping gums....

'Said she wanted to thank us,' Jesse went on in the same sullen tone, 'for sending you home, to run your uncle's cattle property.'

'So you put two and two together....'

'You'd told me about this place, and your uncle.' He shrugged a shoulder. 'I figured something must've happened to him if you were needed back here to run the farm.'

'I see.' She gave a slow nod. 'You thought you'd come crawling back and once again claim a share of my "good fortune".'

'No, I....' The words died in his throat. It seemed he was only making matters worse. Thinking if he stayed silent the fight would go out of her and she'd come around, like she had in the past, he pressed his lips together and stared at her.

Abbey's gaze flicked to a point over his right shoulder and then returned to his face. 'I hate to burst your bubble, Jesse, but there's no fortune to be found here. So there's no point in your hanging around.' When he didn't move she stepped forward and gave him a shove.

The push sent him stumbling backward and bumping against something solid. Whirling around, he stared up at a stern-faced man towering over him.

As surprised as Jesse by Granger's ability to make a stealthy entrance, Abbey looked on with mild amusement.

'What the?' Jesse jumped back as though stung. 'Who the hell are you?'

'You first.' Granger's deep voice rumbled down at the smaller man.

Abbey raised a hand. 'It's alright, Jack. Jesse was just leaving.'

Glancing between the two of them, Jesse snarled, 'Oh *right,* I see what's going on here. You've got yourself a cosy little arrangement with this ... big ... dude, so you don't need me anymore.' His eyes glittered. 'Nice one, Abs. You hook up with *this* gold-digger,' and he thrust a finger at the narrow-eyed Granger, 'but have the nerve to chew *me* out like I'm the bad guy.'

'*You're* the only gold-digger here, Jesse. And as I've already said, there's no gold or fame to be found here, only dirt and hard work, lots of it. You wouldn't like it one bit.' Abbey's expression hardened and she indicated the door with a flick of her hand. 'Go. I'm sure Stacey's waiting for you at home like the good little fall-back she is.'

'Stacey's not in the troupe any more.'

'I don't care.'

'No? Well you *will* care about this.' His face twisted, became ugly. 'Star's not with us any more either.'

She froze. 'What do you mean? Where is he?'

Raising his chin, Jesse fixed her with a triumphant glare. 'J and P's.'

Her hand flew to her mouth. 'No!'

''Fraid so.' He gave a mean laugh. 'Your pal has gone to the knackery.'

'But ... why?'

'He was the same as you, a lame duck. No good after the accident, kept favouring that leg even after it healed. It was like the stupid nag was pining for you.' His lips curled into a sneer. 'So I guess it's *your* fault he's been sent to the slaughterhouse.'

She turned her face away so he wouldn't see her distress. 'You're lying. Margot wouldn't do that to Star ... not after having him so long, and putting in all that training—'

'Shows how well you know her,' he said sourly. 'Mum got rid of the horse like she got rid of you ... without a second thought.'

The insult rolled off Abbey's back. Her only concern was the gelding. 'When?'

'Should be there by now, I'd reckon. Next time you see him, it'll be in a pot of glue.' Jesse's jubilant snigger was cut short by the thump of a large hand on his shoulder.

An instant later he was propelled, swearing, down the corridor, through the door, and onto the front veranda, where Granger gave him one final push and growled, 'On your bike.'

'And Jesse?' Abbey called from the doorway, 'don't bother coming back here. Ever.'

Scuttling to his beat-up panel van, he jumped into the driver's seat and started the car. Thrusting out an arm as he accelerated away, he raised a middle finger at them in a rude gesture.

Growling darkly, 'Loser,' Granger turned to see Abbey's welling eyes, and scowled. 'Don't tell me you're crying over that idiot.'

With a disgusted, 'Oh *please,*' she brushed the tears away with an impatient hand. 'He's just a past mistake I thought was history.'

'Then why are you upset?'

'Star ... the horse. He was my regular mount in the troupe.'

Granger stared down at her. 'Means a lot to you?'

'An awful lot,' she said brokenly. 'Star ... always took care of me. Even saved my life.'

He nodded his understanding. 'J and P's?'

'The abattoir.' She blinked hard and swallowed. 'About two hours south-west of here.'

'Yeah, I know the place ... had another name back then, though.' He studied her face, his eyes softening. 'Ring them,' he finally said. 'See if the horse is still there.'

'And if he is?'

'We'll go get him.'

'You mean ... *save* him?' At his nod hope flooded her face, and then doubt clouded it. 'They'll want money for him, but—'

'Don't worry about that now. Get on the phone. I'll hitch up the float.'

'But—'

'Go!'

22

'I hope they keep their word.' Abbey threw him a worried glance. 'It'd be horrible to turn up there only to find he's already been....' Her voice trailed off and she bit her lip.

'Don't worry.' Granger kept his eyes on the road and a firm grip on the steering wheel. With the float in tow he had to take it easy on the rutted and potholed gravel. 'There's money heading their way. They'll wait.'

At his mention of money she eyed the bulge in his shirt pocket, the reason for their brief stop at the auto teller in Miriam Vale. Why was she surprised he could withdraw that much cash so easily? Had she assumed he was a penniless drifter simply because he was living rough?

'Assumptions can be dangerous things,' Bill used to say. 'Smarter and safer to rely on facts.'

And the fact is, Jack's living rough but he's not broke.

'I *will* pay you back,' she said stiffly. 'It just ... might take a while.'

At his indifferent shrug, she turned to stare out the window again. They travelled in silence for kilometres and then she asked, 'Were you close to your brother, before...?'

Granger took his time replying. 'I 'spose.'

'His name's Jonathon, yeah?'

'Yeah.'

'But you refer to him as Johnno. What does he call you?'

'Jax. The whole family does.'

'Jax.' She smiled. 'I like it.'

He flicked her a glance. 'What about you?'

'I've always been just plain old Abbey, or Abs.' She grinned. 'Only Gero calls me Girlie.'

After his grunt of acknowledgement, silence fell once more.

A few kilometres later she looked over at him again. 'How did your dad die?'

'His heart gave up the ghost one day.' Granger kept his gaze ahead. 'Dropped him where he stood, working in the shed.'

'Who found him?'

'Mum.'

'That must've been an awful shock for her.'

'For all of us. He'd always been strong as a bull.'

She nodded and lowered her gaze. 'Uncle Bill was made of tough stuff too.' She fiddled with the hem of her paint-spattered work shirt. 'He died in an accident. Was out riding and fell off a ridge.'

Granger said nothing.

'Gero thinks there's something fishy about the accident.'

'Oh yeah?'

She lifted her chin. 'I'm going to look into it, find out some more details.'

'How?'

'I'll start by talking to the local copper. I've left a message for him to call when he's back at the station after doing his western rounds.'

'Will knowing the details make things better for you?'

'I don't know ... maybe?'

Silence fell once more in the ute's cabin.

This time Granger broke it. 'Knowing the cause of Dad's death didn't stop us all being cut-up by it.'

Abbey eyed him. His posture was more laid-back than usual, and something told her he might be more inclined to talk. She sat a little straighter in her seat. 'I guess each of you had different ways of dealing with the grief?'

He nodded.

'You said you went away?'

Another nod.

'And when you came back?'

'I didn't.'

'You didn't? You mean ... you stayed away?'

'By the time I was due to return, the farm was past saving. No point in my going home, nothing I could do there.'

'What had happened?'

Granger exhaled. 'Johnno had some bad luck – a long drought followed by fires – though nothing all that unusual for primary producers.' He paused, thoughtful.

From her side view Abbey noticed the length of his dark lashes. They shaded and softened his smoky blue eyes, allowing a glimpse of the man beneath the tough exterior.

He went on, unaware of her scrutiny. 'The worst fire went right through the property, scorching the paddocks and destroying our entire stock of hay. The house was saved, thanks to the rural firies, but we lost the bulk of our herd. When I think about the trouble Dad and I had gone to, establishing those breeders and the improved pasture....'

'Oh, Jack, that's terrible.' She continued eyeing him, unsure how he would take what she was about to say. 'Not entirely your brother's fault, though? I mean ... natural disasters can hit anywhere, any time.'

This met with an aggrieved snort. 'Yeah, but that was only part of the problem. Johnno and Sandra had been living high, playing the wealthy pastoralists, and ran up a mountain of debts. They expected to pay off their creditors after the next bull and cattle sales, but the drought and fire put paid to that plan. They got desperate. So when the electricity board approached him about running high-voltage towers through the property, Johnno grabbed at their offer of monetary compensation without even negotiating the best payout figure. Nor did he give any thought to the impact construction of those damn towers would have on the already struggling farm.'

'Did the payment get them out of debt?'

He shook his head. 'I think they underestimated how much they owed. Anyway, when debt collectors started coming to the house, Sandra went ballistic. She was pregnant with their first child by then, and in a delicate condition. It was all too much for my brother. He took the easy way out.'

'I just don't get why he didn't call on you for help.'

'I was overseas, and hard to reach at times.' He blew a resigned breath. 'But I suspect what it *really* came down to was Johnno being too stiff-necked to admit to his "younger brother" what a mess he'd made of things.'

'Pride comes before a fall, Uncle Bill used to say.'

Granger nodded.

'How long ago did all this happen?'

'Coming up for five years.'

'*Five* years? That's a long time to be angry with someone, especially a close family member.'

Then again ... who am I to preach?

A few kilometres later she broke the protracted silence. 'Have you met your little niece or nephew?'

'There's one of each now.'

'So ... you've met them.'

'No.'

'Why not?'

'My brother and I are not on speaking terms.'

A crease formed between Abbey's brows. 'Your choice or his?'

'The time for talking was *before* he did what he did.'

'Is that how he feels too?' When Granger didn't reply, she persevered. 'Has he tried to talk to you?'

After a pause, Granger gave a curt nod.

She reached across to put a hand on his firm, sinewy arm. 'Jack, he's your *brother*, and his family is *your* family.'

He tensed in his seat and stared ahead, tight-lipped.

She withdrew her hand. 'I envy you.' Seeing his perplexed frown, she said wistfully, 'I'd give *anything* to have a brother or a sister of my own ... *any* family for that matter. I have no one now Uncle Bill's gone.'

This time when he glanced at her, his eyes held sympathy. 'You have old mate.'

'Gero?' She gave a half smile. 'True, but even he has a sister, so he's doing better than me in the family stakes.'

Granger once more fixed his gaze on the road ahead.

'If I had a brother,' she went on, 'I don't think it would matter what he did, I'd still be glad to have him.'

Granger's stare became a frown. 'So ... you think I should forgive and forget, even though what he did cost me everything?'

'Is he your only sibling?'

'Yeah.'

'Then that makes him all the more precious.' Turning to gaze out the side window, she folded her hands in her lap and said softly, 'Material possessions and careers can be replaced. Loved ones can't.'

While listening to her, it occurred to Granger that his mother would like the plucky young woman sitting arms' length from him. He let his eyes rove over her profile, taking in her lightly tanned, makeup-free skin, naturally full brows, and smattering of freckles over a longish, straight nose above full lips. Her mane of dark hair, tied in a practical ponytail, lay between a set of slender but firm shoulders.

He heard his mother's voice in his head. 'Find yourself a nice country girl, Jax, and settle down. You've been drifting too long.'

And she was probably right.

Frowning, he fixed his gaze to the front again. It didn't pay to chase thoughts like that, they could lead into territory he had no wish to revisit.

Staring ahead, he said gruffly, 'Turn-off's coming up.'

Abbey peered through the windscreen at the faded sign approaching on the left. Behind the blistered lettering it displayed peeling images of fat cattle and well-fed, contented horses.

In truth, most of the beasts that found their way to J and P Abattoirs were far from fat or contented. Even those that were, didn't stay that way long.

She shuddered and threw Granger a pained glance. 'I hate this place of death.'

He dipped his head in agreement.

Turning to the front again she took a deep, fortifying breath and murmured, 'Hang in there, Star. We're coming for you, boy.'

23

Chestnuts, bays, roans, greys, piebalds; pacers, brumbies, grey-muzzled ponies, gallopers, even a draft horse or two milled about in the metal-fenced pens, some frantic and wild-eyed, others with heads low as if aware what fate awaited them. Some had ribs visible beneath their flea-bitten coats. Others were well fed and glossy as if recently stabled and pampered ... until deemed of no further value by their owners.

Floats and trucks came loaded and left empty amid a constant babble of noise. The air was filled with the piteous cries of penned animals, the clang of gates and scrape of hooves against steel grating, the yells of workers as they herded the next lot up the raceway and individually into the killing box.

From where there was no return.

Over everything hung the stench of rotting manure, spilt blood, terror ... and death. In every way, the slaughterhouse was an assault on the senses and the psyche.

Cupping a hand over her nose and mouth, Abbey tried

not to breathe in the terrible smell as she and Granger walked toward the pens. Still it invaded her senses, feeding the nausea in her stomach. Images of Star's bloody, butchered body flashed across her mind, and she made a choking sound.

Granger glanced at her, noting how ashen her face had become. Reaching for her clammy hand he wrapped his warm, bear-like paw around it. 'I can look for the horse,' he said, compassion in his voice and gaze, 'if you want to wait back at the car?'

She shook her head, not trusting herself to speak.

'A grey gelding, right?'

She swallowed the rising bile and nodded.

Stretching his neck to sweep a glance around the pens, he asked, 'Fine-boned or heavy?'

'More on the heavy side,' she replied, her voice husky, 'with darker points and some dappling ... and a big, noble head.'

'Think I see one like that.' Granger turned to face her, bending to gaze into her eyes. 'Wait here.' He gave her hand a squeeze before releasing it. 'I'll take a closer look.' He jogged away, leaving her standing staring at the ground, and then at the sky – anywhere but at the pitiful creatures with their soulful gazes and stoic stances.

She heard Granger call, 'Star!' and saw a pale head rise above the others in one of the pens closest to the race. And then it was gone.

Granger jogged back to her side. 'I might've found him but he doesn't recognise me. Come on.' Grabbing her hand, he led her closer to the pen. 'Try calling him.'

'S-Star?' Her voice came out as another croak. She cleared her throat and tried again. 'Star? Is that you, boy?'

The pale head rose again, and a pair of large, dark eyes found her.

With a cry of, 'Star!' she rushed to the fence. 'Star! Here, boy.'

The milling horses parted as a grey gelding pushed his way threw the crush toward her, muzzle outstretched, making soft whickering sounds. When he slipped his muzzle through the gap in the rails, she reached in to press a hand to each side of his grey head. 'Oh, Star.' Resting her cheek against his velvety nose, she murmured, 'You're safe now, boy. We're here to take you home.' Throwing Granger a watery smile of gratitude, she said, 'Let's get him out of here.'

'Oy!' The loud call came from one of the pens momentarily emptied of doomed inhabitants. 'Whad'ya think you're doin' with that animal?' The man climbed through the rails and marched toward them.

Granger strode to meet him. 'We're here for that grey gelding.'

The man eyed him, frowning.

'We rang and spoke to the boss this morning,' Granger went on. 'Now we've come to collect the horse.'

When Abbey came to stand at Granger's side, the man ran his eyes up and down her and flashed a gap-toothed grin. 'Love that 'orse, don'cha lil' lady?' At her wary nod, he puffed out his chest. 'Was me you spoke to, I'm the boss 'ere. And as you can see, I lived up to me promise to keep the 'orse safe for ya. Now you keep yours and cough up me askin' price.'

She squared her shoulders. 'Five hundred, right?'

He stared at her through narrowed eyes and ran his tongue over his lips in a way that made her think of a lizard. She stifled a shudder.

'Thousand.'

'*What?*' Her head jerked back. 'No! You said five hundred on the phone.'

'Was thinkin' of another grey 'orse. That one's a thousand bucks.'

'You can't be serious!'

The boss's tongue darted across his lips again. 'Heavy brute like that's worth a lot to me in pet meat 'n glue.'

As the colour drained from Abbey's face, Granger stepped forward. 'There's no way you paid that much for it.'

'None of your business how much I paid.' The man's mouth hardened. 'The price for the nag is one thousand bucks. Take it or leave it, but be quick about it. That lot's overdue for killin',' and he indicated Star's pen with a lift of his unshaven chin.

A tiny, strangled sound issued from Abbey's throat. Granger gave her arm a reassuring squeeze before tugging the wad of notes out of his pocket, making sure the boss saw it. Greed glittered in the man's eyes and his lizard tongue flicked in and out of his mouth.

'Here.' Granger held out the cash. 'Take your money.'

Snatching up the wad, the boss half-turned away to count it for himself, licking his filthy fingers after every few bills. The count finished, he squinted at Granger. 'Where's the rest?'

'That's it, the price you agreed on.'

'Not for that there 'orse.'

'I gave you his brand details over the phone,' Abbey managed to squeak, 'and you confirmed we were talking about the same horse.'

The man gave a phlegmy cough and spat on the ground. After dragging a filthy hand over his nose and mouth, he pointed to Star's pen and yelled to one of the nearby workers,

'Get 'em ready.' When the worker climbed into the pen and began bunching the horses toward the raceway, the boss flicked Abbey a sly glance. 'Like I said, the price is one thousand bucks, or you can say goodbye to your grey buddy.'

Sweeping Abbey aside with a protective arm, Granger moved in close to the boss. 'That,' and he tilted his chin at the wad of notes still clutched in the man's grimy hand, 'is the agreed price. And more than the going rate for killers. So I'd take it if I were you.'

'You hard of hearin', mate? I *said,* it's not enough.' An instant later the man gave a yelp as he was hauled onto his toes by the collar, thrashing and grabbing at Granger's hands.

'We paid you the agreed price,' Granger growled, 'and travelled all this way to collect what we bought, fair and square, from you.'

He proceeded to drag the indignant, puffing man behind a stall, out of Abbey's sight. Shoving him up against the rails he said through clenched teeth, 'It's a *done* deal, *mate.*' After eyeballing the man, who merely stared, slack-jawed, back at him, Granger released his vice-like grip and shoved him away. 'We're done talking about this. I'm taking the horse. That's the end of it.'

The man stumbled back, holding his neck and gagging. He kept his frightened gaze fixed on Granger, who glared back at him, the picture of restrained but obvious menace. After silent, tense seconds ticked past, Granger took a step toward him and the man managed a frightened nod. With a cursory dip of his head to acknowledge sealing of the deal, Granger turned on his heel and made for the pen where Star stood at the rear of the jostling horses. At his approach, the wide-eyed worker hastily climbed the opposite fence and skulked away, wanting to keep a healthy distance between himself and the towering, fierce-looking man.

When Granger undid the chain around the heavy gate and heaved it open, the nearest horses made straight for the gap, followed by the mob. 'You'll need to grab him as he comes through,' he shouted to Abbey above the noise of frantic escape and workers' yells. 'You ready?'

Shouting back, 'Yeah,' she positioned herself at the side of the open gate.

The gelding was one of the last to burst from the opening.

'Star!' Abbey stepped forward and put out a hand. 'Here boy!'

The horse's ears flicked, and then he saw her. Whirling around, he came to a sliding stop right in front of her. With a laugh of pure joyful relief she flung her arms around his neck. Burying her face in his normally well-groomed but now tangled mane, she wet it with glad tears. Snorting, Star wagged his head up and down, before lowering it as if to tuck her against him.

Granger allowed them the tender moment before striding up to put a hand on Abbey's shoulder. 'We better go.'

Pressing a final kiss on Star's warm, grey neck, she lifted a glowing, teary face to Granger and nodded. After slipping the rope halter over the gelding's head, she led him on a loose lead toward the float, noting only a slight favouring of his 'bad' leg. She gave a sardonic huff.

Even a slight disability is enough to earn eviction from the Boyce's select circle.

'Does he travel alright?'

'Oh ... um ... yeah. He's an old hand.' She threw an arm around the horse's neck. 'Aren't you, my beautiful boy?'

'Right then.' Granger glanced behind at the bedlam they'd caused. Newly freed horses careered around the yard, snorting, pig-rooting and kicking up dust as red-faced workers, yelling and waving their arms, tried to round up the escapees. 'The sooner we leave here, the better.' He went ahead to lower the float's ramp, and watched as Abbey led the gelding up to it.

Flinging the halter rope over his withers, she slapped Star on his broad rump and commanded, 'In you go.'

And the horse calmly walked up the ramp and into the float.

Abbey glanced behind and saw Star tugging at the hay net she'd hung in the float for him.

With a contented sigh, she turned to Granger. 'I seem to be saying this a lot lately.'

'What?'

'Thank you, Jack.'

He gave a dismissive grunt, his eyes fixed on the road.

'You're a handy man to have around.'

Another grunt.

She stared at him until he turned to her with a frown. 'What?'

'Can I ask you something?'

After a loaded pause he nodded and returned his gaze to the road.

'You're camping out, roughing it, but can whip a quick five hundred out of the air whenever you like?'

The frown returned, deeper this time.

'I don't mean to put you on the spot, just....'

'You thought I was a penniless hobo?'

'No! That is ... um ... well....' She shrugged and grinned an apology.

One side of his lips tipped upward. 'Who's to say I'm not some eccentric billionaire wanting to get back to nature?'

'Are you?'

He gave a humourless snort. ''Fraid not.'

'I didn't think so. You're too practical, too good with your hands to be a desk-bound money-grubber.'

'I'll take that as a compliment.'

'That's how it was intended.'

When he didn't say anything more, Abbey turned away.

He surprised her by breaking the silence. 'I haven't always lived rough or worked for no pay, so I'm not destitute, I have money.' Emotions ran beneath his usual poker face. 'Since losing the farm, I've been saving most of what I earned.'

When his voice trailed off she prompted, 'To replace it, the farm?'

He nodded.

'So you still want to pursue a life on the land?'

'I did.' He heaved a sigh. 'Until reality set in.'

'Oh?'

'Even if I slaved and saved for the rest of my life I couldn't afford a spread capable of supporting me.' He flicked her a quick sideways glance. 'And any family I might be lucky enough to have.'

What she saw in that smoky-eyed glance made her insides spin and flip, like a street dancer on speed. Excited and nervous at the same time.

Once more gazing ahead he went on. 'The best I could manage would be a hobby farm. Hardly better than a suburban block.' His distaste for that option was obvious in his voice.

'Once I realised that, I decided it was time to take a hike – literally – to clear my head and consider the future.'

Staring out the window, trying to rein in her bolting emotions, Abbey murmured, 'And here you are. Considering your future.'

As they rattled to a stop near the yards Abbey saw Flip standing at the fence, chatting with Gero. Flip raised a hand in a smiling wave, and when Abbey jumped down from the cabin and headed for the rear of the float, Flip sauntered over.

'Already buying some new blood, Abs?'

'Not really.' Abbey threw her a rueful smile. 'This was a rescue.'

'Oh?' She peered in at Star, pulling contentedly at his hay net. 'Looks a good type ... too good for the knackery. That where you rescued him from?'

Abbey nodded.

When Granger strode up to undo the habitually sticky tailgate latch on that side, he didn't notice the coy smile Flip gave him.

Abbey did, and her insides clenched.

'Well,' Flip purred, moving closer, 'aren't you today's heroes.'

Abbey arched questioning brows at her just as Granger released the latch. She hastened to grab the other side and between them they lowered the tailgate to the ground.

When Granger lifted his head and his gaze fell on Flip, she flashed him a coquettish smile from under long, fluttering lashes. A v-shaped crease formed above his nose as he stared at her, clearly taken aback.

He was the picture of puzzlement. It was almost funny.

Almost.

Abbey snapped her mouth shut as Flip danced fingertips along the float's raised trim line.

'I was just telling Gero,' Flip said in the same silken voice, 'about the bush dance that's on tonight, at the hall.' Stilling her hand, she fixed Granger with a winning smile. 'Are you planning to go?'

When he maintained the silent stare, Abbey said quickly, 'I'd forgotten that was on. Did you say tonight?'

'Mm hmm. Starts at seven. Should be fun too, the local band's playing and Jeff's doing the calling.'

Abbey bit back a snort. That a semi-effective local policeman could be a highly effective dance caller was something of a local joke. Casting a sideways glance at the tight-lipped, clearly disconcerted Granger, she said, 'Thanks for the heads-up, Flip. Right now we'd better get Star unloaded and settled.'

'Oh, sure. Well,' and Flip sent a final smiling bat of eyelids Granger's way, 'hope you make it tonight. Seven o'clock, don't forget.' With a theatrical flick of a hand, she strode off, slim hips working overtime in snug denims.

They watched her go and then Granger turned to Abbey with raised brows. Swallowing her unease, she gave a wry 'who knows' shrug, and stepped up the ramp to Star's side. 'C'mon, boy, let's get you out of here and settled in your new home.'

Alone in the yard, she had almost finished rubbing down the horse when Gero spoke from the other side of the fence.

'You young'uns plannin' on going to that dance Flip was yabbering about?'

Abbey frown-smiled at him. 'By "young'uns" you mean me and Jack?'

The old man pretended to glance around. 'Y'see any other young people here?'

She grinned and continued running the brush over Star's already gleaming coat. 'It's been a long day,' she said slowly, 'I don't really feel like going dancing.'

'All the same, you should make an effort.'

'Why?'

'You know why; to join in, be part of the community again. Not to mention show support for the organisers. It's not easy putting on these events out here in the sticks y'know. Some folks have gone to a lot of trouble.'

'Point taken.' Blowing a resigned breath, she rubbed the curry comb over the body brush to remove the collection of silver-grey hairs. 'Alright, I'll go, but I won't be staying long. I can't speak for Jack, though.'

Gero gave a grunt and was about to move away when Abbey said, 'Say, do you have any idea why Flip's acting like a ... flirt ... around him, when she's already spoken for?'

He paused to eye her. 'Around Jack, you mean?'

At her nod he gave a snort and rocked back on his heels, tucking his thumbs into imaginary vest pockets. 'Well, that explains it.'

'Explains what?'

'Why she was grillin' me about you and Jack. Whether....' He shrugged. '... you know.'

Heat flooded Abbey's face. 'And what did you tell her?'

'That far as I know there's nothin' going on between you two.' He fixed her with narrow eyes. 'That's right, isn't it?'

After a fraction of a second she blustered, 'Of course it is.' At his drawn-out, doubt-ridden, 'Riiight,' in response she snapped, 'What?'

'If there's nothin' going on between the two of you, why are you bothered about her flirtin' with him?'

'Oh ... it's just ... um....' Colour bloomed in her cheeks. 'I don't like to think of her going behind Banjo's back.'

'I see. So it's *Banjo* you're worried about, is it?' Gero twitched an eyebrow at her. 'Well, he's been stringing her along for years. Flip's a good'un, doesn't deserve that. So who can blame her for lookin' elsewhere? Jack strikes me as a dyed-in-the-wool country bloke who'd make a fine husband for a country lass.' He locked eyes with her. There was a definite twinkle in his. 'Wouldn't you agree, Girlie?'

'You're a handy man to have around.'

With her own words replaying in her mind, she dipped her head so he wouldn't see her rising colour. 'Sure,' she said briskly, dusting off her pants. 'So good luck to her.'

Gero's meaningful chuckle followed her as she headed to the stables to return the grooming kit.

The old man was too damn perceptive sometimes. He also had an over-active imagination.

She came to an abrupt stop.

But was the flare-up she'd felt at Flip's come-on to Granger imagined?

Searching inside herself, she found a smouldering ember.

Not imaginary.

Disturbing.

24

The foot-tapping beat of *Cotton Eye Joe* greeted them as they walked up to the balloon and bunting-festooned Weerong hall. Golden light spilled from the open barn-style doors, punctuated by bright flickering from the disco ball turning above the crowded dance floor.

With a rumbled, 'After you,' Granger gestured for Abbey to go ahead of him into the hall.

She dipped her head in thanks, trying to ignore the tease in his half smile. All the same, heat once more flooded her cheeks.

Why was she so flustered? All she'd done was casually enquire if he wanted to come along to the dance, nothing more.

Of course blushing so hot my cheeks could've fried eggs kind of contradicted the casualness I was shooting for. What an idiot! It wasn't like I was asking him on a date *or anything. Though I could hardly blame him for thinking I was, given my ridiculous performance.*

She groaned inwardly.

Well, nothing I can do about it now, except pretend it didn't happen.

Lifting her chin, she proceeded to march up the hall's steps, the burgundy skirt of her sleeveless, Audrey Hepburn-styled swing dress swishing over the layers beneath it.

She had forgotten about the dress until she came across the box of performance outfits in her wardrobe. Tailor-made for her, the mostly western outfits were unlikely to fit anyone else. That was no doubt why Margot had 'gifted' them to her, leaving the box with the other gear for her collection from the Brisbane unit.

Unwilling at first to have anything to do with those remnants of her old life, she had shoved the box into the back of the wardrobe. It was only during her fruitless search for a bush-dance-worthy outfit that she found it again and reluctantly lifted the lid. After shaking out the dress she held it at arm's length, admiring its pinched-in waist and polka-dotted panels, and remembering....

Margot had visions of the girls doing drill team formations, incorporating ballet-style dismounts and pirouettes, in the pretty outfits. Abbey recalled trying on the dress, and practising the movements on a colour-coordinated Star. But before the performances became part of the show, she was injured.

And subsequently abandoned....

Her eyes refocused and she stopped inside the entrance to scan the room, her eyes skimming over the admiring glances being sent her way. As Granger came to stand beside her, he too was subjected to close scrutiny from a number of quarters.

Gero had done something similar before they left home. After giving Abbey a proud thumbs-up, he had praised Granger for 'scrubbing up well', saying he 'looked dapper' in his best blue jeans, spit-polished boots, and long-sleeved white shirt. Abbey had said a silent thanks to Bill for the shirt, rustled up from his boxed collection of outgrown – or kept for best and barely worn – clothes. A little on the too-large side for Bill, the stylish shirt only just fit the taller, broader Granger.

Marion Bolton's grinning face and wildly waving hand above the bopping heads caught Abbey's eye. Then her roving gaze fell on Dave and Rhonda Graham boot-scooting on the dance floor, before landing on Flip's gleaming pixie-cut. Their eyes met and Flip said something to the man beside her – Abbey recognised Banjo – and skipped over to them.

'You came!' She smiled into Granger's eyes before casting Abbey a quick glance. 'Super.'

Abbey marvelled at how different her friend looked all glammed-up. The short-skirted, blue floral dress complemented her fair colouring, and the skin-coloured high-heels gave her muscular legs an alluring shape.

Tucking her arm through Granger's, Flip led them with a swing of skirts to where Banjo leaned against the bar, talking to his mates.

As Abbey trailed behind, feeling like a fifth wheel, she heard Flip announce gaily, 'Banjo, this is Jack Granger, the bloke I was telling you about.'

Banjo's casual glance over one shoulder changed to one of grudging admiration as he took in Granger's size and appearance. Straightening to his – sadly less impressive – full height, he turned to face the stranger his girlfriend had been going on about.

'Gidday, mate.' They shook hands and Banjo said affably, 'So ... Flip tells me you're workin' at *Clearwater*.' When he noticed her hand resting in the crook of Granger's arm, his eyes narrowed and he fixed the other man with an interrogative gaze. 'And you're from Granger Farm over Lowmead way, I believe.'

'Not any more.' Granger was saved from more stilted conversation by an announcement over the PA system.

'Grab your partners, folks, 'cos our dance caller is ready to get them boots a-scootin'!'

Abbey glanced toward the stage, to see Jeff Thompson take the band leader's place at the microphone.

'Right, let's get moving!' Thompson flashed the audience a broad grin. 'There are already some twosomes on the floor so we'll start with an easy closed couples, the Brown Jug Polka!'

After extracting his arm from Flip's hold, Granger extended it to Abbey. 'Shall we?'

Smiling, she tucked her slender hand in the crook of his elbow. As he led her onto the dance floor, she leaned in to murmur, 'Do you know how?'

'To dance?' At her nod, his eyes crinkled in the corners. 'I grew up in the country, remember? Where attendance at every social event is compulsory.' They shared a grin and took their place among the other couples on the dance floor. When the band struck up a spritely jig, he brought her around to face him and took her in a ballroom hold.

His proximity and the warm hand at her waist sent all her nerve endings zapping, as if she'd run full-tilt into an electric fence. She managed to put an unsteady hand to his broad shoulder, hoping he wouldn't notice her other hand trembling in his gentle but firm grasp. Not knowing where to look, she fixed her gaze on his shirt. Beneath the whiteness mere millimetres from her face, she could see shadows of a manly shape, and a darker line of hair heading south....

More heat radiated up her throat and into her face.

'Everyone ready?' Luckily, Thompson chose that moment to launch into his sing-song call. 'And ... here we go, with a heel and toe, heel and toe....'

Feeling like chiffon in Granger's arms, Abbey floated into the turns in time with the music. She couldn't help smiling as he led her through the promenades, the hand clapping and knee tapping, and soon they were laughing together.

'... and a left arm turn and finish!'

As the music ended, Granger kept hold of her hand. 'Up for another one?' At her eager nod he smiled, a real, lop-sided smile that set her face aglow ... again.

'Now you're all warmed up,' Thompson announced, 'we'll go straight into a Dashing White Sergeant....'

This was followed by a Postie's Jig, and a Blackwattle Reel. When the reel ended, Abbey and Granger twirled to a stop, puffing and grinning at each other.

Keeping hold of her arm, he bent to murmur in her ear, 'I had to wing that last one, didn't know it.'

At the caress of his thumb over her skin, the deep timbre of his voice close by her ear, and the breath against her cheek, she experienced a whole-body shiver. Afraid he would notice, she gave an overly bright smile and extracted her arm to run both hands over her hair. 'It was a brave effort,' she said in a rush. 'And you didn't crush my toes once.'

'Kind of you to say.' He glanced at the bar and back at her. 'Time out for a drink?'

She nodded and they headed to a vacant bar stool. Nearby, Flip sat slumped over a wine glass, face pinched with disappointment. Banjo was right next to her but half turned away, beer in hand, guffawing at one of his mate's jokes.

On seeing her friend's expression, Abbey pulled Granger to one side. 'How about you dance with Flip next?' At his raised brows, she tipped her chin toward her dispirited friend. 'She's bored, poor thing. I don't think Banjo's much of a dancer.'

After a cursory glance at Flip, Granger turned back to Abbey. 'What will you do?'

'Savour my drink, take a breather, and be ready to corner Jeff on his next break.'

'To ask about your uncle's accident?'

'Not directly, this isn't the time or place for that. But I do want to give him a heads-up that I'll be seeing him officially, so he has time to gather the details beforehand.'

Granger eyed her silently before running a hand over his chin. 'Right then. I'll get our drinks. What would you like?'

After a quick scan of the chalk-scrawled blackboard behind the bar, she said, 'A white wine, thanks. And next round will be my shout.'

'Right-o.' With a dip of his head at her, he strode to the quick-service area.

She saw him rest a boot on the scuffed metal footrest, and lean his elbows on the towelling runner while waiting to be served. He was certainly right at home in the country hall surrounded by country folk. Then she noticed the men on either side of him grow edgy, as if intimidated by the tall, well-built man in their midst. Swallowing a grin, she settled herself on the barstool as Gero's voice rang in her head.

'... would make a fine husband for a country lass.'

She gave a start when another voice hissed in her ear, 'Have you finished monopolising the only available man in the room?'

Spinning around, she frowned at her friend. 'I'm not monopolising anyone, Flip.'

'Really? You're telling me that wasn't you dancing with the same bloke ever since you got here?'

'So you think I'm monopolising Jack.'

Flip gave a huff and clicked her tongue.

'We did come here together,' Abbey went on, keeping her tone calm and level. 'And asking a stranger to dance is a tough call for a bloke, one likely to end in fisticuffs with a jealous husband or boyfriend.'

'I'm not a stranger. Jack knows me.'

'Well, he's *met* you ... briefly. And why are you so antsy, anyway? The dancing has only just started.' Abbey narrowed her eyes at her querulous friend. 'What's up?'

Flip's gaze slid away. 'What d'you mean?'

'Don't play coy with me, you know what I'm talking about. It's not like you're making a secret of tipping your cap at Jack.'

Flip gave a nervous giggle before meeting Abbey's eyes again. 'I checked with you beforehand,' she said defensively, 'and with Gero. You both said there was nothing between you and Jack.'

'And there isn't.'

'So you've got nothing to worry about.'

The two women eyed each other.

'So,' Abbey said tentatively, 'you're serious about wanting to ... get together with him?'

Flip glanced over at the man in question, standing square-jawed, broad-shouldered and narrow-hipped at the bar. 'Why wouldn't I be? He's a good catch, though not as handsome as Banjo....' Her voice trailed off, and then strengthened again. 'But he's big 'n strong and knows his way around a farm.'

Turning back to be met with Abbey's sceptical frown, she stepped in closer and lowered her voice. 'I want Banjo to know there are other fish in the sea, and that I'll throw my line in the water unless he gives me a reason not to. It'll either give him a push to move our relationship forward, or a shove to get him out of my life.' She bit her lip to stop it wobbling. 'Either way, I see it as a win.'

Abbey's frown deepened. 'So you'd just be using Jack to test Banjo's affections?'

'Well I ... um....' Flip winced. '... guess you could say that. Then again, we might be meant to be together, me and Jack. Who's to say we're not?' Noticing Granger heading their way, a wine glass in one hand and a beer in the other, she flashed him a bright smile. 'And I wouldn't be too sad about that.'

Abbey stared at her friend.

Where did Flip get off, using another man to manipulate Banjo?

Resentment and concern for Granger's feelings further entangled her already smarting emotions.

What if Flip was right about them being meant for each other?

Not that Abbey had any reason to be bothered by that outcome.

Of course not!

Then why was a perplexing competitive urge, and something akin to fear, lurking beneath her other emotions?

Unless...?

She searched her feelings, a frown burrowing into her brow when an inner voice whispered the findings.

No ... surely not?

She double-checked.

Same answer.

But ... how had this happened?

Was she simply on the rebound from Jesse? Maybe suffering a bad case of heart-felt appreciation for all Jack had done for her, the farm, Gero, and now Star? Or was it familiarity, morphed into something more profound by her overactive yearning for family? Something deeper, wonderful, intimate ... and perilous?

'Abbey?' Granger was gazing quizzically into her face.

'Oh ... um ... thanks.' Hastily taking the glass he was holding out to her, she gulped a mouthful of the chilled wine. It went down the wrong way and left her spluttering and coughing.

I'm acting like an idiot.

Get a grip!

She gave one last cough and forced a wry grin. 'Thanks for the drink, but I might try swallowing it next time. Inhaling didn't work.'

He nodded, amusement crinkling the corners of his eyes in the way that made her stomach fizz and flip....

'Okay, folks.' Thompson's announcement boomed over the sound system. 'Grab your partners for a Colonial's Quadrille.'

When Granger sculled the last of his beer and then asked Flip to dance, Abbey's stomach sank. It plummeted further when she recalled suggesting he do just that.

Great. Now I'm pushing him into her arms, to be used and possibly thrown aside.

Clutching her wine glass in both hands, she watched the couple join the groups on the dance floor. As a spectator she was able to admire Granger's strong bearing and ease of movement as he led Flip in the dance.

'... couples cross and ladies chain,' Thompson intoned, slapping his knee in time with the music.

'My, my.'

The smarmy voice close by her ear gave Abbey a start.

'Don't you scrub up well, Miss Miller.'

Forcing herself to turn casually, she met the speaker's condescending gaze. 'Hello Mr Pearson.'

'Vince, please.' His tone was oily, sycophantic. 'We're neighbours after all ... Abbey.'

The hairs on the back of her neck stood on end.

Go away, Pearson.

Managing a forced smile, she turned her back on him to watch the dancers. When Granger guided a beaming Flip into a spin, she wondered if Banjo was catching the performance. Glancing toward the bar area she found him standing, stony-faced, staring over his beer glass at the dancing couple.

Was Flip's plan working?

'So, how are things on the farm? Getting the place ship-shape again?'

Her nostrils flared at his effrontery.

What are you hoping I'll say, Pearson, that you were right? That the farm's too much for me to handle alone and I'm just DYING to sell it to you?

Even if selling would be the quickest and easiest option....

Quelling that traitorous thought, she said tightly, 'The farm's just fine, thanks.'

'Good, good.' His tone implied it was anything but, and she got the feeling he wanted to say more.

Well, she certainly wasn't going to help him.

'... now polka the room....'

She watched the dancers twirl and swirl around the dance floor like an ex-cyclonic low.

'Say, neighbour, you haven't had anyone ... interfere ... with your farming equipment by any chance?' At her raised eyebrows Pearson hurried on. 'It's just that some of my ... ahem ... irrigation equipment has been tampered with recently. I was wondering if you'd noticed anything untoward at your place?'

You're fishing, hoping to catch me out.

She stifled a derisive grin and shook her head. 'I guess having Jack and Gero there makes any would-be trouble-makers,' and she stared hard at him, 'think twice about trying anything on at my place.'

'... and finish.' At Thompson's call, the dancers jostled to an enlivened halt, clapping, puffing, laughing, and milling around the floor.

Abbey noticed Granger glance her way and scowl when his eyes fell on Pearson.

He caught the scowl too. Muttering, 'Well, I'm glad things are going okay,' he touched her forearm. 'But my offer stands if that changes any time.' Letting his fingers slide off her arm and leaving a clammy sensation on her skin, Pearson tipped his head at her and moved away, into the crowd.

Wrinkling her nose, she swiped a hand down her arm as though removing a slime trail.

Granger strode up to her, his gaze following Pearson. 'Every-thing alright?'

'Yeah.' She gave a shudder. 'That man really does give me the creeps, though.' Spying Thompson climb down from the stage, she exclaimed, 'Ooh, that's my cue,' and hurried over to him.

.   .   .

Later, in a break between the dances – during which Abbey grew increasingly comfortable *and* uncomfortable with Granger's physical nearness – she saw him check his watch.

'They'll be winding up soon.' His forehead creased. 'Guess I should get Flip up for another dance.'

So now she's Flip, not Philippa.

Abbey felt a stirring of unease as she eyed her friend sitting slouched on a stool, elbows on the bar, chin in her hands. By her side Banjo was busy yarning with his mates again. 'Yeah,' she said quietly, 'I guess you should.'

'Well folks,' Thompson announced a few dances later, 'sorry to say we've come to that time of night.'

He was met with howls of protest.

'Yeah, I'm sad too. But we can trust our band to end the evening on a high. Let's hear it for the talented *Scrub Turkeys* who've kept our boots scootin' all evening!'

Amid the applause the band leader stepped up to the mic. 'We've had a request for the final song of the night, so take your main squeeze in your arms for the romantic old classic, *All I Have to do is Dream.*'

As Granger accompanied Flip off the dance floor, an impatient-looking Banjo stepped forward to grab his girlfriend's hand. His face a picture of determination, he led her straight back onto the floor.

Abbey's lips twitched.

Oh yeah, Flip's strategy is definitely working....

Feeling a touch on her arm, she turned to see Granger extending a hand.

'May I have the last dance?'

Dipping her head, she gave a coy smile. 'You may.'

'Dre-ee-ee-ee-eam ... dream, dream, dream....' The singer's Glen Campbell-esque croon and accompanying mellow bass riff flowed around and over them as Granger led her onto the dance floor.

This time he brought her in close against his firm body. It felt natural to sink into the embrace, rest her head against his chest, and close her eyes. They wound their way slowly around the dance floor, and she found herself wishing the song would keep going on a permanent loop.

Of course, it didn't.

Realising they were no longer moving, she drew back to find him gazing down at her, his poker face gone. Something in his eyes set her insides quivering. She sucked in a quick breath as he bent his head, and when he touched his lips to hers, heat exploded within her. An instant later he straightened to gaze at her again, this time with uncertainty.

She stood, eyes closed, her whole body alight and showering sparks like a bushfire. When he spoke she opened her eyes to watch the movements of his mouth as the words rumbled in his chest.

'That wasn't ... inappropriate ... I hope?' At her shy smile and whispered, 'No,' he let out a breath. 'So, are you ready to go?'

An unsteady nod was all she could manage.

They didn't say much on the drive home, but shared occasional smiling glances. When he stopped at an intersection and reached across to stroke her cheek with the back of his fingers, there was more meaning to that touch than words could convey.

But when they arrived at the farm and walked up to the homestead, Abbey's steps faltered as awkwardness set in.

Did Jack have ... expectations? If so, how should she respond? Their mutual attraction was obvious but *very* new; no way to tell how far it would go. And she was effectively his boss; shouldn't she be keeping a professional distance?

And then she remembered Gero, and winced. The old man was still sleeping in the guest room while waiting for his quarters to be ready. And the internal walls in the old homestead were one-layer thin.

As if guessing at her discomfort, Granger stopped and put a hand on her arm. 'Abbey?'

The thrill she got from hearing her name spoken in that deep, gravelly voice would never get old. It was almost as stirring as his touch, his kiss ... almost.

When she looked up at him, he said, 'I enjoyed myself tonight.'

He didn't add that it was the closest to fun he'd had for a long time. That was, until he kissed her and changed everything.

Or nothing.

It wasn't like this *thing* between them could go very far, considering their different circumstances. Abbey owned a farm, while all he had of any value were the savings he'd tucked away in the hope of one day buying his own spread.

The *vain* hope.

'I did too.' She was smiling shyly at him.

Taking a step back he mumbled, 'I'm making an early start in the morning, got that feed to spread in the lower paddocks. So ... I'd better turn in.'

His poker face was back.

Reality rushed in, dousing the rising heat between them and dissolving her smile.

Had she said or done something wrong?

Gathering herself, she said crisply, 'Of course. Goodnight, Jack.'

Dipping his head and murmuring, ''Night, Abbey,' he turned and stepped off the porch.

25

Abbey rose late the next morning, heavy-eyed and groggy after only a few hours' sleep. Wrapped in her dressing gown she dragged herself to the kitchen. Stopping in the doorway, she took in the homely scene before her.

Gero sat at the table, a steaming mug of tea and a week-old newspaper in front of him. On a paint-chipped cast iron trivet at his elbow, the teapot sat under a hand-knitted cosy stained tannin-brown at the spout opening.

She swept a glance around the room, down the corridor, and out the open front door.

No sign of Jack.

Blowing a breath through pursed lips, she allowed her tense shoulders to slump.

Having brooded over him all night, re-living the thrill of his touch, his kiss – and then berating herself for being so pathetic – the last thing she wanted this morning was to run into him.

Raking fingers through her tousled bed-hair, she shuffled

across the room to the shelf where the cups and mugs hung from tiny brass hooks.

Gero's shrewd eyes followed her. 'You're up late, Girlie. Out shakin' a boot 'til the wee hours, eh?'

Pointing to the teapot, she croaked in morning voice, 'Anything left in that?'

'Enough for another cup.'

From off the shelf she grabbed her favourite mug, a much-loved if rather ugly stoneware floral, one of Bill's last gifts to her, and sank into a chair at the table.

Over the rim of his own cup Gero watched her pour the tea, add a splash of milk, and wrap both hands around the steaming mug. After some grateful mouthfuls of the rejuvenating brew, she set the half-empty mug down and sagged back in her chair.

'Right. Out with it.'

She sniffed, blinked, and mumbled, 'Out with what?'

'What's buggin' you.' When she just stared at the table, he prompted, 'You look terrible, and not just late-night terrible. Has somethin' upset you?'

She gave a humourless snort.

'I'll take that as a yes. So, what was it?'

Her expression soured. 'Nothing I care to talk about.'

'Ah.'

'What's that supposed to mean?'

'All I said was "Ah".'

'I heard what you said.' Noting the twinkle in his eyes, she sat forward to fix him with a penetrating gaze. 'I want to know what it means.'

'Nothin' really, just....' He shrugged a shoulder. 'I get it.'

'Get what?'

'I saw the way you looked around when you first came in.'

He gave a sage nod. 'Checkin' for Jackson would be my guess, and relieved to find he wasn't here. So I'd reckon you 'n he have had words.'

'Great.' Slumping in her chair again, she scowled at the ceiling. 'I clearly suck at keeping my feelings to myself.'

'Only 'cos I know you so well, Girlie. Have done since you was a little 'un.'

When she remained silent, he set down the newspaper and sat forward. 'Why don't you get it off your chest? Won't go no further than here,' and he slapped his own chest with an open palm. When she didn't respond, he swallowed the last of his tea and waited.

Finally she tipped her head forward and sat upright. 'Gero....'

'Mmm?'

'You're a man.'

He gave a wry grunt. 'Last time I checked.'

'I mean ... you understand how men think.'

'Not all of 'em, not by a long shot. Some blokes are downright bag-o-cats crazy.' Seeing her bite her lip he assumed a milder tone. 'But I'm happy to offer an opinion, if that's what you're after.'

She nodded. 'What do you think would make someone like Jack ... um ... back off from someone suddenly?'

'From a woman, you mean?'

'Um ... yeah.'

'A woman like ... you?'

With a barely audible, 'Yeah,' she hung her head.

'Well now, it depends. I'm assumin' this all happened last night, so how about you tell me what went on beforehand?'

'Okay. So he ... *we* ... had a good time at the dance. He got

Flip up a couple of times, but danced mostly with me.' A smile twitched the corners of her lips. 'He's quite the twinkle-toes.'

'His parents were too, if I remember right.' A faraway focus crept into Gero's eyes. 'And towed them boys along with 'em to every knees-up within cooee.' He snapped back to the present. 'Anyway, carry on.'

'So, after the last dance....'

'Yeah?'

'He ... well ... um ... kissed me.'

Gero grinned at the colour infusing her cheeks. 'Think I'm gettin' the picture. Sure does sound like you two had a good time. So, what changed?'

'We came home and ... I wasn't sure....' She screwed up her face. 'Not that I ... well....' Shaking her head to clear it of the more embarrassing details, she plunged on. 'Anyway, he just suddenly went all distant for some reason. Said he had to get up early to spread feed and marched off, leaving me standing there like a pathetic twit.'

Mumbling, 'I did hear the tractor start up before daylight this mornin',' Gero drained his tea cup before speaking again. 'Could be he just got the wrong signals from you, or was worried he'd misread 'em.'

Her colour deepened.

'Maybe the kiss was his way of showing you how he feels,' Gero went on, 'and bein' a gentleman, he's leavin' what happens next up to you.'

'Maybe.' She cleared her throat. 'But I get the feeling there's more to it than that.'

He gave a thoughtful nod. 'Overall, young Jackson strikes me as a good type, like his father was. Proud like him too. But if I'm any judge of character, he's carryin' some baggage.'

'I think I know what that baggage might be.'

'Oh?'

'It's the family property, Granger Farm. Jack was supposed to be joint owner of it after his dad died, but his brother got into financial trouble and sold the farm out from under him.'

'Ah, yes.' Gero rubbed his grizzled chin. 'I remember hearin' whispers back then about the Granger boys fallin' out. Didn't give it much credence, was never one for town gossip.'

'But why would losing the farm stop Jack from getting ... close ... to someone?'

'You need to see it like he does.' The old man fixed her with a level gaze. 'I'm sure you know what farmin' types value above almost everythin' else.'

'Land?'

'Yep. And in Jackson's case he not only lost his share of land, he lost his home and livelihood as well.' The old man paused to stare into the distance. 'So now pride comes into the equation. And if he lets it, a man's pride can play a major role in his life.' After taking a breath he went on without looking at her. 'If he believes he has nothin' to offer, pride can make a man feel inferior, and unworthy of bein' loved.'

'Nothing to offer? But—'

'I'm sure nowadays it's considered an old-fashioned belief, but a lot of country folk still hold to it; that a man should have more to offer a woman than just himself.' His eyes refocused and he fixed them on hers again. 'And when it comes to the two of you, Girlie, it's obvious who's holdin' the higher cards.' He paused for effect. 'Not only do you have more than him, you *have* what he *lost*.' When she merely gaped at him, a hint of exasperation crept into his voice. 'The farm. You own a workin' farm.'

'Oh ... of course ... right.'

'So, considerin' all that, what conclusion d'you reckon most folks would jump to if they knew he was chasin' after you?'

'That he's....' Her eyes widened. 'A gold-digger.'

Gero clicked his fingers. 'Right on the money.'

Staring into mid air, she frowned. 'Jesse even called him that when he was here.'

'There you go, he's copped it already. Now do you understand what might be holdin' him back?'

At her slow nod, the old man gave a grunt and pushed himself to his feet, dangling his empty cup from a wrinkled finger. 'So, Girlie. Assumin' I'm right about all that, and assumin' you want to change the situation, I'd reckon the next move's yours.'

Abbey took a breather and stretched her back. 'It was Pearson.'

'What?' Granger kept his focus on the nozzle of the caulking gun, pressing it to the crack in the aged but solid Blackbutt floorboard.

After their first stilted exchanges following the night of the dance, both acted as though it never happened. They continued working on the final touches to Gero's quarters, and for Abbey, keeping busy helped gloss over the awkwardness between them.

'Pearson found Uncle Bill after ... the accident.'

Finishing that run of gap filler, Granger sat back on his haunches to squeeze the caulking gun, readying it for the next run. He didn't look up. 'So you've spoken to the copper.'

She nodded. 'Story goes Pearson was out "riding the boundaries" and noticed disturbed ground on the edge of the ridge.'

'Isn't the ridge on your property?'

'Yeah. Apparently he told Jeff he spotted the disturbance from his side of the fence, though I very much doubt that. It's too far away to see with the naked eye, especially with thick scrub in between. At least ... there *used* to be scrub there....'

After a weighty pause he asked, 'You haven't seen for yourself?'

Hit by a wave of self-reproach, she turned her face away and shook her head.

'You should.' He caught her uncertain frown as she busied herself unwrapping a new paintbrush and fanning the bristles against her hand. 'I could come with you,' he said slowly. 'Would give me a chance to check the fences over that way, the only ones I haven't got to yet.'

She nodded without looking at him and bent to dip the brush into the paint. 'What about you? Been for a look at the family farm since coming here?' She felt a chill settle around them and straightened.

He was staring at her, his eyes hooded. 'Why would I do that?'

'Because....' She took care to position the dripping brush over the centre of the paint tin. 'You lived there, it was your home.'

'So?'

'So, aren't you curious to see what it's like now?'

'Not in the least.'

'Why not? I would be.'

A flicker of something like pain crossed his face at the prospect of seeing his old home, established with such care by his father and the repository of their family history, looking neglected or worse. 'Because,' he said tersely, 'there's no point dwelling on past history.'

She eyed him, and after a lengthy pause said, 'You're saying I should go to the ridge.'

He nodded.

'For closure, right?'

Another nod.

'Well, it looks to me like you could use some too ... closure, that is, on the subject of Granger Farm.'

When he bristled, she hurried on, using his own words. 'I could come with you.' She threw him a bright smile. 'It's a pleasant ride from here, one day to get there and back. Goes through some pretty country....' Her voice faltered. 'As ... you probably remember.'

He gave a non-committal grunt and began resealing the gap filler cartridge in the caulking gun. After a drawn-out silence, he cast an eye around the restored living area. 'Didn't take as long as I thought to get these quarters up to scratch.' Lifting his chin at the paint tin by her side, he asked, 'You nearly done?'

'Just this last section to do.'

With a firm, 'Right,' he rose to his feet. 'I don't have anything pressing to do after this, so we can head to the ridge once you're finished.'

Abbey remained where she was, staring at the paint dripping from her brush, mulling over his offer – which, to her annoyance, sounded more like a directive. She understood the need for closure but dreaded what awaited her at the ridge. Still, it wouldn't pay to be precious about it, she just had to tough it out. Couldn't afford to neglect that section of the property by forever avoiding one *awful* place.

Where the agony of loss waited to assault her anew.

A shadow fell across the paddock as rain clouds gathered above them. The breeze dropped and a hush fell over the land, broken by the thud of hooves on sparsely grassed ground. Cooper and Gordon ambled side-by-side, close enough for their riders' legs to occasionally bump together with a clang of stirrup irons. Whenever it happened Abbey would nudge Cooper sideways to increase the gap between them, taking care to do so discreetly.

While she wanted to avoid physical contact with him, and the intense reactions it brought on, she didn't want Granger thinking she resented him, or worse, was repulsed by him. Especially as her feelings were heading in quite the opposite direction, at full gallop. And if Gero was right, Granger's reticence to pursue a relationship he could materially profit from revealed honourable intentions, which only increased his appeal. And her respect for him as a man.

But while she could acknowledge this growing attachment, the rest of her emotions remained scattered, like a mob of wild cattle on an unfenced range. And like how she would treat that mob, she was leaving them to calm down and sort themselves out ... for the moment.

His gravelly voice broke into her reverie. 'We must be getting close now.'

Her stomach did a flip and then sank.

He was right, they were almost upon it.

The spot where Bill Miller drew his last breath.

Granger stood a safe distance back from the crumbling edge, staring down at the rock-strewn ground some thirty metres below the escarpment. Emergency Services offices had retrieved Miller's broken body but left his mount where it fell, chestnut neck twisted, limbs askew, teeth bared in a deathly rictus. The crows flapping and jostling around the decaying carcass looked, from above, like cockroaches gorging on fallen food scraps.

Stepping away from the edge he squinted at Abbey standing well behind him, eyes huge in her ashen face. At his urging she had taken a rushed glance at the scene below before stumbling back, smothering an anguished cry with her hands.

Now, fixing him with a piercing, tear-filled gaze she ground out, 'Th-there, I've done it.' Her voice rose and cracked. 'I've seen where he d-died.' Sagging to her hands and knees in the dirt, she sobbed, 'Are you *happy* now?'

As her sobs became open-mouth howls, Granger rushed to squat beside her and wrap her in his arms. Pressing his lips against her hair, he murmured, 'I'm so sorry, Abbey love.'

Her muffled words rose from where she huddled close against him. 'I was doing okay before I s-saw....' Grabbing his shirt tightly in both hands, she thumped a fist against his firm pec and cried, 'W-why did you m-make me come here? Why?' She thumped him again before sagging against his chest, sobbing.

He held her tighter, stroking her hair with a large hand.

'I c-can picture him ... down there.' She shook her head as if to dispel the traumatic imagery. 'D-don't want to remember him like ... *that*.'

'Then don't.' Granger's words rumbled beneath her ear. 'You can *choose* how to remember him.' He felt her stir, and heard her sobs become hiccups.

Uncurling her hands, she let go of his shirt and drew away.

Gazing at him with watery eyes above flushed, tear-soaked cheeks, she croaked, '*Choose* how I remember him?'

He brushed the hair from her damp forehead with gentle fingers. 'Remember I told you it was Mum who found Dad?'

She nodded.

'Well, although I've seen more than my share of death, Mum....' He frowned. 'It was awful for her to see Dad that way.' He blew a long breath. 'When I asked her how she was coping, she told me she refuses to remember him like that. Instead, she chooses to picture him as he was, an alive, vital and proud man. The husband she loved.'

Abbey sniffed and ran a hand over her eyes. 'Is that what you do too? Choose how you remember him?'

'Yep.'

'Does it bring you comfort?'

He nodded. 'It will for you too, if you picture your uncle the way you loved him best whenever you think of him.'

They gazed at each other, and then Abbey let herself sink against him once more. As he wrapped his arms around her again, she murmured, 'Thank you, Jack.'

He held her until finally she drew back, sniffing and rubbing her eyes. Even then, he kept his hands at her waist.

Throwing him a shy smile, she murmured, 'Guess we should be getting back.' When he gave a grunt of agreement and dropped his hands, she was hit by a revelation.

It was as if Bill were there once more lending her his wise advice; telling her that every moment was precious, that it was foolish to assume there'd be time later to make things right.

And with that revelation, the emotional haze cleared and she felt words building in her throat, impatient for release. She blurted, 'Jack, wait! I ... want to talk about something else for a minute.'

About to rise to his feet, he paused to eye her.

'The ... night of the dance. And what happened after.'

His shoulders slumped and he settled again, a resigned expression on his face.

'Would you ... um ... we....' She blinked hard and tried again. 'If our roles were reversed, would things have been different?'

'Different?'

'You know, between us. You and me.'

Gazing levelly at her, he said slowly, 'You mean if the farm was mine and you were....'

'A blow-in who just turned up one day. Would that make a difference ... to us?'

He gave a wry snort at the blow-in reference, and then frowned. 'Why are you asking this?'

'Because I think we ... feel something ... for each other. Something more than friendship.' She sucked in both lips and stared nervously at him. Relieved when he didn't contradict her, she went on more boldly. 'But you're holding back from taking it ... *us* ... further, and I think I know why.'

He stared mutely at her.

'It's because you're proud, and assume you have little to offer me; that a gold-digger, what Jesse called you when he was here, is how you'll be seen by everyone, including me. That's right, isn't it?'

When his only response was a narrowing of eyes, she charged on. 'I'll take that as a yes. So now, here's how I see things. Firstly, you could've taken advantage of the situation – and me – but you didn't. That tells me what kind of man you are.' She swallowed, gathering her courage, and tipped her face upward and closer to his. With a soft, 'And here's how I feel about that,' she pressed her lips against his firm, dry mouth.

After a slight backward twitch of his head at the unexpected move, he quickly recovered. Putting a hand to the side of her face and wrapping his other arm around her, he pulled her closer and deepened the kiss. A long time later he drew back, breathing heavily, to rest his forehead against hers.

She blinked, sucked in a breath, and made herself carry on despite the unsteadiness of her voice. 'And secondly, the ... um ... farm means a lot to me because it meant a lot to my uncle.' Her voice grew stronger.

Sensing the importance of her speech, Granger lowered his hands and sat back to eye her levelly.

'It's also my home and now my livelihood. But in the long run, the farm is just a house and animals on a piece of land.' When he gave a disconcerted frown, she said, 'Don't get me wrong, I love the place. But if I had to live here alone for the rest of my life I wouldn't be happy.' She put a hand on his arm. 'What's important to me, Jack, is the *people* living here. Family. That's what I value most after losing the last of mine,' and she inclined her head toward the drop-off, 'down there.'

He gazed back at her. 'What are you telling me?'

'That with you and Gero living on the farm with me, I ... sort of have a family again. You couldn't offer me anything I'd value higher than that. So it's really *me* with the most to gain; *me* who could be called the gold-digger.'

He continued staring at her, his normally inscrutable face working, before rising to his feet and holding out a hand. 'Come on,' he said gruffly, 'let's head back.'

26

T hey rode in companionable silence. Abbey risked an occasional peek at Granger and each time found him staring straight ahead, poker face firmly in place. Now and then he reined in an over-eager Gordon to match Cooper's more sedate stride. Apart from that, he could've been riding alone.

When they pulled up at the yards he helped her down from the saddle, and then surprised her with a question.

'Plans? No, not really.' She gave a shy smile. 'Unless you call putting on a roast "plans".'

'Don't worry about cooking tonight.' After clearing his throat of an uncharacteristic tremor he said firmly, 'I'd like to take you to dinner.' His lips twitched. 'If you'll lend me the ute, that is.'

'Of course, you can borrow it any time.' Her smile widened. 'And going out to dinner would be lovely, but could we make it tomorrow instead? It's just ... I promised to cook Gero's favourite dishes for his last night in the homestead. Roast lamb with Yorkshire puddings, and lemon delicious for dessert.'

'He's moving into the quarters tomorrow?'

At the look in Granger's eyes, her heart gave a body-jolting bang and her cheeks flushed bright pink. 'F-first thing in the morning. He's one happy camper right now.'

'And he's not alone.' After a quick glance around, Granger moved in close to put a hand at her waist. Tilting her chin upward with a finger, he gazed into her eyes and said in a husky voice, 'I've wanted to do this for a while.' Bending his head, he pressed his firm lips against her quivering ones.

The kiss had her buzzing all over, weak at the knees, and longing for it to never end.

As if sensing the undercurrent between them, Gero didn't linger over his usual after-dinner cup of tea on the veranda. Rising stiffly from the squatter's chair, he dipped his head at Abbey. 'That was a damn fine meal, Girlie. You'll make some lucky bloke a fine wife one day.' With a wink at Granger sitting quietly in the shadows, he exhaled in a contented whoosh. 'Right, I'm hittin' the hay. Got a big day tomorrow. Night, you two.'

As the old man shuffled off they called, 'Good night,' at his back.

With him gone, the air around them thickened.

Granger rose from his chair without speaking to take the one Gero had vacated, beside Abbey. She watched him pull out his wallet.

'I was telling you about my Dad.' His tone was low, intimate.

'Mmm.'

'Would you like to see a photo of him?'

She sat straighter. 'I'd love to.'

As he tugged the rough-edged photo from his wallet, a card came with it and clattered to the floor. He passed her the photo before bending to retrieve the card.

She stared at the man in the picture, an older version of the one sitting beside her, if a little more wiry in build. Standing tall, chin up and chest out in saddle-stained moleskins, checked shirt, and battered Akubra hat, Jim Granger stared into the camera lens. While his expression gave nothing away, his eyes held a kind light.

'Oh yes.' She smiled. 'You're *so* like your dad.'

'Thanks ... I guess.'

'Was this taken at Granger Farm?'

He glanced at the peppermint green weatherboards in the photo's background. 'Yep.'

'Cool.' She studied the picture again before saying carefully, 'Have you thought about what I said?'

'You've said a lot of things.' His lips twitched.

She gave a mock-annoyed huff. 'About going to see your old home.'

'Oh, that.'

'Yes, that. So have you thought about it?'

'I have, as a matter of fact.'

'And?'

'And ... I think we should go some time.'

'You do? Well, that's great. I reckon your Dad,' and she waved the photo at him, 'would be glad to hear it.' As she passed him back the photo she noticed he was still holding the card he'd retrieved from off the floor. Something about it made her ask, 'What's that?'

'This?' He held it up. 'My Veteran card.'

The blood chilled in her veins. 'Did you say *Veteran's* card?'

'All returned servicemen get one. It's no big deal.' He turned it over in his fingers. 'Haven't had much cause to use it—'

'It's *yours?* You mean you ... were in the *military?*'

'Yeah, the Army. Five years as sniper. That meant sitting around waiting for something to happen most of the time, but it made Dad happy. He liked to take credit for our skill with rifles, Johnno's and mine.'

Unaware of her anguish, he slipped the card and photo back into his wallet. 'I only joined up to please Dad. He said young men should do their patriotic duty ... unless they're in line to inherit a farm of course. I suspect the old man liked spruiking to his mates about having a son in the military.' He gave a fond headshake and raised his eyes. 'I was only intending to do the minimum stint, but after the farm was sold—'

Unable to stop herself making a choking sound, Abbey gripped her chair's armrests with claw-like hands.

'Hey, what's wrong?' When he leaned closer, she recoiled. 'Abbey!' He put a hand on her arm. 'What is it?'

Cowering and shaking off his hand, she rasped, 'Y-you .. *you* were in the Army?'

He frowned, baffled. 'I just told you I was.'

Don't let it be true. Please.

'*You,* not your brother?'

'My brother? What—'

'A soldier.' Dread replaced the shock in her grey eyes, and a flat, resigned note crept into her voice. 'You're a soldier.'

'*Was* a soldier. For a short while.' His frown deepened. 'I don't understand—'

'Is ... was ... same deal either way.' Her mind filled with clouded, frightening childhood images. An enraged man in camouflage fatigues roaring and lashing out at a huddled female form on the floor. His whimpering victim cradling her head with bruised and bleeding arms, feeble protection against the next rain of blows. A quivering arm falling away, exposing the victim's swollen and bloodied face.

Leah Miller's swollen and bloodied face.

With a strangled cry, Abbey jolted upright and rose unsteadily to her feet. 'You ... need to ... leave.'

'*What?*' He leaped up. 'Abbey, look at me!' Gripping her shoulders, he spun her toward him and froze at the sight of her pinched face and clenched jaw.

She stood stiffly, arms jammed against her sides, curling and uncurling her fists. The condemnation in her eyes, while really meant for the soldier in the scene playing out in her mind, sliced through him.

'No, *no* ... Abbey love, don't do this. Tell me what's wrong.' He tried to pull her close only to have her thump both hands against his chest and shove him away.

'DON'T you touch me.' The words came out as a hiss.

'But—'

'Leave. Now!' Her voice, her insides, her whole being, shook. 'You're no longer w-welcome here.'

He stared at her in stunned disbelief. 'Abbey, no.'

'I said GO! And I want you packed up and g-gone by m-morning.'

This last volley caught in her throat as, with an agonised sob, she stumbled inside and slammed the door.

Morning saw him waiting on the veranda when she finally emerged. One glimpse of her stony face told him nothing had changed, he was still *persona non grata* for some reason.

After spending the night mulling over the inexplicable change in her attitude toward him, he reached the only possible conclusion. Her discovery of his stint in the military – not that he made a secret of it, just didn't proclaim it from the mountain tops – was behind her sudden change of heart. But why would knowing that effect such a radical change? She didn't strike him as bigoted.

And yet....

'I trust you're here to inform me you're leaving.' Her voice was flat, dry, cold.

He stared into her red, swollen eyes. 'Abbey....'

When he made to move closer she thrust up a hand. 'The only word I want from you is goodbye.'

'Well that's too bad, because I have something else to say.'

'I don't want to hear it.' She turned toward the door.

'I love you, Abbey. And I think ... hope ... you feel the same about me.'

She paused with a hand on the doorknob and bowed her head, but didn't turn around. Squaring her shoulders, she said brokenly, 'Goodbye ... Jack. Thank you for ... all the work you did for ... um ... us.'

In her words he heard sorrow, regret, and anguish. 'Don't *do* this, Abbey.' He took a step forward, his voice rising. 'Talk to me! Tell me what's wrong so I can fix it.'

With a sad shake of her head she risked one final, stricken glance at him, before stepping inside and shutting the door behind her with a firm thud. When her knees threatened to give way, she slumped against the door. Pressing her forehead to the timber, she felt the shudders as he knocked again and again, calling her name. Then the knocking stopped, replaced by a sliding sound as he rested his open hand against the door.

She touched her own palm to the timber so their two hands were only separated by the door's thickness. The thump that came next might've been his forehead against the door's outer, for she heard a long, frustrated breath blown close by her ear. A moment later his hand slid away, followed by the scrape of boots on floorboards and the trudge of booted feet across the veranda and down the stairs. They crunched across the gravel, and out of her hearing.

He was gone.

Turning her back to the door, Abbey slipped down it to the floor, mouth open in a soundless, tortured wail.

Why hadn't she known before this? She should've been able to guess, should've picked him as a soldier when they first met and avoided all this hurt. Instead she had to go and fall for him, a military man, and repeat her mother's terrible mistake.

The ache of loss engulfed her. She curled into a tight, anguished ball on the floor.

Did she *really* have to push away the man she loved, the man who had just admitted to loving her back?

Who'd also admitted to being a military man.

And was therefore not to be trusted.

27

Was it a case of history repeating itself, this time robbing him of the perfect girl? A country girl, whose grey eyes, freckled nose, and beautiful smile made his heart race in a whole new way.

A girl who, out of the blue, turned him away without an explanation.

Granger gave a frustrated grunt.

Had he come to the right conclusion? That her change of heart was simply because he had served in the army? If that were in fact the case, how could she let such a minor detail derail something so promising?

Something so ... wonderful.

He paused, rolled-up jeans in his hands.

But *was* it a minor detail? Look what happened with Laura. Given half a chance their relationship might've developed into something more, until his stint in the military killed it as sure as a bullet to the head.

With a dismissive huff, he pressed the jeans into a tighter roll.

Bottom line? It's over with Abbey.

End of story.

Shoving the bundled jeans into his already firmly-packed duffel, he sat on the bag to close the zip and then finished bundling the remaining gear into his backpack. After one last look around the loft that had come to feel like home, he shrugged on the backpack, grabbed the duffel, and descended the ladder. As he strode off he kept his gaze ahead, away from the homestead.

This was just another chapter in his life to relegate to the past.

Taking a deep breath, he shrugged the backpack higher and lengthened his stride.

Gero came inside, a notable spring in his step, and headed to the kitchen.

'Well, Girlie,' he announced jauntily, 'you two have done wonders with them quarters. And thanks to you not lettin' me help with the inside rennos, I've managed to plant out me market garden.' Beaming, he slapped the back of a chair with both hands. 'Even got some seedlings startin' to poke their heads up.'

Grateful his eager, break-of-day inspection of the renovated quarters had given her time to regain a measure of composure, Abbey bent to open the oven door. 'Glad you like the place.' She kept her face turned away, certain the eagle-eyed old man would see through the thin veneer of calm.

'Like it? I *love* it! Why, it's almost as swish as me old place, and that's sayin' somethin', comin' from me.' Sniffing the air as he took a seat, he said to her bent back, 'Sure smells yummy in here.'

She lifted the tray of freshly baked jam-drop biscuits and nudged the oven door closed with a knee. For now, baking was the only activity she could face, the only task that brought a glimmer of comfort. 'These'll be cool enough to eat shortly.'

He eyed the golden-brown biscuits as she transferred them to a cooling rack, and licked his lips. 'That Jackson's a marvel with hammer and nail. Has given the old place a new lease on life. Went to tell him that, only I couldn't find him anywhere. Did he head out early this mornin'?'

She stiffened.

'Did y'hear me, Girlie? What's Jackson up to today?'

The still-hot baking tray slipped from her grasp to clatter into the sink. Her shoulders drooped, and she put both hands on the counter to support herself. 'Jack's gone, Gero.'

'Gone? What d'ya mean, "gone"?'

She stared unseeingly into the sink. 'What does "gone" usually mean?'

'He's left the farm?' The old man frowned at her back.

She nodded.

'But ... why?'

Straightening to wipe her hands on her floury gingham apron, she steeled herself before turning to face him. 'His services are no longer required.'

'No longer required?' He stared at her, perplexed. 'I don't understand.'

'He helped catch up on the jobs around the place, which is why he was here.' She continued wiping her already clean hands, her movements hurried, jerky. 'I can't afford to pay wages, and couldn't expect Jack to go on working for food and lodging only.'

'But it's all so ... sudden.' The frown in Gero's wrinkled brow deepened. 'And I thought the two of you had sorted out—'

'We did.' Realising she'd snapped at him, Abbey took a breath and said more calmly, 'And after that we had a good ... working ... relationship.'

'*Working* relationship?'

'That's right.' She whirled back around, squeezing her eyes shut and leaning against the sink. 'Jack and I had a *working* relationship, nothing more.' Hearing Gero rise to his feet behind her with a grunt, she cringed. Any sympathy he might show was sure to tip her over the edge.

If I could just be given time to recover properly....

Taking hold of her arm and turning her to face him, Gero stared into her dark-ringed, puffy eyes. 'That won't do, Girlie.' He gave a determined shake of his head. 'I want the full story.' When she tried to free her arm he tightened his grip and guided her to the table. 'So take a pew and tell me what happened.'

The dreaded tears welled in her eyes as she sank into a chair. 'Gero—'

'Don't argue, just start talkin'.' He crossed his arms and stared her down. 'You know anythin' you say won't go no further than here.'

What little fight she had left melted away. Bending her head, she blinked hard before finally mumbling, 'He was a soldier.'

Gero took a seat beside her. 'Who was?'

'Jack.'

'Yeah?' Gero's already wrinkled brow furrowed as he thought back. 'I knew one of them Granger boys joined the military, just didn't realise it was Jackson. But so what? That's no big deal, unless....' His voice trailed off as something nipped at his memory. After catching the elusive recollection, his tone softened. 'This is about your dad, ain't it? Him bein' a military man ... and what he did to your ma 'n all.'

'I've tried to conjure up positive memories of my "real" father,' she murmured through stiff lips, 'but....' When her voice dropped to a hoarse whisper, Gero had to lean in to hear. 'All I can ever recall is him being angry and abusive. Of Uncle Bill having to save us from him, Mum and me.'

'Yeah,' he nodded sagely. 'Was a tough time, and you were such a scared little mite. It's no wonder you got bad memories.'

'Mum made a terrible mistake when she got involved with *him,* and she'd be horrified if she knew I'd made the same mistake.' She raised welling eyes to meet his. 'I swore long ago to never get involved with a soldier, serving or ex.'

'Understandable.' Gero nodded gravely. 'So ... when you found out Jackson was one, you gave him his marchin' orders. Even though you have feelins' for the man.'

Her only answer was an angst-ridden silence.

With a sigh, Gero stared down at the table. Neither spoke for a while, and then he sat straighter in his chair and eyed her again. 'Girlie, I'm gonna do somethin' now that I hope won't be goin' against me old mate's wishes.'

She raised her eyes to see a flicker of uncertainty cross his leathery face. It settled an instant later into stoic resolve.

Lifting his chin he said slowly, 'Your uncle Bill, he ... never spoke about a certain time in his life, not even to you. Only 'cos it was too painful, and he wanted to leave those memories in the past, where they belonged. He also didn't want his past deeds to colour how others thought of him. Back then they were more likely than not to think badly of him ... of *us*.' He gave a sad shake of his head.

She frowned. What was Gero talking about? Bill wouldn't have kept any secrets from her. And why would anyone have cause to think badly of him?

'Bill 'n me, we....' The old man took another deep breath and cleared his throat. 'Fact is ... we're Vietnam Vets, both of us.'

Seeing her mouth drop open, he gave a wry grunt. 'So, now you know, what'cha gonna do, Girlie? Chuck *me* out too?'

His hastily dismantled campsite appeared much as he'd left it. Even the tarp roof remained in place, along with the emptied camp cupboard. He hadn't worried about dismantling them, had expected to return sooner than this.

And then a lot happened that he hadn't expected.

But now he was back.

Granger swept another dull-eyed glance around the site. It felt ... foreign ... like he was trespassing on someone else's patch. His shoulders slumped and he blew an exasperated breath. Bending his head to trudge under the tarp, he dumped his gear in the back corner and squatted beside it, rubbing his dry, grainy eyes.

Abbey Miller.

She had made it clear she didn't want anything more to do with him. Didn't even trust him sufficiently to explain the reason for her change of heart. She simply refused to talk to him, despite all his efforts. What more could he have done?

He stared off into the distance.

Was there any point in hanging around? After all, the only reason he'd come here was to take a breather before moving on again.

He got to his feet.

It was time to return to the nomadic life.

The one he should never have left.

She stared at Gero, tongue-tied, her face working as she took in the startling revelation.

Uncle Bill had kept a secret from her, and what a secret! Wise, kind, Bill Miller had been in the military and never told her.

Why keep it a secret? Was he worried it might change my regard for him? As if!

Hang on....

She sucked in a pained breath.

Wasn't that exactly what happened with Jack? I didn't throw him off the farm because he was a lowlife, sleaze, or a bludger. In that quiet way of his he did a lot for me, Gero, Star, and Clearwater. And things were good – becoming better than good – between us ... me and him.

It was because I discovered his military past ... and now, not just his.

Jack.

Bill.

Gero.

The three main men in my life, all ex-soldiers.

The blood drained from her face.

'I can see this has been somethin' of a shock to you, Girlie.' Gero put a gnarled hand on her shoulder. When she raised distressed eyes to his, he soothed, 'Just you sit there quiet while I make us a pot of tea. We've got more talkin' to do, and that's always best done over a cuppa.'

He kept up the conversation while busying himself in the kitchen. 'Considerin' what's goin' on, I reckon it's important you know what your uncle did durin' and after the war.' When the kettle sang, he took it off the stove and filled the teapot. 'Bill was a young sapper when he first went to 'Nam in the sixties. While he was away fightin' the Vietcong, his wife, Beth, died in childbirth. The news knocked him around somethin' rude, as you can imagine.'

'Mum told me about Aunty Beth and their son,' Abbey said quietly. She sniffed and swallowed. 'I didn't realise Bill was away fighting a war when they died.'

'Yeah, he didn't like talkin' about it, and he never really recovered from their loss. Certainly never tried to start over, family-wise, that is. Reckoned he'd used up his share of happiness and didn't deserve another chance at it.' After pausing to shake his head sadly, Gero went on. 'As a sapper, your uncle was tasked with clearin' minefields.' He shifted his gaze to stare out the kitchen window. 'So many of our mates were killed or horribly injured by those mongrel things.'

Rousing himself, he slipped the cosy over the teapot. 'Once, after an Anzac Day session at the pub, Bill admitted there was a time he hoped he'd be killed in the performance of his minefield duty. So he didn't have to go on livin' with the pain of losin' his family and close mates. Of relivin' their sufferin' in his dreams....'

Heaving a sigh, Gero carried the teapot and cups to the table. 'Needless to say, he returned to Australia badly scarred. Even after buyin' this place, from an old digger who'd scored the land under the soldier settlement scheme, Bill couldn't handle civilian life. Same as me and other Vets like us.' Going to the fridge he found the milk jug and returned to the table, where he pulled out a chair and sat opposite her.

'We all found ways of coping. Some beneficial, others ... not so much.' His gaze slid away from hers, and he got busy pouring their teas. 'For your uncle, it was returning to Cambodia to put his old skills to use clearin' the forgotten landmines litterin' the countryside. He told me that work brought him peace.' After splashing some milk into his cup, he sat stirring the tea a while before continuing.

'Anyway, by the time he returned home from there, he was ready to immerse himself in the wholesome farmin' life. He knew I was strugglin', so he tracked me down and brought me here too.' The Adam's apple bobbed in his wrinkled throat and his voice took on a choked sound. 'He encouraged me to buy the place next door 'n helped me get my head right again. As right as such a wreck could be, that is.' He gave a wry huff. 'And so my best mate Bill became the good, solid man you knew 'n loved.'

Refocusing his faded hazel eyes, he met Abbey's riveted stare. 'As far as not deservin' another chance of happiness, he reckoned he got one anyway, when you and your ma arrived at the farm.' He watched her wipe away tears. 'And he gave you a second chance by leavin' his farm to you, Girlie. Then *you* gave *me* one by takin' me into your home. And that grey horse of yours got another chance too, thanks to you 'n Jackson.'

Setting down his cup with a satisfied grunt, he reached across the table to take her smooth hands between his lined ones. 'I'm an old man, Girlie, 'n maybe this is an old-fashioned view, but I reckon just about everyone deserves a second chance. Don't you?'

After scattering the rocks and white-grey remnants of campfire ash into the scrub, Granger swept the compacted area with a leafy eucalyptus branch, tossing the branch into the under-growth when he was done. Taking a final glance around, he moved to where his gear sat waiting and hoisted the heavy backpack onto his shoulders.

His guitar was strapped to the outside of the pack, and his crossbow and bolts, tightly rolled 'roof' tarp and compressed camp cupboard, cooking and other gear, were snug inside. The duffel at his feet bulged with his remaining possessions. With a slap of hands to clean them of dust, he picked up the duffel and strode away from the vacated campsite without a backward glance.

He followed the boundary fence south for a while, and was about to cut through Pearson's property, which would save him time and boot leather, when a waft of breeze brought with it the distant hum of a motor.

He pulled up short.

Did that sound like a pump motor?

Had Pearson re-commenced stealing water?

Taking a quick scan of the surrounding area, he spotted something black lying amid the green undergrowth a short distance away.

Resentment flared hot within him.

But why should I be angry? It's no longer any of my business. Never really was, in fact.

Scowling, he ignored his better judgement and followed the line of poly pipe until he came upon a recently joined section. It ran across the sandy creek bank and into the clear water, where a small whirlpool on the surface indicated the sucking action happening beneath it.

His scowl deepened.

Clearly their sabotage of Pearson's water syphoning operation had proved a short-term solution. The arrogant, thieving prick was at it again, even after receiving what must've been a heads-up that he'd been discovered.

Dragging a hand over his hair, Granger dropped the duffel at his feet. Lowering himself to perch on the bag, he leaned his elbows on his knees and stared at the precious, swirling water.

He had two options.

One: mind his own business and keep going.

Two: stay and do something about it.

Neither course of action felt right.

But only one felt wrong.

Picking up his duffel and shrugging the backpack higher on his back, he stared at the pipeline.

Why was Pearson hell-bent on accessing such a large volume of water? Domestic and stock needs could easily be met with tanks and windmill water pumps.

There's something else going on here, and I doubt it's legit.

Pushing his way through the undergrowth, he found a track of sorts beside the line of poly pipe. Striking out along the track, he followed the illicit pipeline through the fence.

And into *Weerong Station.*

28

Abbey sprinted to the yards, snaffle bridle jangling in her hand. At her approach, Star's grey head shot up and he whinnied.

'Sorry mate, no time to stop.' As she ducked through the fence the gelding jogged over to it, positioning himself so she came up right under his solid neck. Pressing her cheek to his warm greyness, she took a moment to breathe in his earthy scent. 'It's so good to have you here, buddy, but right now I've gotta dash. I've been an idiot, and have an apology to make.'

With a final pat she slipped away, making for where Cooper stood dozing in the next enclosure. Star followed, nudging her in the back with his nose whenever he got close enough. She broke into a jog. He did too. Sliding to a stop when she ducked through the side fence, he pushed his nose between the rails and watched her with pricked, flicking ears.

As she drew near the other horse she pulled up short.

Was that a new mark on Cooper's barrel, just behind his nearside elbow?

Oh-oh.

'Hey, mate.' Running a hand down his dark neck to his barrel, she bent to inspect the sore. 'What's this?' His skin twitched beneath her fingers. Muttering, 'Yep. Girth gall,' she frowned and straightened. 'Damn it.' When he turned his head to eye her, she rubbed the gelding's broad face. 'I'll put some blue lotion on it in a sec, Coop. First, I need to find another mount....' Hurrying to the fence, she leaped onto the middle rail and scanned the horse paddock. With a more vehement, *'Damn it,'* she dropped to the ground. 'Trust Gordon to be right down the far end. May as well be a three day camel journey away.'

At much snorting and pounding of hooves behind her, she glanced over a shoulder. Star was charging around his yard, pig-rooting and shaking his head.

'Well well, someone's full of oats this morning.' Going to the fence, she studied his movements and found no sign of a limp. When she climbed through the railings he raced to meet her, bobbing his head as she stroked his whiskery muzzle.

Chuckling, 'Okay, okay. I get the message,' she ran a hand down his neck and across his body. 'Cooper's gear should fit you.' Returning to his head, which he obligingly lowered as he'd been trained to do, she slipped on the leather bridle and gently settled the Eggbutt snaffle in his mouth. He stood quietly mouthing the bit while she adjusted the cheek straps to the right length. After fastening the throatlatch, she flicked the reins over his head. 'Right then. C'mon, boy.'

He followed as she headed for the tack room. After a quick check of the sky she went inside, to emerge wearing an oilskin coat and carrying a saddle and checked woollen cloth slung over an arm. A bottle of blue lotion poked out from the top of one of the coat pockets.

'Look what I found, Star!' She raised the arm holding the tack. 'My old trick riding saddle. Uncle Bill set it up for me when I first talked about becoming a trick rider. Of course back then he thought it was just a phase....' Sighing, she lowered her arm. 'I haven't used it for years, but I remember him saying he made it big enough for me to grow into. Here's hoping.' As she headed to the fence, the gelding swivelled on his feathered hooves to follow her.

After slinging the saddle and cloth over a railing, she gave the pommel a doting thump. 'From memory it's super comfy, which'll be kinder to my back, and should fit you just fine. But first....' Taking out the bottle of lotion, she climbed through the fence to where Cooper stood dozing. 'Here you go, old fella. This'll take care of that nasty girth gall....'

Star stood tossing his head until she returned.

Wiping her hand against the oilskin coat in a futile attempt to remove the blue stain from her fingers, she announced, 'Right, that's done. Now we'd better get going.'

After a quick flick of the body brush over his already smooth greyness, she spread the thick saddle cloth over Star's withers and back. As she settled the saddle over the cloth, she took a moment to run her hand over the worn leather.

Feeling the tackiness of years of saddle soap and neatsfoot oil, she murmured, 'Thanks, Uncle Bill, for keeping my gear in such good condition.' Swallowing a rise of emotion, she gave Star a fond slap on the shoulder. 'He would've liked you, old mate, and I reckon you would've loved him, like I did. Now, no puffing out your belly when I do up the girth.'

Remembering to keep her movements smooth so as not to strain her back, she reached under the horse's belly to grab the string girth. After fitting and tightening it, she stretched the gelding's front legs to release any folds of skin caught under or between the strands, and led him to the mounting block.

Once in the saddle she checked the length of her stirrup irons.

Spot-on, pretty much. Either I didn't gain any height over the years, or some other adult has used my saddle. Flip, maybe?

She clicked Star forward, and out of habit, bent to open the gate from her high perch. When her back handled the movement without a twinge, she blew a relieved breath.

Did she dare think she might be fully healed?

Dr Hughes had said her recovery might only take weeks....

He also said it could take months, or even years.

Pushing those thoughts to the back of her mind, she once more glanced at the sky as they ambled through the gateway.

'We'd better hurry, it's gonna rain any minute.' When Star sprang into a spritely trot at the tiniest pressure of her legs against his side, a broad grin spread across her face.

My back feels fine, and Star wants to run.

The gelding sprang into a canter the instant she leaned forward and urged, 'C'mon, boy. Let's go find Jack.'

The terrain past the rise dropped sharply into a narrow gully. Dropping his bags at his feet, Granger climbed down to stand at the head of the gully and gaze along its length.

He would never have stumbled across the site if he hadn't followed the pipeline there, to where it terminated at a four metre-wide poly tank. From the tank, a network of soaker hoses fed row upon row of plants tucked amid stands of forest trees. Green shade-cloth stretched between the trees' sturdier branches, providing extra protection for the well-tended and flourishing crop.

And concealment from low-flying aircraft.

Someone has gone to a lot of trouble and expense with this set-up.

Returning his gaze to the rows, Granger tried to make out the leaf shape. Marching up to the nearest plant, he broke off a branch and peered at it.

Cannabis. No doubt about it.

He flicked the branch to the side like it was a filthy cigarette butt.

The man skulking in the bushes nearby took his eyes off Granger just long enough to type and send a text message.

INTRUDER AT NURSERY

Unaware he was being watched, Granger stared at the rows and rows of plants.

Does Pearson know there's an illegal plantation on his land?

He gave a scornful grunt.

Of course he knows. Ten to one this is his operation.

Who else knew about it? Had Bill Miller stumbled across the site too?

Exhaling, Granger lifted his hat to drag a hand through his hair.

The operators of ventures like this are known for being ruthless.

His eyes narrowed and he shoved the hat back in place.

The day I saw Pearson at the roadhouse, one of his offsiders sniggered about Miller's death ... but that only proves the bloke's a lowlife. And Miller had been in Pearson's bad books, for refusing to sell him Clearwater Downs.

He stiffened.

But if Miller had *discovered his dirty little secret, would that have driven Pearson to silence him ... permanently?*

Granger's head snapped up at the sound of fast-approaching hooves. At the same moment, something hard and cold dug into his back.

'Hands in the air,' a voice behind him snarled, 'and keep 'em there.'

Cursing himself for letting down his guard, Granger slowly laced his fingers together and put his hands behind his head. After a few tense minutes, during which the rifle's barrel never moved from its position against his back, Granger spotted Pearson and another of his stockmen galloping toward them.

Hauling his palomino to a sliding halt in front of the two men and showering them in dust, Pearson glowered down at a silent, stony-faced Granger. 'Well well, look what we have here. A trespasser on my land.' Noticing the backpack and duffel on the ground nearby, he pointed to them and sneered. 'You moving on, mate? Had enough of the pretty little thing next door, have you?'

Granger merely glared at him.

'Cat got your tongue?' Pearson gave a snide grunt. 'No matter.' Leaning forward to cross wrists over his western saddle's intricately engraved silver-plated pommel, he said coolly, 'After seeing you with the Miller girl at the dance, I heard on the grapevine that a certain Jackson Granger was working at *Clearwater Downs*. So I take it you're Granger. The only other man next door is that booze-addled halfwit, Alhurst.' He cocked an eyebrow. 'I had been a bit ... concerned ... about all the people taking up residence next door, for purely busi-ness reasons, mind.' His lips tipped into a smirk. 'But now here you are, leaving. Which means one less obstacle to getting my hands on that property and its water.'

The only change to Granger's expression was a further tightening of his lips.

Pearson went on in the same smarmy tone. 'I'm sure you would agree that in the current economic climate, continual improvement and operational expansion is in every entrepreneur's best interest.' He smiled down at his taciturn prisoner as though they were enjoying a neighbourly chat. 'Anyway, now we've been properly introduced, Mr Granger, I should tell you that you've presented me with something of a problem. You see, now that you've stuck your nose into my private business, I can't let you go blabbing about it to all and sundry.'

Straightening in the showy saddle, making its stiff new leather squeak, he eyed Granger up and down. 'From what I've heard you're a drifter, tough, and play your cards close to your chest.' He tapped his lips with a finger. 'I think the best solution for everyone would be for you to come and work for me. I pay well and reward loyalty.' He jerked his head at the man behind Granger. 'Just ask my other employees.'

Drawling, 'You'd be wise to accept ... *mate,*' the man dug the rifle barrel deeper into Granger's back.

Ignoring him, Granger continued staring at Pearson. 'Why drugs?' he finally said. 'You have a nice place here, good facilities and stock. Clearly money's not a problem. Why not just stick to a legit farming operation?'

Pearson's voice took on a sullen edge. 'What was I thinking? Of course a drifter like you wouldn't have a clue about running a business.' He exhaled and rolled his eyes. 'It costs a lot to run a spread like this, Mr Granger. And market circumstances dictate that today's grazier be flexible, ready to diversify, to grab opportunities when they arise. And this particular "opportunity",' and he swept an arm to indicate the crop, 'is helping keep me afloat during the hard times.'

Dropping his arm to his side again, he tapped fingers against the glinting rifle stock protruding from his saddle's leather-fringed scabbard. 'Of course every enterprise has its drawbacks, and I'm sure you can guess one of the main drawbacks for this little venture of mine.'

At Granger's muttered, 'Water,' Pearson nodded.

'The plants need so damn much of it, the thirsty little buggars.' He gave an indulgent huff. 'Which is why owning the property next door is such a tempting prospect.'

'And why you tried to "discourage" Abbey from occupying the farm, and "encourage" her to sell up. By burning down the homestead ... or attempting to. So you're not just a thief and drug supplier, Pearson, you're an arsonist as well.'

'And *you're* guilty of assaulting my men, and sabotaging my pipeline.' His eyes narrowed. 'You have become something of a thorn in my side, Mr Granger.'

'Was Bill Miller a thorn too? Did he stumble on your little "enterprise"? Is that why he ended up dead?'

'My, what an active imagination you have!' Pearson gave a bark of humourless laughter. 'While that nosy neighbour of mine *did* come too close for comfort on one occasion, what happened to the old coot was purely accidental. My men intercepted him before he got a chance to see the "operation" up close.' He fixed steely eyes on Granger. 'As is only right when dealing with a trespasser, my men chased him back over the boundary. They weren't to know Miller's horse would bolt and take a flying leap off the escarpment.'

'Unusual for a horse to willingly throw itself off a cliff,' Granger said in the same flat, emotionless voice.

'The thing panicked, apparently. It happens, especially with green horses.' Pearson arched an eyebrow. 'Not my fault Miller chose to go riding in poor light on an easily spooked youngster.'

Granger's eyes glittered. 'And I can tell you were really cut-up about his death.'

'I did the right thing,' Pearson snapped, 'reported the accident to the police even though it didn't happen on *my* property.' He paused. 'Technically speaking, Miller *had* been trespassing on my land. As you are now, Mr Granger.' As he spoke, he tugged the lever-action Winchester from the scabbard.

A shaft of sunlight through gathering grey clouds flashed off the intricate silver filigree inlay in the rifle's breech and butt. While a beautiful piece, there was no denying the weapon's deadly purpose. Laying the barrel across his other elbow so it pointed at Granger, Pearson inclined his head in the direction of *Weerong's* homestead.

'I think we should continue these discussions indoors,' he said pleasantly. 'So much more civilised, don't you think? So if you'd be so kind....'

When he jerked his chin at the stockman behind Granger, the man growled, 'Get movin',' and poked Granger in the back again.

'Tell your thug to back off.' Granger's voice was low, menacing.

Pearson stared darkly at him. 'Now why would I do that? He's just doing his job. And who do you think you are, giving me orders? Not to mention calling my men thugs, and me a criminal?'

'If you're such a civilised, upstanding citizen, Pearson, why are you frog-marching me to your place with a gun in my back?'

'That's *Mr* Pearson, if you please, *Mr* Granger.' A smirk tugged at his lips. 'You don't know me – yet – so I'll let that little transgression slide. But to be clear, I like to maintain protocol; find it's best to keep all my dealings on a professional level. And to answer your question, you're a trespasser on my property. I have every right to remove you. Just be thankful I'm not the type to shoot first and ask questions later.'

At another shove in the back Granger stumbled forward, while the man behind him kept the pressure on. Pearson and the other stockman waited for them to pass before following behind. All four climbed out of the gully and were about to leave the scrub for open paddock when a rumbling sound reached their ears. As the group stopped in their tracks, a curtain of heavy rain hit, instantly soaking them and turning the surface of the ground to mud.

Seconds later, a horse and rider burst from the scrub and came to a sliding halt right in front of them.

'I thought I heard voices.' Rain gushed from the brim of her Akubra as Abbey took in the scene. She raised her voice to be heard over the drumming of the rain. 'Hey, what's going on here, Pearson?' When her eyes fell on the now dripping rifle in his hand, she gasped. 'Wait, that's—'

'A rifle,' he yelled back. 'Yes, I know, Miss Miller.'

'No, it's—'

'Pointing at your *boyfriend*.' He rolled his eyes. 'I know that too.'

Abbey swiped the water from her face and saw Granger staring back at her through the rain, shaking his head in a silent message.

'Pleasantries aside, Miss Miller,' and Pearson gave an affected sigh, 'I don't recall inviting you, or *anyone* for that matter,' and he arched an eyebrow at Granger, 'to visit me today.' He blinked the rain out of his eyes only to have them fill again. 'It's not like I'm holding an open house or some such thing.'

'Abbey!' His loud call earned Granger a prod in the back, which he ignored. 'Go home.'

'Not without you.'

'Well, isn't that sweet.' Pearson sneered. 'The big man needs the little girl to save him.'

Above the coarse laughter Granger shouted to her, 'I'll be fine, really.' His frown was obvious through the sheeting rain. 'Just *go*.' When he made to step forward, Pearson urged the palomino sideways with a leg yield and made a point of cocking the rifle.

'Nobody's going anywhere,' he growled, ''til I say so.'

At the sight of the cocked weapon being trained on Granger, Abbey's eyes widened and her legs tightened against Star's sides. With a loud, 'Tsss!' she dug her heels into his flanks.

The gelding gave a surprised grunt and leaped forward, barrelling into the palomino's side. The blow knocked Pearson out of the saddle and sent the palomino careering into the horse next to it, catapulting its rider into the air. The startled man hung there for a fraction of a second before falling to the ground, landing heavily with a bellow.

During the melee, Granger felt the pressure on his back ease. Ducking and spinning around, he threw out his left arm to deflect the rifle barrel and knocked the stockman to the ground with a hard right cross to the face. When the rifle flew out of the man's grasp, Granger launched himself at it, snatching it up and training it on the fallen man.

As she wheeled an excitedly prancing Star around, Abbey saw Pearson struggle to his feet and begin searching the ground. Spotting a glint of silver in the mud, she kicked the gelding into a gallop, just as Pearson also spied the Winchester and made a lunge for it.

With his feet struggling for purchase on the wet ground, he flinched as horse and rider bore down on him, each pounding stride sending up clods of muddy dirt. Seeing Abbey swing down the horse's near side to suspend herself above the fast-moving ground by one slender hand and a booted foot, his eyes widened in disbelief.

Blinking the rain from her eyes and dodging flying clods, she extended to full stretch, her open hand mere centimetres above the mud as she reached for the rifle.

With a frustrated roar, Pearson lunged forward but could only watch, open-mouthed, as she scooped up the weapon on the fly.

Clambering back into the saddle, she reined in Star, spinning him in a tight circle. With the gelding dancing beneath her, she caught her breath and firmed her grip on the muddy Winchester. As if anticipating her next command, Star jogged closer to the scowling Pearson.

Levelling the rifle at him, Abbey said through clenched teeth, '*Thank* you for returning my uncle's rifle, Mr Pearson, but I'd like to know how it came to be in *your* possession.'

Pearson scowled darkly back at her while behind him, Granger had the two stockmen on their knees in the mud, hands behind their heads.

'Got your mobile on you?' At Abbey's nod Granger ordered,

'Call the police. Tell them there are three felons to take into custody. And a certain plantation they'll be very interested to see.'

Forty minutes later the sky had cleared and the five were starting to dry out, when Jeff Thompson arrived with a young constable in tow. The recent recruit tried, unsuccessfully, to hide his thrill at being involved in a drug bust.

While initially hesitant to arrest a loudly protesting Pearson, Thompson's first glimpse of the cannabis crop had him reaching for the handcuffs. Then he, the constable, and Abbey all listened intently to Granger's report of Pearson's involvement in Bill Miller's death.

After checking the constable had the three handcuffed men under control, Thompson moved to where he could once more see the crop below. Standing hands on hips, he rocked back and forth on his heels. 'Whee-oo, will you get a load of this!' He shook his head in awe. 'The rumours were true about a drug operation in the area. I better pay more attention to town gossip from now on.' Stepping up to Granger, he gave him a thump on the back. 'Well done, son. You not only discovered this illegal operation, you also uncovered new information about Bill Miller's accident. Wait. Make that *manslaughter*.'

'I didn't do it alone.'

Thompson waved away Granger's objection and slapped his hands together. 'Right. I'll take some photos, then get them blokes to the station for charging and incarceration. We'll come back later to finish gathering the evidence.' He flashed Granger a grin. 'Don't reckon it'll go anywhere in the meantime.'

When the two men re-joined the group, Abbey leaned

down from Star's back to address Thompson. 'Could you do us a favour, Jeff?'

'Gladly. 'Specially after the way you folk have helped us.'

'Could you drop Jack's bags to the farm?'

Thompson glanced at the backpack and duffel still lying where Granger had dropped them. 'Sure. We'll head there once we've got these three on board.' He tilted his head at a sour-faced Pearson and his two worse-for-wear stockmen. They were being loaded into the back of the 4WD paddy wagon by the eager young constable.

Bending to collect the bags, Thompson stashed them on the vehicle's back seat. Turning, he touched his cap in a salute before climbing in the driver's seat.

Abbey watched them go and then rode up to a bemused Granger. 'C'mon.' She wriggled over the cantel to settle herself on the saddle's rear leather skirt. Leaning down, she extended a hand. 'You can ride up front. Can't have today's hero having to trudge all the way back home on foot.'

29

They rode the first half of the return trip to *Clearwater Downs* in thoughtful silence. Above their heads the sweet song of the Butcher birds celebrated the rain, accompanied by the drips of rainwater, Star's breathing, and the drum of hoof beats on dampened ground. Abbey almost gave a start when Granger spoke from his perch in front of her.

'That was some fancy riding you did back there.'

'Well, thanks.'

'Aren't you nursing a back injury?'

'I am ... was.' After an exploratory stretch, she blew a relieved breath. 'It held up, thankfully. Guess it's pretty much healed.'

He nodded and said nothing for a while. Then, 'Thanks for what you did.'

'You're welcome.' Tightening her hold around his waist, she rested her head in the space between his broad shoulders.

When he tensed and barked, 'Why are we doing this?' she lifted her head again. 'Doing what?'

'Riding two-up to the farm. I thought you wanted me gone from there.'

She sighed.

Time to fess up.

Keeping her hands at his firm waist, she sat straighter. 'Well, I ... um ... figured the ride would give us a chance to talk.'

'So talk.'

That cut-to-the-chase approach is another thing I love about you.

She cleared her throat. 'I was wrong to send you away ... like that.'

His replying grunt reverberated through her hands.

'I feel just *awful* about it—'

'So why did you do it?'

Despite having mulled her explanation over and over, she was slow replying. 'Because I ... you....' She swallowed. 'When I heard of your military background I ... felt I couldn't trust you.' Her voice was soft and low, her tone remorseful.

'So,' he said sharply, 'it *was* because I'd served in the army.' After a tense silence, he frowned and said, 'Why the change of heart, if that's what this is? I'm still an ex-soldier. There's no changing that.'

'But you're a farmer first, right?'

'Yeah, so?'

'So that's what matters most.'

'What's that supposed to mean?' His frown deepened and he firmed his grip on the reins. 'And you didn't answer my question. What's changed?'

'I've had my eyes opened.' She chewed her lip. 'Been given cause to reconsider my ... opinion ... of military men. I was lumping you all in the same rotten basket. That was foolish, and very wrong of me.' When this met with another grunt she charged on. 'And I hope you'll forgive me when you know the reason for my....'

'Bigotry?'

She winced. 'I guess I deserve that.'

'Just calling it what it is.'

'You're right, and I'm so sorry for doing that to you, Jack.'

He said nothing.

'So, I'll explain the reason behind my actions. If you're prepared to listen?'

'It's not like I have much choice.' Despite his words, there was a definite softening in his tone.

Right, time for the story of my life.

She blew a breath through pursed lips.

Here's hoping it accomplishes what I need it to, otherwise....

At the thought of what was at risk her heart clenched, and her voice came out at a higher pitch than usual. 'Unlike you, I don't have fond memories of my father. My *real* father.' She swallowed and lowered her voice. 'For one thing, he died when I was only little. And for another, he was a troubled returned serviceman....'

As he listened to her tell of her childhood, of her mother's fraught relationship with Neil Carter and fears for their daughter, and of their eventual escape to *Clearwater Downs,* Granger's whole bearing softened. By the time he climbed down from Star after arriving at the farm, he knew the full story.

Luckily Star was content to stand dozing a while, for after helping Abbey dismount, Granger stood holding her close for the longest time....

~

When he rapped on the bedroom door, Granger heard a chorus of shushes, whispers, and giggles from inside. Then Flip poked her head out, accompanied by a waft of peach blossom fragrance. Arching an eyebrow at him, she rested a hand on the half-closed door. The overhead light glinted off the diamond on her ring finger.

'You shouldn't be here, you know,' she said primly. 'Although....' She ran her eyes over his 'western tuxedo' of black jacket over matching silk waistcoat, fitted black jeans, and long-sleeved white dress shirt with wing-tip collar and western bolo tie. A black cowboy hat dangled from his fingers. 'I must say, you're lookin' mighty fine there, stud.'

He waved a large, impatient hand at her. 'Some guests have rolled up early.'

'*Early* birds! Don't they know it's rude to arrive before the designated time? Who are they?'

'My side of the family—'

'Oh, well, they're excused I guess.'

'—and the Thompsons, Jeff and Emma, along with Dave and Rhonda Graham.'

'Trust them to rock up before everyone else.'

'It's alright,' a woman's voice called from inside the room. 'We'll be out to see to them shortly.'

'Gero hasn't turned up yet,' Granger continued, 'and I'm starting to get worried.' He blew a frustrated breath. 'I suggested he hold off running his market stall today but the old buggar was determined not to miss it. '

Flip's carefully made-up forehead creased. She turned to

address a towel-turbaned Abbey seated out of sight in the room behind her. 'You don't think he'd stop at the pub on the way home, do you?'

The answer came straight back. 'He hasn't fallen off the wagon in ages, and he wouldn't do anything to spoil today.' Setting down her champagne flute, Abbey raised her voice so Granger would hear. 'He only went ahead with the stall 'cos the organisers begged him to, Jack. They said lots of people only come to the markets to buy his eggs and produce.' She checked the time. 'He should be back at the quarters by now, though.'

'Yeah,' he said drily, 'back, all cashed-up from selling out as usual. He'll be good for a loan soon.' The quip met with another round of giggles.

'I wouldn't worry,' Abbey called. 'He's probably busy changing into his special occasion dungers.'

At the childish cry of, 'What are *dungers?*' from inside the room and Flip's droll, 'Pants, you wally,' Granger shook his head in amusement. Turning to him again, Flip gave a mock frown. 'So, are you gonna let us get back to what we were doing? You *do* know we have a wedding to get ready for?'

Flashing her a broad smile, he stepped back from the door. 'I'll go check on Gero.' As he headed outside, the thuds of his cowboy boots across the floorboards resounded through the house.

Calling after him, 'Don't *you* go getting lost too,' Flip closed the door with a firm click and turned to Abbey. 'That big man of yours needs to tread softer when he's inside. He's no Tinker-bell, that's for sure.'

Marion was still clucking around Abbey, making final adjustments to the gown she'd hand-made for the occasion.

After what felt like ages she finally stepped back, pins protruding from her mouth, to run a critical eye over the finished product.

The gown's white and silver-ribbed halter-neck bodice stood out against Abbey's tanned shoulders and arms. From a silver clasp at the pinched-in waist of the A-lined skirt, the top layer of sleek, pure white fabric tumbled from her hip in an elegant, wavy cascade.

'Oh, Abs,' Flip murmured breathily, 'it's simply stunning. *You're* simply stunning.' She flashed an impish grin. 'Almost as glam as me.' Holding out the skirt of her midnight-blue, lace-bodiced bridesmaid gown, she did a twirl before clapping Marion on a shoulder. 'You've outdone yourself, Mazza.'

'Oh Flip! You know I hate it when you call me that.' Marion frown-smiled as a chuckling Flip pulled her in for a one-armed hug. 'But thanks for the compliment. Truth be told, I've been waiting for a chance to use my sewing talents on something like this. These two,' and she inclined her head at her teenaged granddaughters lounging on the bed, 'won't need more than school ball gowns for a while yet.'

'I'm glad you're up for a challenge,' Flip said, "cos I'll be putting in an order for my *own* gowns soon.'

Marion's eyes lit up. 'When did you say you and Banjo are tying the knot?'

'Beginning of June. Was him that set the date, after I said if he hadn't given up the bull riding, and we weren't married by the middle of the year, I was walkin'. Seems it worked, 'cos he rode in his final rodeo two months ago. From the winnings he bought me this,' and she flashed her engagement ring. 'Then told me to go ahead and make the arrangements.'

'Good for you. Sometimes a woman's gotta show her man who's boss.' The three women shared a laugh. Hearing sniggers from her granddaughters, Marion turned to see the teenagers nudging each other. She followed their gazes to their younger sister. The little girl stood in front of the full-length mirror, ogling her floral crown and the midnight-blue tutu skirt of her flower girl dress.

With a clap of her hands, Marion announced, 'Enough of that, you two. C'mon, our job here is done, and we've got early birds to serve drinks and appetisers to.' She tilted her chin at the little flower girl. 'Hayleigh, you stay here. Flip will tell you what to do.'

Saying warmly, 'Thanks so much for all you're doing, Marion,' Abbey put a hand on her arm. 'For these gorgeous gowns, lending me your sweet little granddaughter, making the most beautiful tiered cake in the whole world. For organising just about *everything*.' Her eyes misted. 'I know my Mum would be so grateful you stepped into the role of mother of the bride.'

'Oh, love....' Marion beamed and blinked. 'That makes me so....' She touched both hands to her heart. 'I couldn't be prouder.' With a final doting nod, she ushered the teenagers out.

'Right, Abs,' Flip announced with a clap of hands, 'time's a-wastin'. That man of yours is ready and rarin' to go, and we've still got to do your hair and put the last touches to your makeup.'

As Flip led her to the dressing table, Abbey unwrapped her towel turban and shook out her hair. 'Are you sure a loose back plait will be enough? With no veil or headpiece....'

'I'm *sure*. Now stop fussin'.' Seating Abbey in front of the mirror, making sure not to crush her gown in the process, she threaded fingers through her friend's dark tresses. 'It's gonna look beautiful with some soft tendrils to frame your face.' She demonstrated, and then scooped up a handful of tiny white satin flowers. 'And these scattered through it. Just leave it to me. After all, I *am* a qualified hair stylist.'

Abbey smiled into the mirror as Flip blow-dried her hair, brushing it until it gleamed. After weaving it into a soft, fat plait, she began deftly tucking white blossoms into the glossy braid.

Abbey's smile widened as her gaze moved down to the glowing eyes and radiant face staring back at her. 'Flip.'

'Mmm?'

'If I don't say this, I'm going to burst.'

'Go on then.' Flip gave a mock-resigned sigh and continued tucking. 'Get it out of your system.'

'I'm so happy....'

'You could cry?'

Abbey pressed her lips together and nodded.

'Please don't. I mean it, Abs. It'll ruin your mascara.'

'Gero?' Granger strode up to the quarters, relieved to see fresh tyre tracks from whoever had dropped the old man home from the market. 'You there?'

Gero appeared in the doorway dressed in new suit pants and shirt, and wearing a frown. 'What the blazes are you doin' here, son?'

'Checking you're still coming.'

'Humph! Told you I'd be there in plenty of time and I will be. Got me dungers on and the rest of me bag-o'-fruit ready,' and he pointed to the jacket slung over the back of a chair.

'That the suit Abbey took you shopping for?'

'Yeah.'

'Swish.'

'So it should be for the price.' Pride tinged the old man's half-hearted grouch. 'Just need to finish tyin' *this* damn thing.' He tugged the ends of the crossover tie hanging loose from the upright collar of his crisply-pressed shirt.

'Here, let me.' Stepping in and brushing Gero's hands aside, Granger bent his head to attack the recalcitrant tie.

Gero fixed him with an assessing gaze. 'That brother of yours turned up yet?'

Granger nodded. 'With Sandra and the kids. They brought Mum with them too. They're all staying in town for a few days.'

'So, you have your best man to stand up with you, and a Granger family reunion to boot.' Gero gave an approving nod and continued eyeing him. 'You boys had a chance to talk?'

'Yep.'

'Things okay between you?'

'They will be.' After a thoughtful pause Granger added, 'Given time.'

'Did you tell him Abbey dragged you back to the old farm?'

'He knows I've been to see it.'

'Say, you never did tell me how things were at the old place.'

Granger's eyes took on a faraway look and his hands stilled at Gero's throat. 'It was much the same as I remember. Apart from the electricity towers running through the front paddocks, of course. The new owners have even kept the original colours.' He gave a lopsided grin. 'I'll have to tell Mum the house is still that peppermint green she loves.'

'So you said a proper goodbye to your home.'

'My *old* home.' Granger returned his focus to the knot. 'This farm is home to me now.'

'You and me both, here on *Clearwater*.'

'Only because Abbey's here. *She's* my home now.'

'And that's how it should be.' Gero nodded, earning himself a growled, 'Keep your head still or I'll never get this tied right.'

Making sure to keep his freshly shaven chin up, the old man charged on. 'Our Abbey is a smart girl, encouragin' you to make peace with your brother. She's learned, maybe the hard way, there's nothin' more important than family. And now her family's growin'. It's not just me 'n you any more, now she has your kin as well. And one day, your young'uns.'

Dipping his head in agreement, Granger gave the neatly knotted tie a final tweak.

'Told me she feels like a weight's been lifted, now she has you to share the running of the farm,' Gero continued. 'And I reckon you'd be pretty happy 'bout that situation too.'

'Reckon I am.' The warm smile transformed Granger's customary poker face. 'And with *Weerong Station* coming up for auction now Pearson's been convicted and put away, we might even expand our landholdings in the future. I always intended for my savings to go towards buying land.'

'Yep, you're a farmer alright, just like your father.' Gero gave a smiling shake of his head. 'Reckon me old mate Bill would be real happy right now, knowin' his girl and his farm are in good hands.'

'I like to think so.' As Granger turned down the old man's shirt collar, the strains of Richard Marx's *Now and Forever* reached their ears from the rose-filled garden setting. After helping him shrug into his jacket, Granger commanded, 'C'mon then, "Uncle" Gero. You have a bride to give away.'

'And you, son,' the old man said with a wink, 'have a wedding you can't be late for.'

～

If you've enjoyed this story, I hope you'll consider posting a review on your retailer's site and/or on Goodreads - the folk at Clearwater Downs *will love you for it!*
Alicia :)

OTHER NOVELS BY
ALICIA HOPE

THE LONG ROAD TO LOVING GRAYSON

Uber-capable HR officer Maggie is in love, just not with the man she married - a situation she didn't anticipate ever having to face.

And when engineer Grayson travels to a remote Queensland town to relieve for six weeks, he doesn't anticipate having to summon the Flying Doctors, survive a tropical cyclone, or lose his heart along the road....

The Long Road to Loving Grayson is available in paperback and as an ebook.

THE LONG ROAD TO LOVING MITCHELL

The gift she'd lost, the precious reminder of his promise to return, had somehow found its way back to her. She'd been wrong to believe her treasured garnet bracelet gone forever.

Was she wrong about him too?

The Long Road to Loving Mitchell is available in paperback and as an ebook.

THE CAFE BIRDS

A *literal* chick lit novel!

What does a girl do if she has a soldier husband suffering from PTSD? Or an abusive boyfriend, a recently Goth teenage daughter growing more distant every day, a callous and unfaithful life partner, or a guilty conscience and gluten intolerance keeping her from the man of her dreams? She calls up her BFFs and vents over coffee and cake of course!

A no-fail recipe: in five pretty cafés, blend women friends and their modern day dramas with to-die-for coffees and scrumptious cakes and serve.

Bon appétit!

The Cafe Birds is available in paperback and as an ebook.

MEET THE AUTHOR

Once you choose HOPE, anything is possible....

You can connect with Alicia online at
http://www.aliciahopeauthor.blogspot.com

www.ingramcontent.com/pod-product-compliance
Lightning Source LLC
Chambersburg PA
CBHW050011120726
47903CB00006B/1720